TRUE COUNTRY

*'Is this place real? You wait and see. I've been away for
a couple of years before. When you're away you wonder
if this place is real.'*

*Oh, it need not be real. It is not this reality we are
homesick for.*

Billy is drifting in, looking for a place to land. A young school
teacher, he arrives in Karnama, a remote settlement in Australia's
far north, in search of his own history, his Aboriginality, and of
his future.

Set in a region of abundance and beauty, where the river
meets the sea, Karnama is nevertheless a place of conflict,
dispossession and dislocation. Home to the Aboriginal
community for thousands of years, it is also an eighty-year-old
mission, now in decline, and an isolated outpost of government
administration. The desperate frontier between cultures.

Yet it is here that Billy is able to find his place of belonging.
Gradually the outsider is drawn in, his life, his story, absorbed
into that of the community. From hunting, fishing and simple
friendships, Billy slowly finds himself engaged more deeply,
more intimately, not only with the moments of desolation and
despair, but also with the great heart and spirit of the people.
Finally the exile enters the true country.

Kim Scott's haunting first novel paints a vivid and disturbing picture of a stolen country as its hero makes his tentative and fumbling way towards the true one, the 'reality that we are homesick for'. This vital, often lyrical and always uncompromising novel marks an impressive debut and a challenging direction for Aboriginal writing.

Australian Book Review

... a superb novel, original in conception and wonderfully evocative. The novel is a realistic picture of a disintegrating culture, yet it is exhilarating to read because of the vivid colloquial style. The comic disaster of a corroboree, the savage murder of an Aborigine, the crazed mind of a child in hospital are described with such intense poetic force that we seem to be not merely witnessing them but experiencing them with our hearts and senses.

The Australian

With straightforward prose, which is often poetic in its energy and rhythm, Kim Scott captures the ambiguities, the troubles and the rewards which accompany the brutal and the delicate nuances of relations when particles of one culture pass, as if through a not so fine sieve, into the heart of another culture.

Elizabeth Jolley

... it has the rich feel of real life, of hurling the reader among the dust, the drunks, the swirling heat and the kids with watermelon seeds sprouting out their ears ... an intricate story that comes from the heart.

The Mercury

Kim Scott faces up to some very serious problems, problems about as destructive as any community could have to confront in peace time. But his book is not depressing. He has an honesty and a wholeheartedness which are engaging, and the Aboriginal narrative voice which he adopts much of the time never loses hope. Whatever happens, the country will be there, and it is the country that one remembers when the story is done. It is an impressive first novel, from a writer who already has his own way of speaking.

Randolph Stow

A passionate first novel ... an intricate symphony of voices, all vying to be heard. What is remarkable is that each of them is allowed to speak with supple naturalness, whether it is in the poetic cadences of tribal idiom or in the language of white Australia. This frontier of cultures, allegiances and language has found its 'true country' in Kim Scott's well-crafted evocation.

Sydney Morning Herald

TRUE COUNTRY

KIM SCOTT

FREMANTLE
fine independent publishing PRESS

For
Robert Unghango and Mary Pandilow,
who let me listen.

Author's Note

This novel began with a desire to explore a sort of neglected interior space, and to consider my own heritage. Having turned my attention to that primarily personal territory, and the blank page, I selected some words and images from my little store and scattered them before me. Here, I hoped, might be some place from which to begin.

Actual place names, I thought, would help anchor it all in 'reality' and assist it to become something other than mere personal indulgence. I used details of Kimberley topography, and borrowed from the dialect and past of one community I had lived in.

It is not difficult, for those so inclined, to trace Karnama back to a specific community. But then it's no longer Karnama. In terms of its character Karnama could, it seems to me, be one of many Aboriginal communities in Northern Australia. I created fictional characters that seemed appropriately 'typical' and who would be most able to assist me in my explorations. Many of them ran away from me. None of them bear any relation to any real person.

As I continued to write, the story developed in ways which I had not anticipated. None of the events or situations of the narrative are intended to correspond to any real occurrence. And although in a few instances, aspects of certain actual events are suggested, they are used as stepping off points for the imagination, and this work remains wholly fictional in every aspect.

We carry in our hearts the true country
And that cannot be stolen
We follow in the steps of our ancestry
And that cannot be broken.

'The Dead Heart' — Midnight Oil

(then why) … this sense
of gain and loss, the now I am
not there, then, despite the giveaway
smile? I am a born exile, or they
are tokens of infinity; and distance
like love is a necessary fiction.

'Distances' — Charles Boyle

I

First Thing, Welcome

You might stay that way, maybe forever, with no world to belong to and belong to you. You in your many high places, looking over looking over, waiting for a sign. You're nearly ready, nearly there.

You're trying to read a flat pattern, like the sea, the land from high above. Or you might see your shadow falling upon this page. And maybe that's all you'll see and understand.

Or you might drift in. Fall or dive in. Enter.

Wind drift, rain fall, river rush. The air, the sea all round. And the storming.

You alight on higher ground, gather, sing. It may be.

You listen to me. We're gunna make a story, true story. You might find it's here you belong. A place like this.

And it is a beautiful place, this place. Call it our country, our country all 'round here. We got river, we got sea. Got creek, rock, hill, waterfall. We got bush tucker: apple, potato, sugarbag, bush turkey, kangaroo, barramundi, dugong, turtle … every kind. Sweet mangoes and coconuts too.

There is a store, school for our kids and that mission here still. That's all right. Yes, you might never see a better place. Our home.

When it's rainy season rivers fill up and food and surround us.

Is like we are a forgotten people then, on a maybe shrinking island; a special place for us alone.

You might fly in many times, high up and like reading river, hill, tree, rocks. Coming from upriver and the east, you flying flying fly in looking all the time and remembering; you flying quiet and then you see this place. You see the river. You see the water here, this great blue pool by High Diving where the kids swim. You see the mission grounds all green, and the houses all quiet and tiny from up in the air. You notice the dark mango trees, and the coconut trees standing tall along that airstrip road. That airstrip is like a cross, because there's two airstrips. The old people built them in the war, with the army and the fathers, when those Japanese bombed this place. They make a cross for someone like a sky pilot to land on.

But, first time, you in a plane. You go over the gorge and you see the landing where the barge came in long ago. You see that and you see where the river goes into salt water, and the islands scattered blue offshore. Then the plane banks and maybe you see nothing just sky, or maybe the trees the road the rubbish then in front of you the gravel coming up and bang you are landed.

Welcome to you.

Long White Walksocks

Two white men would have been at the mission workshop, crouched beside a four-wheel drive. They stood up together, looked at their watches, and squinted into the sky. One was tall like a tree, the other one short with a round gut. They spoke, and got into another vehicle.

Many kids and young people, dark ones, were over near the store and the basketball court. One tall boy leapt into the air, hovered, and tossed a basketball toward the backboard. The orange ball gently arced and descended through the hoop without touching it. The boy rolled over onto his back, laughing. He looked into the sky, and pointed up and to the south-east. All the kids stopped their games, and looked, and they pointed too. Their eardrums, even those that were perforated, or congested, or — in one or two cases — hindered by sprouting watermelon seeds, trembled with the drone of airborne engines.

Next to the lumpy and cracked basketball court was a corrugated iron shack with rubbish and graffiti scattered along the wall. People were sitting on the ground there. A man put his head out the door. 'Teacher plane,' he said.

'Teacher plane teacher plane. Gissa ride, gissa ride.' The utility, coming up now, pulled over. Bodies poured in, all sizes. The same was happening to other utilities there. Boys standing on the trays, young women sitting holding their babies, people cross-legged on the roof of the cabs. The old people, sitting around the office and out the front of the houses along the road to the airstrip, watched them drive by. The corrugated iron resonated with the rumble of the plane flying overhead, the cars driving past, the shouts, the barking of dogs.

I am flying. I was coming to a landing.

The plane had flown in low, under the rain clouds, navigating by the rivers and coastline. My wife, Liz, still held the small motion sickness bag and could only smile weakly at me. The pilot shouted, but because of the roar of the engines and the earmuffs I wore I couldn't hear him. He pointed ahead and I saw a small settlement. There were tall, deep-green trees, buildings glinting in the sun, and a blue pool where the river slowed and widened.

'Ah, that's it?'

The pilot nodded. We'd been flying for an hour and a half. In the plane with us were Alex and Annette Seddum and their eight-year-old son, Alan. Alex was to be the principal of the school we were flying to.

The boy squeezed his hands between his knees and wriggled. 'We nearly there?' and he turned and called to his mother, 'At last we're nearly there at this place whatever it's called.'

Annette smiled at him. Alex patted the boy's head and turned his own furrowed brow away.

We flew over a large curved pool in the river, and saw the mission with its lawn and buildings and plantation. There were small huts and large trees, and a scratch of a track that dipped through creeks. It scratched past the powerhouse and the school, turned the corner of the basketball court near the mission gates and continued, lined with coconut palms, past corrugated iron huts to a gravel airstrip in the shape of a cross.

Not far from the airstrip the river flows through a gorge before widening to a mangrove-lined mouth and into the sea. The plane flew low and banked to make its approach to the airstrip. I saw the white ribbons of water which poured from the rocks and were shredded and swept downstream. That river is always a torrent at this time.

As we lost altitude the scratch became a dirt road barely wide enough for two vehicles. It went cautiously through the bush between the gorge and the airstrip which we saw before us, through the settlement and then out the other side of it. The bush was littered with old car bodies, tins, plastic, all sorts of rubbish. We landed with a crunch and the gravel spat at us, the engine roared, and we were taxiing over to a crowd of dark bodies waving from the back of four-wheel drive utilities.

We all waved back from inside the plane. It was very hot and humid on the ground. We shouted at one another over the roar of the engines.

'Quite a reception.'

'Good eh? Friendly.'

'Look how many in each car.'

'Gaw, they're really black aren't they?'

Yes, whereas these people in the plane looked even paler than usual. My wife from travel sickness, the others from what? Exhaustion? Apprehension?

The pilot turned off the motor and said to the mostly pale faces around him, 'What do you reckon? Think you can teach them?' He opened the doors for us.

Annette pointed to two white men. 'Look, Alex, there's two men there.'

'Yeah,' he said, 'that must be the project officer. One of them will be anyway.'

It was. His name was Gerrard. The other was Murray, the mechanic and general tradesman for the mission and community.

We all shook hands, a small group circling in the space between the plane being unloaded and the welcoming crowd. Small children shyly zig-zagged toward the long white walksocks among us.

We new teachers sat in the back of the utility with our few boxes and cases. Our clothes stuck to our flesh. We tightly gripped the sides of the tray, worried we'd fall as the ute bounced along the track. A number of other vehicles accompanied us, and we rattled in a great cloud of dust and noise. We came through the corridor of coconut palms and, smiling stiffy, regally waved back at those who watched from the shade of the huts.

Many of the younger children held lengths of nylon fishing line, the other ends of which were tied to cans dragging behind them.

'Hey, I used to make toys like that when I was a kid. I'd forgotten.' It was true. I'd forgotten.

The half-naked children turned, their faces splitting into grins, and waved also. Old car bodies rusted in long green grass. Clothing was strung out on low barbed wire fences around some of the shacks. In one yard a circle of people sat under a big tree, hunched over a game of cards.

What were they saying?

'Who dem gardiya?'

'Teachers.'

'Look out, 'm fall off not careful.'

'Wave 'em, look at 'm they wave. Think they pope, or what?

'Look at that one, blondie one, that short one.'

'See that hat? That John Wayne maybe, ridin' Toyota.'

'Aiee! That red hair girl, mine!'

Screams of laughter.

Fatman Murray turned into the backyard of the teachers' housing behind the school and the front wheels of the Toyota went through the grass and sank deep into the mud.

'Shit.'

At a card game someone fanned his cards out on the top of his belly. 'Coonce!'

I win.

The Midst of a Battle

So, a beginning has been made, and the person I was then might have wanted to compare it to the beginning of a game; have believed it is like a basketball tossed up to begin a game. But what if the basketball were to continue rising? What if, amazingly, it continued rising, away from the control of whistle and game, and right up past one returning aeroplane? It would startle the pilot, that's for sure, and leave him blinking and shaking his head for the rest of the flight. It would leave him wondering and not knowing whether to believe his eyes, the laughter in his ears, or what. How could he explain it to others?

The ball stops rising, is poised, about to plummet. What would you see now, so removed and high above, up there with that basketball?

My first impressions of Karnama were from above, over a map. I looked at several maps. Karnama was labelled either 'Aboriginal Community', or 'Mission', depending on the age of the map. On each map there was a small red symbol of an aeroplane hovering over my destination. And there were variously drawn lines; lines of different colours, of dots, dashes, or dots and dashes, each indicating a different path, whether it be 'unsealed one lane road', '4WD track', 'river' or 'foot trail'. It was like a treasure map.

And then, the reality. A large 'X' helped mark the spot.

School started the day after our arrival. We hardly knew where to begin. The kids seemed friendly and affectionate. They were all Aboriginal. Karnama had no television, radio, telephones, and only a weekly mail plane. There were few books in the community, but many videos. Few of the adults could read and write, and the students had very low levels of education. We had trouble pronouncing their surnames, and understanding their English. Our students were shy, but curious to know about us, and somehow very concerned for our welfare. One youth especially, Deslie, would even guide us around the large wet-season puddles.

The school, apparently, had a reputation for arranging performances of traditional dancing for community visitors. Alex told us near the end of the first school week that the school would be putting on a dance for some visitors in a couple of weeks. He would get a few of the local adults to come in to help with rehearsals.

A couple of days later the whole school gathered in the shade of the mango tree in the centre of the schoolyard. Some of the elder women from the community dipped chewed twigs or small paint brushes into tins of white ochre as the smaller children clambered over and around them. The children closed their eyes to have their faces painted and stuck out their chests when the ochre was placed there. They were all laughing and chattering, with the women occasionally shouting 'Keep still!' or 'Shut up you, you …' Alex paced around them.

The adolescents were reluctant. The older girls leaned against a fence several metres away on the edge of the shade.

Some of them sat facing away from the rest of us. It was hot. Francis, awkwardly bursting out of his clothes and seemingly growing before one's eyes as his hormones bustled, polished his thick spectacles and looked bewildered. The other teenage boys joked.

Sylvester, one of the tallest, called out. 'Look at little Willy! Proper blackfella Willy.' Tiny Willy stomped his feet furiously as if in a corroboree.

Deslie shoved Sylvester and turned away pouting. 'I'm not dancin'. I don't like dancing. No men here.' I could see Alex glancing angrily over to where the high school students were. I was responsible for them.

I went over to them. Alex wanted the boys to change into the lap-lap things and be painted, to enter into the spirit of the occasion, he said, and not destroy the enthusiasm of the young ones. One of the boys said, mockingly, 'We should do it or we'll lose our culture.'

'Yes Sylvester, that might be right,' I said earnestly.

'But so what? I'll still have me.' Sylvester puffed out his chest and pounded it. 'Rambo,' he intoned in his deepest voice. The others laughed with him. Francis, with his head tilted back to stop his spectacles sliding from the bridge of his nose, gave a loud and high-pitched laugh.

'Come on now boys, you have to join in.' I turned back to the younger children, shouting at them to get down from the tree, off the verandah, away from the school gate, to stop fighting, stop throwing rocks ... I smiled at the old women who were laughing as they watched two small girls hurling fists and tearful words at one another.

One of the senior primary boys swung from a branch of the tree, screaming out 'Ninja!' and fell, with a different scream. Liz tried to help him up from the ground where he lay, beginning to sob. 'Sir! Miss! Look! Cyril fell!' Voices everywhere, yelling, laughing. Through his tears Cyril groaned, 'My fuckin' arm, don't you laugh Willy, I'll lift you boy you you … I'll make you sting.'

On the outside of this crowd, this whole excited school jostling around the tree from which bodies and sticks were thrown and fell, I saw Annette with two small boys. The boys danced around a rubbish bin, pounding the earth with their bare feet and exhaling in noisy bursts. Annette turned away as she praised them, calling to the crowd. 'Isn't that good? I want to see more of this, all of you.' But I think only I heard. She saw the chaos, her words not heeded, and her smile fell. Her face became a pale tissue, crumpled.

One of the old women lifted her eyes from painting a small face, and I heard her say, with a little smile, in all that noise, 'We doin' your teachin' for you.'

Liz and I met Alex as we were walking across the school lawn from our class late in the day. It was almost sunset and the air had thickened. Everything was deep and rich in colour as the day turned overripe.

Alex stood bare chested before us in his thongs and sagging shorts. 'It's a shambles, a bloody farce.' His brow furrowed again.

'Yeah it wasn't too good.'

'Ha! They don't teach. They expect the kids to just do it!' He tilted his head to one side. 'Could you work it out, step by step?' Alexander pounded his feet rather feebly on the lawn.

He stopped, and looked at his feet. There was a little silence. 'No. No, not quite, mate.'

'What a mess. There's no teaching method.' Alex turned away, shaking his head.

'But,' Liz tried to insist, 'that's their way, maybe.'

I said to him, 'Alex, what about the men? How come only the women came?'

'I don't know. The AEWs — Aboriginal Education Workers — said the men would come, but apparently they were playing cards or something. Commitment eh? Anyway,' he turned to go once more, 'there's a meal on at the mission tonight, for us. About six. Everything supplied.'

He walked away, shaking his head on his rounded thin shoulders. Alex moved like a puppet on strings; high-stepping and as if hesitating just before each foot fell. His pale skin gleamed, and then faded away as he passed under the mango tree where the darkness first gathered.

We sat at a long table in the courtyard of the mission monastery built, Father Paul assured us, some fifty years ago. Brother Tom mentioned, as we admired the illuminated courtyard and the solid walls made of stones from the riverbed, that the natives weren't much help building this place. They helped as they could.

A fan whirred overhead. We were surrounded by palms and tropical greenery. Father Paul introduced us to the others: Sister Dominica, Sister Therese, Murray, Brother Tom, Gerrard, Jasmine.

The loud fizz-static of insects dying as they hit the insect electrocuter punctuated the whirr of the fan. It seemed an appropriate accompaniment to the prickling heat, the sensation of sweat trickling beneath my fresh clothes.

The tablecloth was white and the Sisters were dressed in

white. Everyone was clean and scrubbed. Knives and forks scratched, glasses clinked, jaws masticated.

Annette sighed and settled her stout body in the chair. 'A week in Karnama seems like an eon. Suddenly, here we have it again. Civilisation.' She raised her arm as if proposing a toast, a wine glass in her fist.

Father Paul leaned forward. 'So, you're finding it a bit difficult then?'

'Oh, it's so frustrating. Kids that don't know how to sit still, and not getting to school until recess time. What are their parents doing? Do they feed them? No, they're playing cards. Alex goes out to see them, like to get them to help with the dancing, and they're all yes sir no sir but as soon as he's gone they forget.' She drained her glass.

Alex glanced nervously at his wife and tried to catch her eye. The other conversations around the table had lulled. Brother Tom called from the far end of the table. 'Ah yes, it can be trying, working here with the Aborigines.'

Annette lifted her chin. 'Well, we were in a little town in the Wheatbelt last year. Alexander was the principal there. When you were the principal's wife you were somebody. And there was sport to play. It wasn't so far from Perth. But here! People laughed at us, other teachers, they couldn't believe that this was a promotion for Alexander. They didn't understand that.' She smiled at her son, Alan, beside her.

People looked around the courtyard, listened to another insect electrocuted.

Liz tried to joke. She tapped her temple and made faces. 'Well, a thicko like me is going to learn a lot here. The kids might not, but I'm sure I will. I need to!' Everyone laughed with relief.

'Oh, they're lovely, friendly people,' we agreed, all nodding and sipping at our drinks.

'Everyone in the office is lovely,' said Jasmine. 'They might not work too hard, but they're sweet, really. This lovely old lady came over today, the first baby born on the mission she said.'

'That would be Fatima,' said Brother Tom.

'Yes, I think so, very tall and heavy. Quite old I think. Well, she'd have to be if she was born …'

'The mission moved here from out at a bay past the river mouth, Murugudda,' Father Paul interrupted, 'about fifty-odd years ago, she was born at the old mission. In the middle of the yard I understand.'

'Fatima, ah yes, she likes to talk, very much!' offered Sister Dominica. Her skin was tight and lined as if she was too tightly tucked into the folds of her white habit. She spoke with a strong Spanish accent. The mission staff chuckled at the sister's comment.

'We see her a lot. We feed the very old people, and her. She helps. Her husband lives with the old people, he's sick. They're a very strange couple, very strange.'

'She must have some interesting stories to tell. She would have seen a lot of changes in her life, when you think about it.'

'Yes, that's true. She might even colour things a bit, ham it up if you give her enough attention for it. They're like that,' smiled Father Paul.

'Okay, just improve the story.'

'She seemed nice. Proud of herself too,' said Jasmine.

'She's among the last of them with any understanding of their culture, you know, 'though lots of them believe parts of mumbojumbo,' said Brother Tom.

'But some sort of new culture must evolve, surely?'

Father Paul snorted. 'But look at what it is,' he said. 'You'll see. I don't think it's very creative or promising. When the mission first came here they were dying out, in terms of numbers. It's only in the last couple of decades that the numbers have started to increase. There's a lot of children now.'

'As a people they can't last,' said Alex. 'They need to organise themselves. Set some sort of goals. Face up to the way things have to be done nowadays. A management plan. And look after finances.'

'There've been a couple of project officers run off with the loot. It's quite common in these sort of communities. It doesn't help.'

'At least they look okay,' Annette offered her wisdom. 'In the Wheatbelt … well, you know. What a way to be. Better not to last if you end up like that.'

'But they've been here, everywhere, in Australia, for such a long time. Maybe they'll still be here, long after we've gone.'

Some of those who heard Liz's comment appeared to be in pain. They winced. But Jasmine nodded enthusiastically at Liz, and said, 'Yes! Maybe not quite the same, but …'

'Like cockroaches you mean?' suggested Alex, and small laughter circled the table.

He turned back to Jasmine with a sharp little movement of his head. 'You're new here aren't you?' he said. 'Bookkeeper, that right?'

Gerrard spoke for her. 'Yep. And I'm the new project officer, so Jasmine and I form the team at the office. That's the shed near the basketball court.' He leaned forward, resting his heavy forearms on the table.

'Some basketball court.' I think Annette hiccupped as she said this. She gave a wan smile, her red lips stretching to reveal her teeth. Her lipstick had spread to her teeth and glass.

'It's unusual to have so many new people, white staff, arriving at once,' said Father Paul. 'It's a coincidence that the previous staff left at the one time.'

Murray called out from where he was serving himself more dessert, a lavish salad of tropical fruits grown on the mission plantation. 'So, it's pretty well a new bunch all round.' He waddled back to the table.

'And a wet bunch we'll be too, if this rain keeps up,' said Liz. 'I bought white shoes to wear to school, and they're nearly ruined already.'

'It'll probably get wetter,' said Father Paul. 'It's not unusual to flood at this time of year. The river comes up, and the creeks the other side too, and we turn into a sort of island.' He waved his arm around to indicate where the water would surround them, and the smoke trailing from his cigarette marked the arc he made.

More insects stuttered and exploded above us. The whirr of the fan was louder. We sat around the table, looking at one another, as if in the midst of a battle. Huddled in the light, within these walls, in this courtyard, in the great expanse of night.

Brother Tom returned to the weather. 'It really upsets things here when it rains heavily. The Aborigines just sit at home, because there's no work for them, and play cards. Play even more than usual, that is. Play guitar. Talk. The kids can't come and work here straight after school when it's too wet. So they get up to mischief, and cause trouble. Everyone gets cranky, very cranky.' He had a soft voice, and spoke slowly. His skin was covered with red patches.

'More wine anyone?' Murray asked, holding up a new bottle. He filled Annette's glass first and she sipped at it before placing it back on the table. Murray tossed the bottle into the bin before he completed his lap of the table. The Sisters had gone to bed. Brother Tom excused himself also.

'You get thirsty living in this heat. Well, I seem to anyway,' I said, and my voice seemed to echo. I took another sip.

'Much drinking among the natives here?' Alex leaned forward as he spoke, and placed his elbows on the table the better to pivot his swinging forearms and hands. His chin went into one of those hands and kept it still. I wondered whether he was about to tie himself in some sort of knot.

'Sometimes.' Father Paul leaned back in his chair, his large working boots propped against the legs of the table. He didn't look like a priest. 'It's a bit of a bloody cock-up really.' He didn't sound like one either. 'Officially, there's to be no drinking, that's the council's decision. But, it happens. Most of the councillors drink, but at the same time they say they oppose allowing it.'

'The Aborigines like their drink,' said Father Paul, as Gerrard handed me a beer from his great height.

'The school gardener, Milton, he's a pretty good worker.' Something in Murray's voice seemed to indicate that he had definite ideas on who was, and who was not, a good worker. 'That's relative to this community,' he added, 'they're none of them real top workers. Can't rely on any of them really. Rather have a good time, and be with their mates, fishing, playing cards, talking.'

There were only the four of us left.

I think I went home very late. The darkness smelt of mud and rotting vegetation as I picked my way through the puddles and heat. Even at that late time of night, and in all that darkness, I heard a ball bounce among the cowpats on the basketball court.

Kidnapped

I saw Jasmine and an old Aboriginal woman under the school mango tree. I watched them from the classroom window. At that distance I couldn't hear their voices and their legs had so dissolved that they, and the tree, sat upon the wavering heat waves between us. Their heads were close together. The older woman held her hand palm up, as if in offering, and Jasmine nodded her head.

Jasmine lifted her face to me as I approached, weak-kneed from the heat. She flicked her hair back with a shake of her head and lifted her right hand to me, half waving half pointing, and bracelets slid down her arm like railway cars shunting.

The old woman slowly turned and peered short-sightedly. The lenses of her spectacles were very thick and her eyes moved behind them like dark fish in a bowl. Her hair hung in thick grey ropes and stopped just short of her shoulders. She gave a small, diffident smile.

'Good afternoon, Jasmine,' I said, very formally. Jasmine leapt to her feet and curtsied. 'Good afternoon, Mr Bill, sir!'

She laughed at me and I saw the old woman looking at the two of us with a puzzled expression for a moment. She grinned.

'This lady,' Jasmine held her hand toward her, 'is Fatima, the person I told you about.'

Fatima remained seated, but shifted about on her buttocks. 'You like stories? You want I tell you stories, about old people, long time?'

I nodded. 'Yes. I'd like that, if you don't mind. I'm interested, and it would be good, I think, for the kids to read. To learn to read about things to do with here. And read it the way you speak, sort of.' I felt awkward.

'I can do that. I can give you that.' Fatima was positive. 'Not today but,' she added hastily, apologetically. 'Today I help the sisters, and feed some people. I see them. I will get someone bring me, when you finish school. Or what?'

We agreed and she began to get up. She twisted her body, put both hands palm down on the bench to her left, and levered herself to her feet. Jasmine and I attempted to help her. She was a very big woman, much taller and heavier than either of us. Her skin was cool and soft. 'Ooh, my knees. I am too old.' We still held her arms. 'Thank you.'

I watched the two of them walk away. They left the shade and went across the wide yard toward the gate. Next to the lumbering bulk of Fatima, Jasmine looked sickly white, tiny, and as if about to fade and dissolve in the powerful sunlight.

Fatima came to the house the next afternoon. I came out when I heard voices. A youth was helping her up the steps. He held her forearm, and she lifted one foot, rested it on the next step, paused, then brought the other foot up beside it. She stopped again, her free arm holding the verandah support, and puffed at the strands of hair across her face. 'I am too old.'

The youth with her nodded a serious greeting. Fatima waved him away. 'Go.' As he walked away she said 'Alphonse' to me by way of introduction. He turned and flashed a smile.

Now that the steps had been conquered she held herself erect and solid on her bare feet. Her arms hung loose at her sides and the fingers on her large hands were splayed. 'I can tell you stories, about the old ways.'

I made tea and we sat opposite one another at the kitchen table with a small tape recorder between us.

'… then I'll listen to the tape and write it out for the kids to read, or me to read to them …'

'Oh no!' Fatima gasped. She put her hand to her mouth and dropped her head. 'I feel shame.' I thought she didn't want me to do this. But it was merely that she had put the wet teaspoon back into the sugar bowl.

'No problem, Fatima.'

'Oh, I'm stupid. I know all about that. I know that.' She shook the spoon and clumps of wet sugar fell onto the tabletop.

'Is a nice house, eh?' She looked around the beige room, appraising it.

'Yes it is a nice house. Yeah I think so.' I thought of how it must seem compared to her own home. 'It was only built a little while ago, wasn't it?'

'Yes,' she said. 'Last year. They should make one like this for me. But with no step,' she added. I joined her laughter as she said this, perhaps because I was relieved she was not bitter about the difference in our housing.

She became serious. 'What we, what is it you want me to tell you?'

'Oh, I'm not sure. Just things. Like what you know, what you remember about Karnama.'

I pushed a button and we stared at the red light on the tape recorder. Fatima took a big breath, and began.

'My name is Fatima Nangimara. I am the first one born in the mission …

'I grow up in the mission. I grow up by the Spanish monks, you know, the Fathers.

'When I was bigger they sent me to school because there's no school in here. No sisters or no anybody to teach anybody.

'Myself and Mary we went to Beagle Bay school by Kuringa, by big ship.

'They didn't tell us nothing, they hide the clothing. They pack it up, gave it to one of the Fathers, and tell us that we were just going to see the people on that boat, Kuringa.

'But it wasn't true. They play tricks on us. We might cry, or my mother might take me to the bush and hide me, see. So they didn't tell anybody.

'So. We went on the boat, we met the crew. They were unloading and Father told us to go up so we went up. We were in that ship and the lady brought us cake. That's Mrs Johnson and Mrs Thompson, they look after us.

'We thought that boat was moving, maybe. But we thought, they said, we were stopping in there, in that Pako Bay. But it wasn't Pako Mission, we were in Wyndham already, you see. Or same as.

'We were thinking of Mummy and Daddy and sad because I didn't say 'bye to Daddy because Daddy was fishing. And Mummy was at home. So.

'We were in that boat with no good air. Then, when it sun setting time, we came out of the place to see outside, you know, and they told us, "This is Wyndham." Those two British nurses, they look after us. They did not let us off the ship. We stayed inside long time. They thought we might jump out of the boat I suppose.

'We were scared of it.

'Out on the water we used to dance corroboree for them. We were happy to do that. I used to sing, Mary dance. She used to sing for me, and I used to dance. Well we were children. We didn't feel shame or anything like that you know.

'I think the lady told us. You know the nurse, from us? She told us to dance, so we dance corroboree for them.

'They used to be happy with us you know, make us not to think for our parents, you know? And they used to be with us, clapping their hands when we danced.

'There were many ladies in the ship. This was big ship. They used to come and make our beds, clean nice undywear, shower. They used to be good for us. Nice food they used to give us, nice bed. They were nice people.

'And from there we went to Darwin. We were only crying for Mummy and Daddy, still crying. We were in Darwin in the morning time. We saw one Aborigine woman, and man. They talk in pidgin you see, they told us, "Where you come from?" And we told them we come from Dresfield. "We know that place. Where are you going?" We told them we didn't know where we were going.

'See, we didn't know where we were going.

'On the ship they thought we might jump out I suppose. But they were nice people. Gave us nice food, nice bed.

'But this Darwin. That Aborigine man was talking with us. He said, "I am from that side too, from this part of the country." But we don't know, see? We were not big people to know everything.'

Again again again. Out on the blue sea, them ladies in their many dresses, their pink skins scrubbed, they clap chapped hands at the two dark girls dancing dancing dancing like shadows in the hard sun. The sun and sea hurt eyes, the sea slaps at the hull. The ropes and timbers creak.

Splinter of wood, scrap of sail, tiny zig-zags across all that blue. We can hear the singing, little bit. Just faint, you know.

'We left Darwin, we went back, and we started to go to Broome. And there we get out.

'The lady told us, "You are going out now, with this man here." We said "No!" many times. We didn't know he was Bishop, Bishop Somebody. He told us, "I'll take you." We used to say "No!" We used to say no.

'After all he took us for a train, from the jetty you know. We went on the train, we get out, and one of the nuns was working in the garden just watering the place. Stop us. Then she take us to the girls. We take two, three days in Broome. Then after Brother took us to Beagle Bay Mission.

'There were three boys there waiting for us that was from Pako Mission. They went in front of us, before us, you know. One of the luggers took them there. They didn't know.

'Like we didn't know. We didn't think. I didn't know anything. Nothing!

'We met one boy, one Aborigine boy, in the road. Give him a letter. It was a letter to that Bishop and when the boy said, "Yes Father," we just looked at each other, Mary and me. We said, "This is Father who we say no no no?" We said to one another, you know, "This is Father?" Oh no, we made a mistake, he's a Father and we just say no no no for him.

'We went to Beagle Bay. We stayed there. We used to be sorry, but too many girls there so that make us happy.'

'We came back here, we were grown-up girls, like the big girls you teach. We got out of the lugger and Mother, Father, uncles and anybody, they were waiting for us. They were waiting for us. Some people in the camp, they said, "The two girls are coming back." They just knew.

'So they were ready for us and they cried for us. We didn't know how to speak the language. We forgot about our language. We talk in English. I couldn't understand my mummy. I forgot all about our language. We forget about it.

'Back then, you would be able to talk their language in no time. They would get sugarbag, bush honey, and sing it and give it to you to eat. When you had eaten that honey you would be able to talk their language just the same as they do. But with us we did just forget, so after a time we getting it little by little so we can talk now.

'My mummy said that she cannot understand, to other people. Telling them that we cannot understand them and that they cannot talk, when they were talking to us in language. Mummy told them, "They don't talk, they forgot about their language."

'Mummy took me to the dormitory where we have to live. I was already a big girl, see, because I couldn't stay with them. In the law of the Aborigine, from the bush, you know, their fathers don't like big girls to live in their mummy's place.

'They don't like me to stay with them. Not like here now they live with their parents.'

I have a photograph of Fatima which I took at about this time. It is in black and white and I processed it myself in the crudest of circumstances. The photograph was taken on the front verandah of our house. Fatima has taken her spectacles off and concealed them in her hands, which are clasped in her lap. She is smiling and looks confident, leaning back in the spindly chair. Looking at it I am struck by her capable feet and hands. Her ankles are crossed, her knees apart, and behind her the sun makes small diamonds in the timber lattice work, and softly spotlights her grey hair. The young girl, Beatrice, is standing beside her. I don't remember her being there. She stands, one hand on Fatima's shoulder, balancing on the ball of one foot. The other foot is held just above the ground. She seems to be almost floating, perfectly poised upon a so-thin leg, her head tilted and her thin cotton shift falling from her shoulder.

It's a messy verandah. At their feet are coils upon coils of what must be rope, or perhaps a water hose. It looks almost, in such a bad photograph, like a large but slender snake spiralling around their feet with its head disappearing out of the frame at the bottom of the print, heading for the photographer.

I asked Fatima about Walanguh, her husband, who I knew stayed over behind the clinic, with a couple of the other oldest people in the community. I knew he was very frail, and not well. Fatima told me that they had never had what she called a proper marriage, but she helped look after him now. They were married soon after she arrived back from her schooling.

'I didn't know what was going. Sister put the veils on us and we went in there to get married, but I was pretty scared. True, I was worried. What is going to happen to me?

'So, we married. They took me, with him, to a little house. You know my house now? Same one but smaller. They took me and him to there and we went in. He was older than me, see. I was frightened. What was going to happen? I was frightened, see.

'The first day I went out. I just run away. I run away, to the dormitory again, mind you.

'So I went again and they bring me back again. They say, "He's frightened." So my sister-in-law, that's Moses' mother, got the key and locked the door, to make me stay with my husband. And you know what I did? I just climbed the window, jump over, and run away and stay with my mother. Not stay, but spend the night, you know?

'My mother and father used to growl me. You know. "Why you don't stay one place? Why you come here, not small girl, or not a baby," Mummy said to me.

'But the other one, Mary, she got married same time, she not frightened. She's all right, but me? No.

'In proper old days, well, they didn't do like that. See? I don't want to, you know, embarrass you. Old men would teach young girls, and other way; old women show young men. Yes?

'But for us, even then when I was young, it was already different. Lucky Walanguh was a special man. He tell me he not angry with me, but with missionaries. He spoke soft to me. Tell me stories and sing to me all night long, until when the light come and I was happy and ready for him. But we never had no children …

'In the proper old days people did all that and like a game.

'But today they marry anykind. Mothers, daughter, take them anyway. People are going a bit like dogs now.'

Preparations

Fatima made regular afternoon visits, and we talked into my tape recorder. She liked the attention, I think.

She welcomed the anthropologists who came to see her, and was happy to advise tour guides researching the area. She received mail from the Institute of Aboriginal Affairs. I read it to her.

I ordered a book which had been written up from the mission journals and read to her the sentence which described her birth in the mission courtyard:

> The missionaries had the opportunity to observe the performance of three 'doctors', two men and a woman, who used the best of their craft on the poor sufferer. The baby survived her own and her mother's troubles and the monks observed the mother applying a few drops of her own milk to the afflicted eyes of the new-born child.

Fatima wept. Two sentences. She'd not heard them before.

We looked through the book and she named the people in the old photographs and identified locations. I read the captions to her. She was pleased by examples which confirmed her memory, gratified by those which corroborated it, annoyed with those which differed. The captions rarely named the Aborigines.

The next day she brought another book with her. It was also written up from mission journals. We looked through it as we had with the one the day before.

'Fatima, why not tell me the history of Karnama? Sort of like what these books do, but more what you remember, or what you know.' The tape recorder was on.

She took a deep breath, and exhaled noisily through her nose. You can hear it on the tape. It was a preparation, I suppose. It occurred to me later that it was almost as if she was taking on a burden, or a duty. I don't know if it was an affectation, or to what degree. A film came over her eyes and she looked into an imaginary distance. She began speaking, slowly and hesitantly.

'The monks, they landed in Loual Bay, that's the anchorage, and they went up the river to Dresfield River. You see, they follow the river right up to Brockman Plain and they saw this Nangimara, that woman. First thing, they gave him ... they gave her something to wear.'

I remembered that I'd read this in the book I'd borrowed. 'A dress I think it was, yeah.' I began skimming through the book trying to find it, flying over fluttering pages.

'They gave her a red material.'

'That's right, yeah, that's what it says in here somewhere.'

'Yeah, red material,' repeated Fatima, 'and the other ones, they run away, see?'

A year or so later, when I finally got around to listening to this tape, I was surprised to hear how obsessed I seemed to be to find that passage in the book. I merely grunted a reply to Fatima's query. On the tape you can hear me turning the pages.

Fatima asked me, 'Did they talk about that?' There was an edge to her voice. Not that I noticed it at the time. Perhaps she thought I was checking the accuracy of what she said. She may have thought I didn't really believe her. She may have even been a little impressed that I had access to something to which she believed herself the custodian. She wanted to know the author's interpretation.

Again, on the tape, my voice is little more than a mumble. 'Yeah, I think so, and this girl tricked them.' It's a bad recording. They all were. There's a loud rumbling in the background on all of them.

I remember noticing that she smiled at the thought of the trick, and then suddenly frowned. It was probably out of sympathy for the obsessiveness with which I was trying to locate that passage in the book.

You can hear the pages turning as I say, 'Um, can't find it now, but this girl, they call her Mary, tricked them. She pretended she was friends. And then the others, it says in here, the other men could sneak up toward them, and they threw spears. Something like that. I can't find it now. But they found her dress many years afterwards where she'd left it somewhere.'

I must have glanced up from the pages. Fatima was leaning forward on the stainless steel and vinyl chair which seemed very small beneath her bulk. Her eyes were intent, her heavy arms hung between her knees and her hands were clasped loosely together. She began to say something, I looked up and saw her mouth open. She closed it, set her lips, and said, 'They say that Nangimara — Mary they say — he died here, in Karnama.'

I grunted a reply. Fatima corrected herself again, and continued. 'She died here. But her sister, she run away and they want to frighten her. You know? But they got 'im and shot 'im!' Her voice had changed, was impassioned. I suppose she sat upright. As the tape reveals to me, I didn't notice.

'Ah, yeah.' Still searching through a book, not listening properly, still removed and hovering over the text.

Fatima repeated herself, spat out the words, 'Shot her!' I didn't notice the change in her manner, and spoke as if to the book. 'Yeah, that's right. Yeah, something like that. I've only read this book once, so lots of things I forget, from it.'

'I never read it,' said Fatima. 'I can't read, so good.'

Her voice sounds dispirited. She would have looked around the room, and through the window to the mango trees in the front yard as I continued, still, skimming across the pages. I said, 'Yeah, when I read it I didn't know any of the names, so I don't remember it very well.'

Fatima grunted, 'No?' and yawned. She said, 'It's not in this book but, the shooting, not in this mission book.'

I found the passage I'd been searching for. And never followed up the story of that particular shooting. My voice is soft. 'They gave her a scarf, not a dress. Yeah.'

Fatima gave a little sigh. 'Yeah.' She shifted herself on the chair, lifted her breasts with her hands, and then let them fall as she sighed again.

I realised she had been telling me all along that it was not a dress. I had ceased skimming the pages, and had settled. I said, 'That's what you said, isn't it?'

She nodded shortly, once, and her chin remained on her throat. 'Red one, yeah.' And then, surprising me, she rippled her fingers in a wave, and said, 'Read.'

I paraphrased from the book. 'There were three Aborigines. There was the Father with some boys. This is a long time ago.'

Fatima agreed. 'Yeah. Yeah. This is really old. I don't remember, my mummy told me.'

I continued. 'And they saw three Aborigines on the other

side of the river. The Abbot ordered two of the boys to go and bring them across to him. They only got one, who came with them, not scared or anything. The Abbot gave her the scarf and she put it around her shoulders.'

Fatima grunted in confirmation of the story so far. I continued to paraphrase.

'She followed them to where they stopped to have something to eat and drink. They gave her some meat and bread which she took but wouldn't eat.' I stopped and said to Fatima, 'That's like what you told me the other day, people didn't know what bread was, they took it to be polite.'

Fatima laughed, 'Yeah, and we thought rice was maggots. People thought these white ones was ghosts, we thought them monks in their habits was like djimi from the caves; white skin, you know, and black clothes floating around them.'

On the tape you can hear my voice becoming more animated. Each time I paused Fatima murmured for me to continue.

'After the meal, she just kept watching them. She just kept watching them like this.' I remember this well. I stared at Fatima, then turned my face slowly, keeping my gaze upon her the whole time. It is not like me to do such a thing, and I was surprised at how positively Fatima reacted to it. I continued to mime as I read. 'Her eyes without resting on any one of us in particular kept moving one to another.'

I paused and said to Fatima, 'She was probably really frightened.'

Fatima's hands were clasped at her chest. 'Yeah yeah,' she said, nodding vigorously. And then, suddenly, we both burst into laughter. I think we were enjoying the re-creation of the story. It is hard to explain this. We were like two demigods perched on a mountain top, or cloud, and the two of us narrating a story as it was simultaneously performed by the tiny mortals far below us.

Fatima stopped laughing and said, quietly and seriously, 'She was frighten I think.'

We were silent for a moment. Human.

I continued, paraphrasing. 'After they'd had their food they said you can go. They gave her some more food and supplies and said, "You can go." '

'Mmm,' mumbles Fatima. She does this often, you can hear it softly on the tape, both to encourage me to continue and to confirm the truth of what I am saying.

'They tried to tell her that they'd be happy to see her come back with some of her family. And then she went away quietly, and she looked happy, they thought. Later on she came back. Instead of three or four Aborigines, there were lots of them.

'The Abbot, and Fathers and that went up to them, showing they were friendly, giving them meat and bread and things like that …

As I was giving these things out I noticed they were becoming more restless and even daring. Twisting, turning, and jumping from place to place, upsetting any order that could have been expected in the group.

I paused, and looked at Fatima. I shifted around in my chair, to show the twisting, turning, jumping. Fatima nodded vigorously.

I counted twenty-six. Only five women, no old people, no children, the rest all strong, well built, and some very tall. Someone said drop the weapons and they all put their weapons down, about forty steps away and came towards us.

'Yes,' said Fatima, slowly.

I qualified what I was about to read. I was oddly defensive, apologetic. 'And then, this is what they say here. This might not be true, because it's just the way they remember it:

Then we noticed that some of the boys with the Fathers were becoming restless and looking a bit frightened. Four of the aborigines went back to where they'd left their spears.

Fatima was enthralled.

Peter, one of the boys, came up to the Abbot saying, 'Father, they want war.' Then the Abbot realised that he was right. They had circled us.

'Yep, make a circle.' Fatima sounded impatient for me to continue.

'Then one of the Fathers. No, it's one of the boys. Liandes, Lianches ...' I attempted to pronounce the name.

'You mean Lianjes,' said Fatima.

'Huh?' I asked. I couldn't hear the sound correctly, let alone re-create it.

'Lianjes,' she said, impatiently.

'Liantes. Liandes. I can't say it.' I sound confused. I was, and I was offended by Fatima's curt correction. 'Anyway, you should be telling stories, not me.'

Fatima smiled when she realised the turnabout in our roles. She offered, 'Well, you read it first. I'd like to get your … words you see. I'd like to get those words.'

I was placated. 'Okay. You want me to read through it all? And I'll just change, you know, I'll just make sense of it.'

Fatima nodded again, keen to continue and to smooth my ruffled ego. 'Yes, oh yes. Yeah.'

'So … Nothing. There were about thirty Aborigines who'd taken part in the attack. That's it. No one mentions the woman here, Fatima.'

She slumped, and grinned wryly. 'No. 'Nother time, too, there was a fight. Big fight like a war, you know, in the mission itself. They talk about that in that book there?'

'Yes, I think so. When the men attacked the mission with spears? There was something about it. The Fathers didn't know why. They thought it was for food, or women, or just nastiness. They fought them off, and they were real exhausted. They were bruised and battered. And very frightened for a long time.'

Fatima shook her head grimly. 'In the mission, in the mission itself, the dog came. They had fish, cooking and frying them. And the dog came on one of the person, on one of the man from there, Father or somebody. They shot it. Shot it. They thought it was …'

I supplied the word, 'Wild.' Now I was the one impatient to hear the story.

'… dingo, you know. Wild dingo.' She graciously incorporated my word into her narrative. 'So they shot it. And the people, they say, "Oh, they kill my dog." This person say they kill my dog. And they all round them up, big mob, and one of the mans throw a spear and got Father Vega here.' She poked her finger into her thigh, and repeated the word. 'Here.' We both looked at her finger as she repeatedly jabbed herself with it.

'Yes, I read that. The Fathers were very frightened.'

'I wasn't born yet,' said Fatima, 'they told me, the old people, when I was little.'

'In the book they didn't say anything about the dog being killed.'

Fatima shrugged, 'Yeah, well.'

'They didn't mention that.' I laughed.

Fatima laughed with me, then stopped. She said, suddenly in earnest, 'I am just telling you. Because I know, because people told us. Father Rosenda told us once, about what it said in his book, about what was happening in there and it was not right. We didn't say, but …'

On the tape you can hear my excitement as I continue, attempting to pick up the line of her thoughts, 'Yeah, see that's why I want to talk to you, and the others maybe, because the book doesn't … it just tells you what one eye saw, they don't tell you the background, like about the dog …'

Fatima said, curtly, 'Yeah, because they don't want to.'

I considered it a moment and returned it as, 'Well, they don't know. They don't want to, and they don't know.'

Fatima accepted this. 'They don't know. The dog came in because they were cooking whitings, and that dog smelled the fish and he came to them. And they shot one dog from that man. There was a big fight in there and they was shooting, shooting, shooting …' Her voice trailed off. 'You know, firing?' It seems she felt unsure of herself, talking like this. And it hurt, imagining it again.

'And got some of our people in the leg. But they didn't know. So one man got the spear and he killed Father here, right here.' She pounded her chest. 'Father Garaldi. So he was wounded, and he went to his home monastery and he died in there.'

It's hard to say. Dislocated? Yes, I felt dislocated by her tone, her sincerity, the nervousness she displayed in talking about this. And, suddenly, still calmly seated at the table, and with the pages fluttering about us, it was as if we were both wrapped in her memory and ascending into the stratosphere like one of those paintings of the Ascension in one of Liz's books.

But no. Not yet. There may have been a small jolt. Fatima shifted in her chair.

'Well, it should be like I say it in that book,' she continued. 'That book might tell you different, this one or this one might tell you 'nother way.' She pointed to the books on the table. 'If you find it, it might tell you that way. So I tell people, like I do now, to you, the right way it happened. The true way, and what we people think. You can do that too, maybe.'

'I hope so.' Quietly.

'But you might find lies in this book. Or you might find things true. I don't know which one, in this book maybe. I don't know, because we don't read sometimes, you know. We only go by the pictures to see. Some of us are not really fond of reading, see? Some are not true, what he says, the books.' She patted one of the books on the table before us. 'These ones, you can have it because I got too many libraries in my room.'

'Wonderful,' I said, 'thank you Fatima, wonderful.' It seemed a significant offering.

'You can have it.' She patted the books before her. 'You know more better, you. You might read. And this tape machine, I take that eh? I can listen on it, maybe do some talking on it. You can write what I say, what we say, all together. Some of us? So people will read it, and know.'

'If I can Fatima, if I can. I'll write it. Yeah, I'll do that.'

I helped her down the stairs. She leaned on me and we walked to her home slowly, at her pace. I left her at her door with her dogs leaping all around her, and strode home through the school grounds.

I was taking huge strides, barely able to keep myself from breaking into a run, and leaping for the joy I felt within me. I felt I was about to take off, and soar. That's what I thought, even then.

Communion

A knock at the door. The child Beatrice stood there, puffing. 'Aunty Fatima said to come now.' Urgent, arms swinging from her shoulders, trying not to run on the spot. Excited.

'Come in Beatrice.'

Beatrice came into the kitchen, looking around and up, at the cupboards, the clean stove, the jars of spices.

'It's cool in 'ere, eh? Mr Seddum's house cool too, like this one. I been there.'

She leaned her chest against the kitchen counter and ran her palms along its top. Beatrice watched her hands circle and skate and spoke, suddenly, to Liz.

'Aunty Fatima said, Aunty Fatima said you bring some plates and like you have, like gardiya have with soup, you know, you say, spoons and stuff.'

I moved and stood beside Liz. On the other side of the kitchen counter we could see only Beatrice's head and arms. She was a glove puppet performing.

Then she swirled before us, was transformed in the open space beside the door, and left. She leapt from the back verandah, her long skirt like a sail filling on the mast of her bare black body, and skimmed across the grass to the gate. She turned and called back, 'Youse are eating at Fatima's aren't you tonight, and she's got food for you?' She ran back to us. 'Hurry up she said I was to get you and to hurry up.'

We walked across the small school grounds, the grass under our feet soft and still wet from the afternoon rain, and Beatrice running ahead and back and all of us laughing in the warm moist air as the sun crashed and slowly exploded.

The school gate was locked. We climbed over it and jumped into the red dirt on the other side. Beatrice grabbed Liz's hand as if to lead her. Before us was a corridor of corrugated iron huts, and scattered in front of each were blankets, pieces of foam mattress, and a few old beds with wire bases. Long green grass grew beside and between the huts, away from the walkways. Scrawny dogs curled up near the bedding growled as we walked past. There were old tins and plastic, large stinking turtle shells, and fires flickering here and there. Behind, coconut palms were silhouetted against a sky darkening and growing stars.

Fatima lived close to the school and next to Milton's family. Milton was the school gardener that Murray had said was a good worker. His old Hilux was parked on the track between his family's and Fatima's hut. A gas lantern perched upon the car's tailgate gleamed in the deepening twilight.

'Good evening.' Milton's voice came softly from the shadows, the deepening darkness of a hut door.

'G'day Milton. You eating with us?'

'No, no …'

Beatrice released Liz's hand and, two steps ahead, said, 'Wait,' shouted, 'Fatima I got 'em.' Liz and I stood holding hands, smiling bemusedly. Beatrice leaned against the tall fence around Fatima's hut and, with her nose and fingers through the chicken wire and creeper, talked to the excited dogs barking at her from the other side. The fence sagged a little further with her weight, and rocked back as the dogs leapt against it.

Fatima stood on the concrete at the door of her hut. 'Billy, Liz, you are here. Shut up Patches. Fat Boy I'll sting you. You wait there, near that table, there. Milton you see.'

The dogs cringed around her. I turned and saw, in the lamplight, a card table erected on the sand. Between it and the Hilux sat an old man, cross-legged, on the ground. A woman lay on her side beside him. Milton's voice rushed ahead of him as he approached. 'You eatin' with Fatima tonight eh? This is my father, Sebastian, and my mother, Victoria.'

Sebastian reached out. We shook hands. Victoria turned to us, nodded, mumbled hello. Liz kneeled on the edge of the blanket which Victoria lay upon, and Victoria moved to give her more room. I sat on the ground before Sebastian. We made a sort of small circle beside the card table. Dots, a short line, a square.

Milton crouched with us. He said, 'My father could tell you lots of stories.' Looking at his father he pointed toward me with his lips, then continued, 'This fella likes stories, you never know no one like it.'

Victoria looked at the crumpled comic pages by her side and folded them up into the pocket of her skirt.

'Yes,' I said, 'Fatima's been talking to me about the old days and the old people and that.'

Sebastian's cigarette had gone out, and he placed it behind his ear. His face was lit by the lamp in a way that made his eyes dark holes in his face, his cheekbones high and taut. Despite the awkward light I saw the cigarette butt fall from his ear and catch in his white hair as if in a spider's web, or, in that light, a tattered halo. Victoria shifted onto her hip and glanced at a magazine picture she had taken from her pocket. She tore around its edge, tidying it, and put it away. We cast glances out of the circle.

'Get out! Get out dogs, down! Somebody get this gate now.' Fatima, with oven tray held high, had one of the children who drifted in the darkness around us open the wire mesh gate and let her through. She placed the black enamel dish gently down on the table. The child leaned against the closed gate, watching. Another small shadow came up, perhaps two.

'Fatima, did you, it's great, did you cook this?'

Sebastian clucked his tongue and rocked gently on his haunches, his shaking hand slightly raised. Victoria sat up. We all gazed at the dish which held roast chicken and vegetables.

'No,' Fatima laughed. 'I got, the Sisters, they cooked it for me. I got no oven here and they did it for me. I asked them. I knew you were coming and I wanted good food for you. I asked you. I told that girl Stella for mother, to tell you … You got plates and … we haven't got, so you go first and …'

Liz and I had each brought a soup bowl, dinner plate, and knife, fork, and spoon. The others had no utensils. So we all ate with our hands.

Figures went by on the edge of the lamplight, and came from the darkness between the fires flickering further down the alleyway. Some called out, but Sebastian, Fatima, or Victoria grunted at them and they disappeared. Once or twice an older person came into the circle of light, had a mouthful of our food, and left. Milton joined us in the meal, but only after much insistence on the part of Liz and myself.

Sebastian had some disease, and his hands shook uncontrollably. He spoke more and more, as the night wore on, of old times, and of the mission.

Fatima brought out a watermelon shell filled with fruit salad. We used the bowls and spoons Liz and I had with us for this. Liz and I ate first, then the others, using the same utensils.

'Me, Walanguh, some other fellas, we got rid of Father Pujol. He had to go. He was a hard man but he cared for us Aborigines. In the old days them missionaries look after us. They tried I reckon. Over Dresfield way people had gelignite. That politician's mob, they put gelignite up people's bums, yes. True. Blew them up. People was shot.'

Sebastian was a silhouette in the hard lamplight. Shaking, shaking, sometimes almost shimmering as a fire nearby blazed, and the stars so high above him.

'Early days this lot gardiya been shoot 'em Aborigine, you know blackfella? They been shoot 'im and see 'im. Ah, that man drop. White bloke see 'nother one, 'nother Aborigine, and he go to shoot him too. He running running and the white bloke go to shoot.

'Bang! Bang! Not the gun shooting, a bang like a big bomb, and that Aborigine bloke disappeared. Gone! That was Walanguh that one, Walanguh when he was young, eh?' He looked at Fatima who nodded and grinned her confirmation. 'He had the power that fella. That dead one, Dada that was, nothing. He had no power. With power, they can disappear, fly, you know. Sing things.

'Early days they been make magic. They can sing lightning too. Anything.'

Fatima had cans of cool drink she'd kept on ice. She and Liz sat at chairs by the card table and drank Coca-Cola. Milton and I prompted Sebastian to continue. He spoke on. The dogs moved in closer to Victoria who drew her finger through the dust and occasionally smiled up at one of us. A young couple somewhere close shouted at one another.

Next morning at school Beatrice ran up to Liz and embraced her. 'You ate supper with Aunty Fatima last night didn't you? You had them things? You had chicken, and potato, and cool drink didn't you?' She looked around at the beaming faces of the other small children around her and then back up to Liz. 'And I came to get you, didn't I?' She hugged Liz tighter.

Rehearsal

In the wet season there were frogs everywhere. They were large and bright green. Their bulging, lidded eyes stared back at us from the toilet bowl, from the steps of doorways, from the tightening black fists of children. Partially submerged, they stared from puddles as if playing at being crocodiles. They were pleasant to look at, but slimy to touch. They disconcerted me. I would crouch to study one, and wonder at the delicate hands, and it would remain motionless and seemingly at peace. I would resolve to feel that slimy skin one more time, and before I had even reached out, the animal would be gone. Such startling and sudden speed. I might see it in mid-leap, thin and stretched, nothing like the complacent squatter I thought I knew.

They climbed into the drainpipes and the guttering and they sang. Their croaking was amplified by the pipes and they seemed to croak all the more because of it, as if intoxicated by their voices and the volume of their improvised solos.

So it was noisy. The frogs. The rain. The bellowing of the stray cattle in the evening. The air-conditioners and overhead fans. The powerhouse with at least one of its three diesel engines growling twenty-four hours a day.

One evening I noticed a steady bass line accompanying the frogs. I walked out into the backyard and realised there was an electric band playing somewhere over near the mission.

There was no moon and the darkness made walking across the uneven ground difficult. Something large moved near me as I fumbled with the gate. A cow. One of the many strays which grazed on the flats around the settlement. This one clumsily stumbled off.

The basketball court was lit with four tall floodlamps. Periodically these would be out of action, and it was often weeks or months before they were fixed again. On this particular night they were working and the atmosphere was so humid that they gave a definite circular glow, as if the very white light was working its way out from the globes in ripples. At either end of the court children and youths leapt and shuffled around a bouncing ball. In this strange moist light they were like shadows, and it was difficult to distinguish them. Some called out a greeting as I walked past, but, what with the ball bouncing, and the band playing so loud, it was difficult to hear what they said. Some people were sitting in the darkness by the community office.

The younger children ran in and out of the darkness, skipping, laughing, tussling, touching me as they ran past. They climbed and leapt the small barbed wire fence beside the old kindergarten, in the mission grounds, where the band was playing. The kindergarten was a low corrugated iron structure in the corner closest to the community office and basketball court. The band was playing under a roofed enclosure extending from the front of the building.

I walked past and up to the gate where the darkness began to gather again. Then I walked back along the fence line and leaned against a children's swing just on the edge of the yellow light cast by a couple of small globes above the band. The sound quality was poor, and loud, but they played competently.

One of the primary school children playing chasey in the dark swooped and leapt into my arms. Beatrice. She put her arms around my neck and squeezed, then hung from my neck with her arms straight and her knees bent to keep her feet off the ground.

'You come for the band, Sir?' She named the men playing: Milton, Alphonse, Bruno, Raphael.

It's not just them boys that play though. They all play, or nearly all. They play all kinds: country and western, rock, some Warumpi Band, Coloured Stone, Archie Roach. All kinds. They play noisy and get the young ones dancing and the frogs singing right along with them.

They all smoking. Bruno he sings mostly. Milton, he bending over his guitar, frowning at it, his big hand wrapped right round its neck. He tickle and strangle it at the one time. Alphonse grinning but serious, waving that guitar sometimes like a gun. And Raphael like angry, angry hitting those drums too hard. If he not careful Brother Tom take them away, practice or no practice.

I saw Jasmine dancing with some of the youths, a couple of them from the high school. They were on the opposite side of the pool of light. They were all dancing energetically, even frantically. Jasmine stood out; her paleness, her clothing. She pirouetted, her skirt swirling high around her. I could see her breasts moving under the strapped, light dress she wore. I thought I could hear her bracelets jangling as she shook her arms and head together, down.

Brother Tom approached from the direction of the church,

walking with his short steps, his slightly stooped posture, as if in supplication. He greeted the dancers, Jasmine especially, and continued on, detouring slightly, to me.

'Hello, Bill.'

'G'day, Brother.'

'They are good aren't they? They play in the church, and after singing practice I let them use the instruments, until nine. To just play, what they want. Then I lock it all up, and they go.'

I walked home and a couple of children who'd been holding my hands slipped away. I could see campfires flickering before some of the huts across the other side of the basketball court. With the band not playing you could hear voices all around, intermingling with the frogs. The powerhouse noise was indistinguishable from here, and, outside, no air-conditioner roared. The floodlights were off.

As I came past the office a voice called, 'Hello, Bill.' There was a group sitting on the ground with their backs against the wall of the office.

'Good evening.'

'You like that music?'

'You like that practice?'

I spoke, briefly, across the darkness, with Fatima, Sebastian, a couple of the other older ones. I couldn't see clearly, and nor could I identify them all by their voices. I wondered if they had been there all evening, listening, watching, talking among themselves.

It began to rain and I entered the roaring house.

And It Pours

Them little kids, half-naked ones, they squatting next to the muddy puddles, black skin shiny with rain. They run with the river, at its edge, past trees caught by that rushing, rising water.

Up on the flat you can see the water there too. It lying in sheets there, that same grey colour like the clouds and the corrugated iron shacks sticking up in the long green grass. The muddy track through the camp is lined with coconut trees all moving, moving angry like they trying to get away.

The little ones catch bush mice and small snakes. They squealing, squealing. There's a willy-willy of children there. Beatrice got a mouse up her dress, she's jumping 'round in excitement. It gets down and out and races off into the grass beneath one of the coconut palms and the kids scatter little bit, then they all spiralling into that clump of grass. Catch it. They pass it from hand to hand. It slips. They all after it. They all laughing, catch it again.

Coming home from cards last night Beatrice saw a shape. She thought it was a coconut. It moved. She jumped high, like a ninja. Snake! But Deslie saw it was a tortoise and he got it. He asked everybody who wanted it. Jimmy's pudda got it and she ate it for supper.

Hear the sound of the rain all the time, tapping and dripping. Wind not so much now. Smell the dirty water, black water where the toilet tanks have overflowed.

The gardiya's new shoes begin to rot already, and their thongs spatter mud over one another. They're talking about the mud everywhere, and the mould on the doors. Will the mail plane get in? What about bread, proper meat? The pays?

Brother Tom and a couple of his boys go down to the water pump to fix it. Then they take kangaroo jacks and shovels to help get the Toyota out of the bog in the school. Silly people trying to move it now, can't go anywhere anyway.

Deslie, Jimmy, Sylvester and that mob wade, chest deep, across to the airstrip and jump and run and wave and yell on the high land there. We saw them.

One time, long time, when we were little bit older than them boys, we, Sebastian, Walanguh, Samson, we went upriver just after flood time. And we went across that river just up near that big paperbark, you know, to hunt kangaroos. We got 'em. We had spears, and Samson, one gun. But that water, 'im come up again, come up again. How we gunna get back? One, two, three kangaroos. And one gun, and them spears. So, Walanguh and Sebastian, they cut down one big tree, long tree. We put the wallabies, the kangaroos on it, the spears, the rifle and that. We put it in the water with us all in a line, along that tree. We were gunna go straight across that river, and down it like in a boat, you know.

Boy, I tell you what, we nearly drowned. We lost everything. Kangaroos, rifle, spears. We all sat there on some safe high land and we did laugh. Laugh.

Just like now, too, we go down to them flats where all the kangaroos, bush turkey, snake, everything come to get out of the water. Take spear, sticks, just bare hands. You grab kangaroo by the tail and swing him 'round and smash his head.

The teachers and the new office mob see all the people going down the track and don't go with them when they're asked because they're too busy. Only that new girl, Jasmine, she goes. They laugh when she pulls away from the catches they show her, but the young men hunt harder, and the women notice her there.

Araselli sees the old Holden panel van in those food days. Everyone does. It's mostly orange but with a few maroon panels. It not ever get out of first gear even. Motor roaring bang bang, going that way along the track, through puddles, past houses, past basketball court, powerhouse. Then back again. All Sunday they did that. Got bogged three times. Ran out of petrol late in the day. Just before dark time.

There were plenty of fellas in that car. Alphonse sat next to Milton, the one that was driving.

Alphonse look up, see Araselli. She see him. They looking, looking deep. It's not right, not by our Law. They rumbud, and they bit worried now, true, because it not first time for them.

They worried all right, but they hungry. Hungry, you know.

Resistance

By Monday the floods had subsided. I was standing before the class, lecturing, when I saw their attention move, as one, toward the south windows, the camp side. Three men rushed out from among the houses, armed with sticks, and began searching in the grass.

'Sir, kangaroos hide.'

'Okay everyone, all eyes to me.' It is embarrassing to recall. I was new. I wanted some control. Eyes wavered toward me. But my attention, too, was out the window where the men were searching through the grass. More men came, and some dogs.

Suddenly a kangaroo broke cover. It was a small one. With its body almost parallel to the ground, and visibly straining for speed, it disappeared from the right side of the frame provided by the classroom windows on that wall. The students leapt from their seats yelling, 'Sir, 'ere, 'im this way!' I had moved to the south windows and was peering awkwardly in the direction the 'roo had disappeared, like a child trying to see within a television screen. They beckoned me from the other side of the room, at the other windows, where the kangaroo, having circled around the western end of the building, could be seen coming from that way, left of screen. Some of my students called again, impatiently, ''Ere!'

'Too boggy for 'im that way,' someone explained, excitedly.

'Go Jamesy. Aiee!'

'Ha ha! Get 'im fat man!'

'Throw it. Now. No. Now!'

A middle-aged man, with his big belly bouncing above his small shorts, chased the kangaroo. He had a large stick in one hand. He threw the stick. It missed. The classroom was noisy with the hooting and shouting and laughter. Some of the older men jogged across the muddy ground, way behind the kangaroo. A pack of their dogs raced past Jamesy, spinning him around like a top with their speed and excited barking.

'Look at 'im. Alphonse! The powerhouse!'

Down by the powerhouse Alphonse, by far the youngest of all these hunters, waited, stick in hand, as the 'roo approached. But his dog broke off toward the 'roo, which veered off at right angles and headed for the scrub further to the north. Dogs now formed two sides of a yapping triangle behind it. Our class was silent for a moment. I had been shouting also.

The dogs' barking grew fainter and they fell out of formation. The men strung out further behind them slowed, and stopped. They mouthed excuses and allocated blame, and the kangaroo disappeared into the scrub. The kids agreed that it had got away.

'Righto, back in your seats.' And they did. We did.

Separation

For our first few months in Karnama we had no vehicle. I fancied we were forted, restrained nomads, waiting for the roads to dry out enough for us to bring in a vehicle of our own. It was stinking hot, so hot that the fifty-metre walk from home to classroom sapped us so that we felt our bones would melt. And Liz and I saw one another, the other teachers, the students, the parents, all the time, everywhere. One of our students, Deslie, turned up at our home at six in the morning a few times in the first weeks asking whether it was time for school to begin yet. We, gummy eyed, half naked, milk and cereal on our lips, mumbled, 'Not yet.'

Father Paul lent the school a four-wheel drive. Alex commandeered it and he, Annette, and young Alan used it to look around, and to get out to the beaches.

On weekend mornings we peeped through our curtains as they rattled and rumbled out of the yard.

'Wish the mission had lent us two vehicles,' muttered Liz. 'Still, maybe they need the break more than us.'

So. On the weekends Liz and I walked to the creeks or the river and swam with the kids. We watched as they used grasshoppers and frogs to catch catfish. We would spend a couple of hours outside and then retreat to the roaring air-conditioning, Liz particularly pink and perspiring. We threw rocks at the coconuts, attempting, with little success, to knock them to the ground. A couple of the kids might shinny up the trees to collect some. The younger children ran and tumbled beside us, pointing at all our shadows, stolid, winking, now different, now the same. Occasionally an older student would question us, but they were shyer, and, although curious, had learnt more. They were pushed away before the stream of incessant chatter and giggles, and the demands of the younger ones tugging our clothes and hair and stroking our skins.

We'd sit inside, looking out the windows at the afternoon rain, the red mud and the intense green, the thin bodies of semi-naked children skimming and spraying through the puddles and sheets of water, their black skins glistening and their cries thin in the thunder. The coconut palms and mango trees in our yard writhed against a great grey sky split by lightning. And the solid rain, and the clearing of the air just before darkness. So I remember it.

It was exotic, but it was claustrophobic too, and when Milton invited Liz and me to a nearby waterfall one weekend we were thrilled. We went in the old Toyota Hilux he'd bought from a previous principal at the school.

Milton was a tall, gentle man, much the same age as myself, thirtyish. When he spoke to you he tilted his head to await a reply, and looked carefully at your eyes. His eyes were soft, and their whites were more of a creamy colour.

He and Alphonse, his cousin-brother, drove us to a waterfall. Liz and I took a picnic meal for the four of us. I was surprised at where a vehicle could go. It scrambled up a rocky slope that must have been an apprentice cliff. From its summit we looked back and saw the different green of the imported trees of Karnama lining the river, and the river's pool glinting there, and the narrowing where the rocks began and the river, compressed, drove its force still, even now, and despite the dry weather we'd had for weeks. And that weather, of course, explained why we could drive, just, to the waterfall. We drove through solid walls of grass too tall for us to see over. It was like being a ghost, going through that grass, except that it bent and parted, rising again behind us and rustling and sighing as it did so.

Then we were there. We peered over from the top of the waterfall. There was only a small rocky creek flowing into it, one we could cross using stepping stones, but the flow was strong. It reached the top of the cliff and shot out, smooth and silver, and poured, roaring, down a five-metre cliff. At its base was a green pool, almost perfectly circular in shape, surrounded with pandanus and strong reeds and rocks. We clambered down the rocky cliff, feeling the waterfall's mist upon us. We sat under the fall, and screamed, and yet were silent in its thundering solitude, and we listened to it drum incessantly on our skulls and flesh. We swam in a deep pool, lay in the cool of the cliffs surrounding the pool, and talked until the light softened.

Milton told us he often came up this way to collect white ochre for some of the community artists to use. 'Snake shit,' he said, 'they say it's snake shit, you know, not ordinary snake shit. You sing when you dig it up, and you leave some. When you come back 'nother time there will be more there. If you sing. That's true,' he insisted, 'I didn't believe, for sure, but I tried it that way. It's true.'

Another weekend we went to a cattle station about twenty kilometres away. It took an hour to get there. Alex and his family followed us. From the back of the ute I watched them sliding and slipping through the mud. Fortunately they didn't get bogged.

Milton pulled up outside the station home. 'Mad bastard this one,' said Milton, and then he and Alphonse were silent. The station manager, a powerfully built man in a stockman's uniform, silenced his barking and snarling dogs as he walked out to us. He and Alex greeted one another and introductions were made. The manager turned to Milton and Alphonse and said, 'You blokes can go down to the single men's quarters if you want to hang around, eh?' Milton and Alphonse nodded and did so. The single men's quarters were about three hundred metres away.

Over tea the manager chortled about how the blacks were frightened of his dogs and how the dogs hated them. He was leaving soon. His wife was silent and watched us with large eyes. He told us the Aboriginal community was taking over the station.

'That'll be one hell of a cock-up,' he snorted. 'I'm hoping that they'll make Ricky the manager, he's a good worker, he's worked with me the past two years and I've taught him what I can. One of the other mob reckons this is their country though, so they'll probably grab it and he won't stick it then.

'Face facts,' he paused, snorted, shook his head. 'It'll be a cock-up. They can't work together, they don't know how to work land like this.'

We all went to a rock pool down the river and lay in the rapidly running water there.

It wasn't until the next day, at school, that I realised

Alphonse had stayed in the water the whole time only because when he first went to leave the water's edge the manager's dog had grabbed him by the ankle of his jeans and only let go when Alphonse returned to deeper water. At the time I'd thought it was just play and had laughed with the others. Alphonse had only grinned at us.

An Artist

The school lessons in traditional dancing, begun so early in the school term and in such a burst of enthusiasm, continued chaotically. The date of the official visit, and the dance, loomed. Previous principals had arranged display dances for important visitors and been promoted out of the school. Alex intended to maintain this tradition. But was he worried? Yes. We were all concerned.

The day of the dance arrived. So did the guests. Two educational advisors for the Aboriginal Development Commission sat in the plastic chairs put out for the occasion, nestling their expensive video cameras in their laps. Gerrard and Father Paul, vying as hosts, sat with them. We teachers busied ourselves organising the children, and attempting to organise the adults. Most of the mission staff were there, as was the storekeeper and a couple of pilots. Those of the local population not directly involved in the dance or the school, stayed away on the fringes, under the trees or leaning on the weary wire fence. To all the visitors, at least, they seemed but thin shadows.

Only the males were to dance. I helped the boys into appropriate dress. Alex had found a heap of 'lap-lap' things in the storeroom, all a uniform colour, which we were using. I got all the young boys into line and led them over to where the adults were, behind another classroom from where they would commence.

Today, unlike the earlier practice sessions, all the adult males had turned up. Alex was anxious. Samson, with his long hair and straggly white beard, seemed the leader. But there was one particularly old man among them. He sat on the ground amid the swirl of painted bodies, grinning and laughing, watching, sometimes scowling and shouting. It was Walanguh, Fatima's husband. I thought his mind must be going, but there was no doubt he was taking a keen interest, and Samson regularly went to him.

Alex shouted at the children, and laughed loudly with the men, slapping them on the back. As the dancing was about to begin he walked away, his clipboard again pounding his thigh, his face grim, and joined the others on the plastic chairs.

I remained, trying to prevent the younger boys from running around too much. Then Samson took over. His yelled orders became more theatrical as he ushered the group from behind the building. Most of the young men were his sons or nephews. The high school boys, with the exception of Deslie, had declined to dance. The older women were singing, clapping their hands, and swaying their hips. Some of the schoolgirls joined in with reluctance and embarrassment, and some just buried their faces in their hands and giggled.

At times Samson reminded me, incongruously, of a character from a music hall comedy as he shouted in a mixture of English and his own language at the others, and acted the part of an old woman, or, most melodramatically, that of a man full of spears. Samson was an entertainer, playing to his audience.

The black and painted bodies ranged from those of five year

olds to aged men. The very old men sat and sang, Walanguh at their centre. The women and girls also sang, rocking rhythmically.

Our two visitors, overweight and soft in their cotton pastels, seemed impressed. They held their cameras erect, their jaws flaccid.

'Who them buggers?' one of the dancers asked as he rested behind the classroom.

'How come gardiya don't dance?' asked Deslie.

Laughing and teasing, the men easily persuaded me to join in the last of the dances. 'All safe ones these, nothing,' Samson told me. I took off my shoes and socks. I felt ridiculously free, pounding my feet among them, seeing, across the shoulders before me, the row of plastic chairs, and the pale furrowed brows sweating in the sun. The sound of the tapping sticks that Walanguh wielded seemed unnaturally loud. Fatima nodded at me.

Samson sat on the step behind the classroom and swore. 'I'm a dancer, man! An artist, you know. I need to be paid!' His long grey hair swung as he shook his head in disgust. 'Who them half-castes with cameras, eh? They show that film somewhere, good for them, eh? Maybe make some money, and laugh at us. We stupid blackfellas dance for them. That other principal, last year, he pay us. What's wrong with this fella, eh?'

I was embarrassed. I didn't know. I said I didn't know.

'Well that went all right then.' Alex was so relieved, and surprised, that he couldn't quite make a decisive statement. He was shifting sprinklers around the grounds when I met him in the late afternoon. 'Bit of trouble with that old bastard Samson though,' he continued. 'Thought he was going to have a go at me for a bit. They reckon they want to keep their culture going, and use school time and that, but then they want to get paid for it. Bloody hypocrites! We won't pay 'em. They gotta play the game, do the right thing.'

'Yeah. It's complex, it's a problem …' I began.

Alex drew himself up to his full height and pulled his head back on his shoulders in that strange way he had, of moving like a stringed puppet. He was shirtless in the late afternoon heat. He pulled in his stomach, tilted his head to one side, and pointed a finger at me. 'Well don't you worry about that. It's my problem. You just get that class of yours busy, and learning. Working hard, you know, go go go!' He mimed a student apparently copying notes from the board. 'I'll deal with the community, and these shifty bastards like Samson.'

We may Fly and Sing

Sebastian and Fatima came to the school late one afternoon. The room which Liz and I were in at the time overlooked an expanse of the schoolyard over which they would have walked, but neither of us noticed them until we heard a cough and looked to see them standing in the doorway.

A third person stood between the two of them. A young woman. Her make-up was obvious, both because it was unusual to see it used in this community, and because it was so generously applied. Her clothing was evidently new, and clung to her thin body. She stood facing slightly away, only turning to squarely face us as her name was spoken. She trailed one hand on the doorframe as she entered the room. She was silent for most of the conversation, and, as Liz said afterwards, it was hard to determine whether this was because of her diffidence, or her disinterest.

As soon as we were introduced I recognised the name. Gabriella. Fatima and some of the students had spoken of her. As far as I could work out she had been raised by the Sisters at the mission after her mother was killed. She'd attended a primary school in Perth, but had suddenly, in her adolescence, started getting into trouble and had been shifted from school to school until she had come back to live with Fatima. The Sisters had wanted her to be a nun, and still spoke of their disappointment in her. She had helped in the school here for a few years, and Father Paul had arranged for her to go to university in Melbourne. He knew people there she could board with, and there were special bridging courses available. Gabriella had, apparently, wanted to become an accountant, or a teacher, and to come back to Karnama and live in a house like those the teachers had.

Sebastian said he wanted a woodworking plane. He was making a didgeridoo. We went over to the school workshop to get one, leaving Liz in that classroom full of books.

Gabriella asked me about the tapings I was doing with Fatima. I said that I intended transcribing them for the students to read, when I could find time. And that I simply enjoyed listening, and the idea of writing them up attracted me.

Fatima brought out the small tape recorder I'd lent her, saying that she usually kept it with her. The batteries were flat. We put new batteries in it and I inserted a fresh cassette. Sebastian said, 'So, just turn 'im on and speak?' And he did. Well, the two of them did. And occasionally I, and less often Gabriella, prompted them.

But, later, when I read some of this aloud to the students, trying on the voices, they listened closely and were attentive to the text. They grinned at one another. Sometimes they recognised the original speaker. 'He sounds like ...'

All these stories I tell you happened in true life. Old people used to have black magic. They used to kill or destroy anybody. Or they used to find out what animal killed that bloke and then go after it and kill it, you know. They dream it. They go and they sleep and they dream it and they go kill that thing, crocodile or shark or whatever.

Like Walanguh, maybe. His daddy had the power, that's for sure. When I was a boy I saw that for myself. One bloke, in Pako, he was proper bitten by shark, and you could see the bone in his legs. He pass away, after a time he pass away.

And that old man, the one who is father for Walanguh, he dream he catch that shark. That same shark that bite the man. In his dream he been catch that shark with a big fishing line, and he pull him in all the way, all the way up the beach. High and dry. It was a big one, very long and heavy.

He told the people after, in the morning, 'You go to that beach by barge landing and you see the big shark there.' And all the people, all of them, missionaries with them too, all the people went there. They went to the beach and they saw that big shark laying on the beach. Dead.

Old people, they had that power.

And he die too, that man. Long time, he die. Father of Walanguh. He was a flying fox up Dresfield way. He make himself a flying fox and he there, hanging in that tree next to the river. But maybe he stay like that too long, or stop thinking proper. And a crocodile get him. A big crocodile swim across and wait for him to fall, get him, eat him up.

Walanguh went up there. He was a young man — this is long time you know — he was a young man, strong and laughing all the time. But he stop in the middle of his laughing one day, and he went away upriver and he saw the tracks of his father. He found the tracks of his father, and then, no tracks. He saw flying fox there, biggest mob. He say, 'Oh, my father been here.'

And he look, and he see the spirit of his father sitting on top of that crocodile. Sitting on that crocodile back just like sitting on a log in the water. That dead man show himself like that. So

Walanguh say, 'Ah, that's the one.'

He went back here, he tell all the people, 'Crocodile eat my father.'

All right. Night-time come. He been sleeping. And he dream. He dream he grab that crocodile with a big fishing line, and he walk that crocodile, he been pull him all the way to the marsh and leave him there in the sun, upside down.

Walanguh, he wake up and say, 'Crawl through those little trees at that marsh and see. Maybe crocodile in there.'

Well, they have a look. They see crocodile lying there with swollen guts. And they been find bones, everything in that crocodile guts.

Old days people could make magic. That's true. That's no story, it's true story.

The old people they had a lot of magic in them.

They even fly in the air. Sometimes like a balloon, a bird, like a snake, even just like themselves. And sometimes they have a real snake crawling on the ground and magic one flying above it. And you be watching that snake flying overhead and you wouldn't know a real one is on the ground following it. On the ground just having to come across and bite you.

And when they fly you usually feel the wind blowing, you know. A nice cold wind. Then you know that someone is flying to kill somebody. They usually do that flying in the night, to kill someone, because they can't look down at own shadow. Not even allow to fly when it's moonlight. They fly when it's big dark, no moon around. Special times, or a powerful one, like one who can make himself invisible, maybe he fly just 'bout anytime.

Or they sing a song, you know, a magic song. Then a bloke has an accident in a car, or somebody just has to get silly and hit 'im on the head with a rock and kill 'im. All this they still use today, people like old Walanguh maybe. So there's still a lot around, mainly when everybody get drunk and fight with somebody and hit the wrong fella and then a bloke find out one of his family is dead or the whole family find him dead. So all these stories are true. They still do it today and they try keep getting their culture growing more strong. When they do all this Law stuff, initiation stuff, they get stronger from that too.

Now, maybe initiate bit different. Them young boys, Deslie and them, we send them to hospital to get cut, you know. And ones like Gabriella — girls can make our future too, you know — they wanted her be a Sister for the mission. But she getting educated her own way now. So, maybe the way's bit different to the way we accepted. It's hard to say. We believe there's two, three steps that you gotta go.

But there's not so much around now. It's harder now. Now some people still have their magic, but they don't see anybody looking for trouble with them. They don't see anybody killing one of their family, or breaking big laws. It's not just simple now. There be all kinds of little things. Maybe someone did a bit wrong this way, but he did it because of this other thing, or another way he did good. Or he be just young, or silly. And some of the young people start not believing. Then they do anything, have nothing.

Not just young ones doing anykind. Old ones too. Francis, Franny, you know him have Moses for father? Well, Moses not really his father, he just act like he is. And he love him like a father. That boy not right, you know. Understand? Well his father, real father, he no longer with us here. So ... that's why Franny be like that, like he is. Little boy with a big body, not right and bit silly. Can't see too good and little bit deaf too.

That happens when people got no respect and don't listen to what they're told to, understand?

I looked at Gabriella; her jaw clenched, her stare not here.

But Who's Tellin' this Story?

That short teacher bloke, he bit like us, but — he Nyungar or what? Look at him, he could be. Why's he wanna know things?

He get to school proper early anyway, sun-up even. Sebastian, he say he see him then at the school. Sebastian just sitting making fire, you know, making tea. He see him.

He get one of the kids with him, go out and get the lazy kids that still sleeping. Lazy those kids. Their mums, dads, still sleeping. That teacher, what's him name? Billy? He goes and he gets 'em, the big ones mostly, them boys over in Moses' house.

Dry season: early morning cool, and I left the first footprints in the dew on the lawn. More and more appeared, those footprints increased until there were tracks everywhere, criss-crossing dark green on the silver sheen of the dew.

Deslie was usually the first of the high school kids to arrive. Our prints intersected at the door of the classroom.

A siren sounded each morning, just before seven, to signal that it was almost time to start work. School started at seven. Kids would arrive dream mumbling, stiff legged and stumbling, knuckling their puffy eyes.

Many of the young people wore bracelets made from the rubber sealing rings of opened fuel drums. Pieces of coloured cloth would be knotted around thighs, wrists, or worn as headbands. Fashions changed as far as they could according to what was worn on the videos and what was available in such a small community. Everyone liked to wear bits of army uniform they got from brothers or cousins — it was only ever males — who'd been away with Norforce, the Army Reserve.

We often went to wake the students to get them to school. The school staff discussed whether to begin school at a later time, especially in the dry season when the mornings were cool. It was not like the past when the mission generator supplied electricity and Brother Tom would turn off the generator soon after dark. Now many of the students sat up late watching videos. Some of the newer houses were even air-conditioned. We decided not to change the school hours. Alex pointed out the need to learn to work to the clock. And there were advantages to having long afternoons, especially once we got television reception, courtesy of a satellite dish donated to us because of our status as the most isolated school in Australia. The teachers' houses were incorporated into the school connection.

One particular morning I sat at my desk in the classroom and watched Deslie push open the gate which led to the high school area. It leaned on its hinges and had strands of barbed wire on its upper section. It was difficult to open. Deslie struggled only a little, evidence of years of practice.

He got to the classroom door and stopped. Slowly the door opened and his head appeared around its edge at about waist height. He grinned from his crouched position as he saw me looking at him. He put on his school T-shirt.

'Use the computer sir?' The students took to the computers enthusiastically, especially before school when we let them play games.

A few more students arrived. They read comics, played guitar or Scrabble, or took a basketball outside. Just before seven a.m. I said, 'Let's go, Deslie.' It had become a routine with us.

'Get the other kids, Sir? Sleepy ones?'

'Yep. Children hunting.'

'Sylvester and that mob playin' basketball late last night, Sir. I came home sleepy and they still there. And when it was cold last night, you know, Sir, cold, I found myself a good spot. Good warm spot. I went into the cupboard, you know the one Sir? Big one, and pulled all the clothes over me and shut the door. Nice and warm and quiet.'

Suddenly he said, 'Sir, know what? Yesterday I was walking along, just walking walking. I was thinking of a snake, and I looked and there was a snake. There! Right in front of me. True!'

He commented on who lived where as we passed different huts and houses and if any of the kids were sleeping in a different place from a few days ago. Occasionally he'd shout at a snarling dog and it would slink away, looking back at us. Most of the dogs were silent and merely watched us pass. Some tails wagged.

The housing consisted mostly of corrugated iron huts built decades ago. Each hut sat on a concrete pad and had a smaller building out the back, usually with a piece of hessian or a blanket thrown across its doorway. This was the toilet, and sometimes there was a shower there also. At a couple of separate locations, one by the river and one by the creek, there was a group of tiny huts, each barely large enough to shelter a single body, which were used, at an even earlier date, as accommodation. They were only ever actually slept in when it rained heavily. Some of the very oldest people used them still. Apparently there was also a deserted site across the river. Fatima told me she used to stay over there when she was younger, until the mission successfully discouraged it. Walanguh, her husband, still liked to go over there whenever he was well enough.

Most of the huts had the ashes of a fire, some rubbish, a few blankets, and perhaps an old mattress, or an old wire bed that doubled as seating, spread before them. Sometimes there would be a family group sitting around a fire drinking tea from small food cans. We'd say good morning, speak for a little while, and agree that the kids would be at school soon.

There were also newer houses, like the one Deslie stayed in. They were standard urban bungalows and not altogether appropriate to the climate or the inhabitants. But they were larger, and more prestigious.

One hut we walked past, near a large tree under which important card games took place, had an old woman living in it who sometimes screamed with pain in the night. This morning she sat in the dirt in front of her hut, warming herself in the sun. She stared vacantly into space, her toothless mouth open. She rubbed one plump arm with the other and her breasts hung to the dirty grey blanket wrapped around her lower body. She did not respond to us as we walked by. Deslie glanced at me to see if I was looking at her.

When we were well past Deslie grabbed my arm and whispered, 'Devil lives in that house. She got him, that what they say. See that big tree back there? Casino?' He smiled at the joke. 'They heard the devil there the other night. And she makes devil noises at night-time.' He watched me closely to see how I reacted. No wonder she had the hut to herself.

I nodded and said, 'Where will these boys be? All at one house still?'

'Mostly Uncle Moses' house, Sir. One crazy dog there.'

We stopped at the back door of Moses' house. A number of the older boys and younger men stayed here. The older girls and young women lived in houses over the other side of the village. Deslie shooed a few dogs away. 'Where that crazy one?' he whispered. He waved me back and went cautiously ahead, a few steps, into the house. I followed, several steps behind, equally cautiously. The house had no coverings on the grimy cement floor, and was unfurnished. Deslie stopped at the end of the short passage and, putting only his head through the doorway, peeped into the living room. He tiptoed back toward me, his finger to his lips and his eyebrows raised expressively. He disappeared into a room and re-emerged with a blanket. I saw him step quickly into the living room and throw the blanket like a cast net. There was the sound of a dog snarling, and the snarling turned to yelping as Deslie, kicking at a four-legged blanket, entered and exited across the frame provided by the doorway. A deep male voice called out, 'Gedoutmongrel!'

Deslie looked back, a grin splitting his face, and waved me into the room. The dog, now free of the blanket, was cringing outside. The entire floor, apart from in the kitchen area, was taken up by sleeping bodies. Bruno lay propped up on one elbow under a grimy blanket. He nodded at me, and then rolled over to face the wall and return to sleep. It must've been he who yelled at the dog when Deslie came in kicking at it.

Sylvester was in the food-spattered kitchen. He stood before the stove watching a blackened saucepan warming. It moved me, oddly, seeing this tall boy, his face still emerging from his dreams, look at me with surprise and even something like fear on his face. He was very rarely late for school.

'Come on Sylvester, you should be at school, mate.' I spoke softly.

He put on a show of confidence and replied in a croak, 'Just makin' tea, Sir.'

I began to move around the room lifting the corners of blankets from over heads. 'Oops, sorry mate, you're not one of the school kids.' Eyes closed again gratefully. 'Sorry mate, I'm looking for school kids. But you should be at work by now anyway, eh?' The faces lifted and frowned, smiled sleepily, closed eyes, and returned to the horizontal. Alphonse walked into the room looking dazed. He nodded a greeting, mumbled something about no sleep, and lay down in a corner.

Deslie stared at him for a moment, then continued looking through the bodies under the thin blankets and coats. He whispered loudly, 'Sir, here's Franny. Get up Franny! School. Sir's here.' Deslie was happy.

Sylvester looked into my face. 'I thought it was early still.' I patted his elbow. 'For you, no worries. But you gotta get there now, eh?'

I stepped over the bodies to where Deslie and Francis were. 'Come on, Francis. Time for school, mate, you should be there.' I had to speak loudly because of his poor hearing. He fumbled for his thick-lensed, smeared spectacles. 'We'll give you tea and something when you get there.' I tried to be stern, but it was ridiculous really. And upsetting. They might have been up all night, dropping in and out of sleep. Watching videos. Or playing cards. Or, a large group like this, just talking and telling stories.

It was better walking back to school, in the warming sun, with the boys waking and starting to want to talk and help me spot other kids who were late to school. Deslie whispered, 'Alphonse been with Araselli, Sir.' His eyes were large.

You see them. Teacher out front and them boys sleepy walking behind him sort of in a line waking up. He turn his head back and talking soft to them. He get 'em there. He's all right that fella, good teacher. He Nyungar, or what. Is he?

Someone, maybe Geoffrey, might yell out to him. 'Hey you! Sir. Teacher. Mr Storey. Billy! Beatrice here.' Or, 'Jimmy here. Get to school you!' He laugh, and say, 'Well you get them to school then.' He might point his thumb at them big school boys with 'im and say, 'I got my flock.' Them boys smiling then too.

Walk past that Djanghara mob, they all sitting there and Albert, he not at school no more, he yell out, 'Sir! Cyril here!' and Cyril he act grumpy and don't wanna go to school. He walk out soon enough, walking slow but, and get in that anykind line and he nearly smiling by then with everyone watching him like that. They get to school, and Sebastian he's seen 'em, they're not lined up, they're all round that teacher bloke then, talking touching 'im, that Bill.

His missus, she go and get the big girls sometimes. That other teacher, boss one, he gets the little kids when he goes with 'em on the basketball court and does exercises. Run around the camp singing out for the lazy ones with all the kids running behind him singing out too, copying him. Noisy ones, them.

Ah yes. And that Alphonse and Araselli. You know, Alphonse, that tired one back there. Deslie see him. It's no good, they been together. Everyone know, even young ones like Deslie. She be getting big belly.

Confirmation

After school finished each day most of the students worked for a couple of hours in the mission gardens. After they had finished there some of the older schoolboys would often come over to the school for the remaining few hours of daylight. They came to play guitar, or fix their bicycles in the workshop, and to talk a little. Francis came to sit in the air-conditioned classroom and draw pictures. He drew comic heroes, and characters from popular films whose muscles rippled and oozed violence. He was a quiet and dreamy boy.

The day after I had first met Gabriella I stayed late at school with some of the students who had decided not to work that afternoon in the mission garden. Sylvester came on his BMX. It astonished me that such a tall boy could ride one without chipping away his elbows and knees. He wanted to do some work on it, probably further raise the seat and handlebars. Francis wanted to draw an Aboriginal version of Arnold Schwarzenegger, or Robocop. Deslie looked at comics.

When I got home Liz, Fatima, and Gabriella were there, talking. Fatima had brought Gabriella over earlier that afternoon. Gabriella had a lot of reading to do while she was on holidays, she said. On previous occasions she had gone over to the mission to read. The church was good during the day, but hot.

She liked it in Melbourne. She had friends there, and a

tutor who was very kind. She got homesick the first year, but Father Paul had told her off and frightened her so that she couldn't go home. And then he had brought Fatima to see her after they had been to see the Pope in Alice Springs. That had helped make her stay. And she was glad. That's true. She said she was glad now.

Liz invited her to visit the school while we were holding classes. She could come and go as she wished. She was a good role model, and helpful in many ways.

She arranged to join the older students for sessions in traditional handicrafts, which was when some of the community elders came and worked with the students doing slate and boab nut carvings, making tapping sticks and didgeridoos, or designing silk-screens based on the rock paintings in the area. Not surprisingly, most of us enjoyed the time spent collecting materials, but, until Gabriella volunteered her services and joined us, many of the students were reluctant participants. As Sylvester voiced most strongly, 'This is stupid, this is blackfella stuff', and got Sebastian shouting and shaking with the desire to strike him.

When Gabriella participated it helped the students consider it worthwhile. She was very skilled. Her slate engravings were extremely detailed, the many intricate lines rendering life and depth, and she produced different hues by her use of the various ochres and by scratching to different depths. She worked quietly.

'I like it,' she told us. 'At uni too, I can do painting. It's like this. I get sucked in, and I forget time and where I am. You know, one day I might paint me a little island, a little place for me to live in there. Fly down into it, just go of the end of my brush, and stay there, eh?'

And sometimes, in the evenings, she came to visit Liz and I.

Once or twice she even came to read some of the stories and poems she'd written for her English classes to the students. She liked English classes, she said. She liked writing poems. She wrote a lot of poems about Karnama and what it looked like — you know, the waterfalls in the wet, and the river, and when you were flying in after a time away, and the mangroves on the beach as the tide was coming late in the day.

She said they gave her Aboriginal Literature to read. Her voice inserted quotation marks. She said it was dreaming stories, and they weren't so good to read, not like being told them. Or they were in a language that she didn't understand and then in English which made them sound silly, or as if they were only for little children. Or it was history stuff. Or sometimes just like any old story, but with black people. Or off-white people. We laughed.

We agreed that English as people spoke it here was good for talking, and that the old people told stories well. But it wasn't so good for writing, maybe? There were not enough words, different words. You needed to hear the voice. And other people couldn't do that so well. And you needed other things; like hands waving in space, and lips pointing, and drawings in the sand.

Liz suggested Gabriella might like to work on her assignments and do her reading in our house during the day while we were at school.

Gabriella said that each time she came back to Karnama after a time away she was happy, because she missed the people and the country so much. But she was sad too. In the late afternoon she might sit on the barbecue near the basketball court, and the paper wrappings and plastic bags blew around her with the dust. She played basketball with her old friends, and the others liked to beat her to demonstrate how Karnama was good for you. But it was like going backwards sometimes, and even further backwards each time she met up with old friends. The bridging course she did at uni didn't connect these two worlds. So it seemed. So she said.

Around the camp, she saw the rubbish spilling out of the smelly drums. She saw the kids coming to school late and knew that children elsewhere did homework, and had desks at home and little bags with packed lunches. She saw Brother Tom give the kids money for their week's work on the gardens and the kids gorging on cool drinks and lollies, and clutching twenty-dollar notes. Later in the week they were hungry.

I'd found the school journals which previous principals had composed. I took them home to read, one at a time. Gabriella read them also, when she sat in our house during the school day, in the lonely quiet.

In 1976 an ear, nose and throat specialist visited the community and the principal of the time wrote that, 'He detected no major problems … Several children were found to have watermelon seeds in their ears.'

At night-time cockroaches crawl in and out of their ears.

Pages had stains on them. Tea, whisky, sweat. Tears? Principals sat, in turn, before their ledgers and wrote. They turned to their journals reluctantly, because the bureaucracy demanded it. Their entries were usually short, often confused, angry, bitter, though cautiously so. Who might read this? Without exception each principal's journal concluded with barely disguised relief and a litany of their supposed achievements at the school. These last entries were scrawled, as if in haste.

It startled, what you read, what you saw through those fogged spectacles, those sweat-stung eyes. Wives shouted into your face with the veins on their throats protruding dangerously, and they packed their bags repeatedly, and repeatedly wept, and threw shoes, smashed plates, spat. 'My wife has combined professionally and successfully with me in every way, although we have had some difference of opinion and she finds it difficult living in such isolation.'

Pigs broke out of the mission and trampled down the school fence. Sometimes, perhaps, it was wild pigs. They rooted and trampled through the flowers and over the lawn. You saw the mess early in the dewy morning, and cursed, almost wept. Snakes were killed with blackboard rulers as students watched and cheered. You chased camp dogs out of the school grounds where they'd cut out a foal from the wild horses that came up to the camp surrounds, and had it trapped inside the school fence, bleeding, frothing, trembling with terror. So frightened, so exhausted was it, that it let you touch its warm muzzle.

But the young donkey that staggered around with fat oozing from its wounds where someone had hit it with an axe, and its anus raw and distended from being jabbed with pieces of wood, you shot.

Children broke into teachers' houses and stole jellybeans and were 'dealt with' by parents and the mission. Mothers brawled in the office over a fight their children had been in, and sent books, chalk, pens, rulers, paint tumbling. One of them returns and threatens you with a club. You write to the police, there and then, as she waves the club around your doubtless twitching eyebrows, and you point to the words you are scrawling and keep saying, 'Police. Government.' The children you had dismissed crouch outside the office window and listen to the club whirring past the lips which chant the threats. 'Police. Native Welfare. Government.'

Tiny children throw rocks through windows, and knives at teachers who follow them home hurling feeble reprimands.

Teachers collapse with dysentery, pneumonia, hepatitis.

A principal admits — in a surprising, perhaps unforgivable, lapse from the professional journal self — that he wants to be out of Karnama, that he can't wait until he has 'done his time … It is sometimes hard to stop oneself swearing before the children.'

Generations of children kill countless beautiful birds with gings and unerring stones while hordes of teachers shout at them and write about it in their ledgers.

Father Pujol screams that the school must not conduct traditional handicrafts or do anything that will encourage native ways.

In 1965 an indignant principal writes at length, under a single globe in a hot insect-ridden night, of an eight-year-old girl 'sexually involved with several old men in the old people's camp on the other side of the river where they stay because otherwise the mission shoot their dogs and because of their lack of dress. She apparently enjoys this pastime and many of the children watch their actions.

'I have decided to ban the children from the old camp altogether and with mission help may be able to clean up this mess.

'Those camps are places of disease, filth, and full of uncivilised people. It is obvious to me that for the good of the children's education they must not associate with the old people.

'P.S. Mathematical tables appear to be a big success. Children do know their tables quite well.'

I came home and Gabriella was sitting at the dining table, staring at the mango trees in the front yard. The air-conditioner roared. She was silent, just looked at me as I entered.

'These books,' eventually she spoke, waved her arm over the journals. 'It's interesting to read them. But I don't like them. I don't like the people that write them.'

'No,' I said, 'but I feel sorry for them, a bit. They shouldn't have been here.'

'Why are you here?' she asked me.

'Because I wanted to. I think I wanted, I'm of ... my grandmother ... My great grandmother must have been Aboriginal, like you, dark. My grandmother is part ... my father told me, but no one ...'

'Ah, we thought...'

'So, maybe that's a part. But I don't feel Aboriginal, I can't say that. I don't understand. Does it mean you feel lost, displaced? But doesn't everyone? And I just wanted to come to a place like this, where some things that happened a long time ago, where I come from, that I have only heard or read of, are still happening here, maybe.'

'Some people said that they thought you might be, like when you danced the other day. True. Fatima and Sebastian said. But because you're a teacher we didn't think.'

I gave a little laugh. 'Yeah, well.' It seemed a silly thing to talk about.

'But these books, these journals, I see things a little bit like they do, I can understand it a bit. But they are like devils, djimi, like the old people say when they first saw gardiya, white people. They said they are like the devils that live in caves, with their pale skin and shadows clinging to them. I think it's sad here really, pathetic even maybe. People don't know, and they pretend. They don't know what they can do, or believe in. Little bit of this, little bit of that. But in Perth, Melbourne, Sydney, Aboriginal people don't necessarily think like me either ...'

'Gabriella, I think ... Yes. A breakdown maybe. Could be an evolution of sorts, there's something in common that must be offered ...'

'You think? What can we do? Look at it. Put the little bits together like one of the paintings? You know, how I've been brought up, I don't know anything of the old ways, a few words, this and that. But there's something there, that's what I reckon. Should we try and put it all together and believe in it? Or try and rediscover things, like that Renaissance thing? Do like they say Walanguh could, you know, sing for this new world.'

We each turned away from the other.

Maybe. But why? When you, I, we, don't know quite who we are these days, why try to tell others this, or that something has gone wrong and the world is not quite right? Because otherwise we have to listen to them, be silent, watch their visions, feel our earth vibrate as they hammer it with thick ankles and well-shod feet, probe and jackhammer drill.

A Beginning

In the busy classroom, buzzing with student voices, the telephone was ringing. It was an internal connection only, from Alex's office to the classroom.

I answered it. Alex said, 'I've just received a telegram for you over the two-way, Bill.'

'Oh yeah.'

'Nana passed away last night love Mum.'

The students were all silent and looking at me; except Francis of course, who had taken the opportunity to return to his drawings of dark, muscular heroes threatening to take others, to take life, by the nape of the neck.

Oh yeah, well done Alex. Billy has a classroom full of adolescents. He looks out the window out out out. He doesn't want to be there. He wants it to be a time when he finally spoke to his grandmother, when she wasn't ten years sick and she could answer his questions about her young days, her life. How come she doesn't want people to know she's Aboriginal and how did she get taken away from her family and does she know of many of them still and where is she from really and why did they send Billy's dad away and and and … and Alex stays in his office and forgets what he has just said over the phone and he doesn't know anything of this and he doesn't want to.

Mum says later that Nana was in pain and they had her on strong drugs. She went right back says Mum. She asked for one son, for Dad, no one said that he was fifteen years dead. We let her go. She started to talk in a funny language and she went through all these names and, in the voice of a small child, she started to cry.

But they took her away. And now she is proper gone. And Billy stands in a noisy classroom and knows that all those things he was building up to asking her now will never have answers. And he's doing with Fatima, Sebastian, Samson what he should have with her, and even with his father but that was too long ago and he didn't think then.

So Billy is doing it with us now, and Gabriella too. We might be all writing together, really.

II

High Diving

One hot afternoon Billy, Liz, the high school kids, they all went for a swim. They went to High Diving, which is just down there behind the mission grounds where the river widens into a big pool before it slides among the rocks and into the rapids of Running Creek. They had to walk past the community office, and past the old people gathered there, sitting in the shade; Fatima, Sebastian, some others. Jasmine came out of the office. She decided she was going too.

The group moved in two major clusters, divided according to sex. The girls grouped around Liz and Jasmine, with Jasmine the main focus because she was of greater novelty than the teacher.

They laughed, they shrieked, they studied her earrings and hair. They asked the two women about boyfriends, husbands. 'Mr Storey hit you ever? What he like when he drunk?' It was Friday. Jasmine said she was annoyed with the office, with working there, with the people, the laziness and the fighting. These kids wouldn't be like that when they were working there would they? Oh no, no.

The girls held their guests' hands and put their arms around their shoulders. They led them past puddles and over the rusting barbed wire fence behind the mission. 'See that, Miss?' They pointed to a metal-framed corridor leading to an opening in a tall corrugated iron wall which also served as part of the fence. It looked like a cattle run, but much narrower. 'That's where people, us mob, older ones but, used to get food, line up for food.'

The boys walked twenty metres ahead. They threw rocks at the coconuts as they went past them, then at the mango trees, at birds, into the river. They spoke of cars, ninjas, of whether Russia or America would win a war, of Arnold Schwarzenegger muscles. They quoted whole lines of dialogue from the videos the camp was watching this week, role-playing with their voices. For their first few months here all teachers understand them clearly when they repeat lines from videos in American accents, but are puzzled by the local English.

Imagine, again, seeing all this from above, as if you were flying slowly, just drifting, quiet, way above them. They are walking along, walking along on a narrow two-wheeled red dirt track. Long grass in the middle of the track and long grass around them stretching to the rocks of Running Creek as they walk past it. You are up high so you don't hear their voices too well, just some little shouts, and the wind sort of singing, and the clank clank of the old windmill there. You are invisible, you cast no shadow. Their clothes are just spots of colours in the vast green which gets drabber as you go higher and see the land away from the river. There is the blue of the river near them, the big green of mango trees and the plantation in the mission. The kids are mostly tight in around those teachers. Black skin looks good in the sun, shiny. Then, nearly at High Diving, the kids break away and start to race to the river. They shed clothes on the run. They dive. They spear the water. They disappear and surface among the reeds by the bank. They climb a tree, and jump. They swing out on the rope there, and drop. They dive. Silent splashes, blossoms of froth, circles in the water. There're white patterns, different colours in that tiny part of the river where they're jumping and making bubbles.

'Aren't they beautiful people? Look, such big smiles,' said Jasmine as she and Liz sat on the bank. 'The boys are so spunky, aren't they, really?'

'I'd say they're all nice looking.'

'And the babies. So cute! Really! So cute!' Jasmine clasped herself with the pleasure of their cuteness.

Billy climbed up the sloping trunk of the great tree which leaned over the river. It was wet and slippery where the kids had been climbing it. He'd watched them virtually walk up it before he'd decided to do so himself. But it was so slippery, and high. He felt a surge of panic. He was bent over like a chimpanzee, using hands and feet. He wished he had claws to grip with. If he slipped here he'd bash himself on the tree, and then on the bank because he wasn't yet out over the water. And the tree kept sloping up and out. The kids behind were getting impatient.

'Okay, I'm an old man, remember?' He forced a grin.

'C'mon Billy, move along.' Liz called out to him.

He managed the grin again. 'Hey, I'm frightened,' he attempted to joke. His joke was taken. He hadn't realised the tree would seem so high. Liz was already far below. When he was a child he'd always dreamt of flying, but hadn't known about heights. He'd experienced vertigo one day walking around some cliffs above the sea. From then his childhood dreams included the terror of heights, of falling from cliffs into the sea, falling falling falling; then entering the water without a disturbance, and going down and down past curious fish that watched him, and the bubbles leaving his mouth for the light, shrinking, above.

He grasped the tree trunk between his knees and continued shinning along it as if it were vertical. The tree moved with his weight as he got to the branches from where the kids leapt. There, Beatrice grinned at him, and, levering her weight with her knees, made the tree branch spring and sway. He grinned back at her, wished she wouldn't. He sat with his arm firmly around a smaller branch and dangled his feet. Kids pushed past him, rocked and leapt, their dark bodies plummeting and exploding as they hit the water, making a moment's dark opening in the centre of a circle of white spray and bubbles in the water. He smiled with Liz, kilometres below him.

Sliding off the branch, he suddenly became incredibly heavy, the water at his feet drawing him. There was an explosion as he hit the water, but he was still intact, himself, and lightened. Brown water around him, bubbles. He swam up elated.

As he surfaced his eyes met those of Francis. Or rather, his eyes met Franny's thick-lensed spectacles, which reflected the river water itself and in which Franny's eyes swam like dark fish. Billy smiled, Franny nodded. Franny very rarely swam. His health was poor because of some trouble when he was very young. Now he smiled back, and Billy duck-dived into the dark water.

'What are they like at school?' asked Jasmine, still smiling at the cuteness of the youngest children, who were also starting to arrive at the river and leap into the water.

'Well, they're way behind most kids in schools. Not all of

them, the best are maybe a weak average for their age. But look at the place. Parents don't read; there's none of that back-up at home. Why maths? What's science? You know. Some things, generalising, they seem extra good at though. Special strengths. Maybe like telling stories, joking, sometimes miming. And visual literacy … I sometimes wonder what we're doing here.'

The older boys swam with the river's drift, and took Billy with them. The pool ended in a clump of pandanus and rocks and became rapids. They climbed out of the river just before the head of the rapids and walked across logs and rocks.

The boys explained to Billy that, by swimming hard, you could get across the rapids to a large tree which hung over the river about fifty metres along the other bank. They demonstrated. And were swept away laughing at one another, looking back at him as their heads bobbed in the sinewed, sharp-edged water. It seemed the tree and they leaned together, and they clasped it, each boy stretched from hand to foot with the torrent, and sometimes hand-in-hand with another boy. They climbed the tree gracefully, they flowed up it, and leapt into a still and deep pool in its lee. They duck-dived back into the current at the edge of the pool and somehow, underwater, swam against the river back to the base of the tree.

Billy watched for a time. He entered the river and struck out for the other side, stroking as if sprinting but going sideways. He got close to the other side, and lined up the tree. The river buffeted him, pulled him under its surface, tossed him up, came into his throat, and then the boys grabbed him as he came to the tree reaching up with his hand and his head going under again. Teasing him, their laughter bubbling with the river, they pulled him to them.

They showed him how to move against the current underwater.

In the strange and changing sepia light he clasped the reeds on the stony river floor and pulled himself along with them. The dull roar in his ears, the sharp slippery reeds in his hands, his body stretched by the same current which pressed his hair to his scalp. Quite alone for those moments, calm and moving against the current, beneath it.

Then rocketing up into the noise, white light, the laughing faces greeting his reappearance.

They played hide-and-seek in the river and reeds. Sylvester would duck-dive and disappear. Long minutes later, in a stiller part of the river, Billy would hear a voice calling him, but would not be able to find the speaker until, there, Sylvester parted the reeds and Billy saw just his nose and twinkling eyes above the surface of the river.

Billy followed Sylvester underwater. In the yellow river light Sylvester pointed to passages under trapped trees, and where you could surface for a breath and not be seen because of the twisted branches and reeds knotted together.

Billy, his lungs straining, followed Sylvester as they pulled themselves along the bottom of the river. He watched the pale soles of Sylvester's feet as they waved, flapped, glimmered before him.

'You know, Sir, they call me crocodile. I was a crocodile.'

Billy returned to the pool with some of the younger children who'd come down to the head of the rapids. He picked his way across the boulders to the other bank and took them back to the still water, but allowed the older girls to join the boys in the rapids. After experiencing the competence of those he'd just been with, he could hardly disbelieve the girls' assurances that they were capable swimmers.

Jasmine interrupted Liz. 'What about Milton's kids?'

'Oh, they're probably the cleverest, school-wise, for their age. They're only young though, yet,' Liz said.

'Yeah, Milton'd only be in his late twenties. Spunky, don't you think? And his wife, Annie? They both seem impressive. Well educated, they seem.'

'Relatively,' said Liz. 'They went to private schools. Perth, Darwin, Broome. Maybe it helps to be sent away, have your world opened up. Like Moses. Almost like, maybe it helps to be taken away from your family and that. Not like they used to do, but … this place is so tiny, so insular and isolated. To go away is an education, important, and if you know you're coming back and still loved …'

Billy swam gently to the bank to keep an eye on the youngest kids. In this heat he felt he could stay in the water forever. Tiny children, five and six years old, emulated the older ones by leaping from smaller trees. Billy swam with a younger child holding his shoulders, floating behind. Little Louella, standing on the bank, called to him. 'Me too?' He held out his hands, and she leapt into them. He let her into the water, chest deep to him, and she struggled and spluttered. Someone called out from way up in the tree, 'She can't swim, Sir, that one.' And Billy, tardily realising this, grabbed at her and lifted her into his arms again. He taught her to float on her back. Tiny children climbed up into his arms, stroked his cheek, feeling the stubble there. They drew their fingers through his hair, pulled at his earring, investigated him; the difference in smell and touch between him and their adults. The similarities. They did the same with Liz and Jasmine. They dived off Billy's shoulders into the water, and he picked them up and threw them into the air so that they landed in the water, splashing anykind.

The young children swam in knickers or shorts. The eldest boys in their jeans. The older girls swam fully clothed. Jasmine and Liz came in and swam in their bathers and the little children draped from them as they did from Billy. The kids noticed the women in their bathers. All that flesh. Like swimming in your undies, the older girls said. That's what those people do.

When they all left the teachers came along last, shepherding stragglers. Some of the older ones — Deslie, Jimmy, and others — helped collect up clothes the little children had left behind. They sniffed them, and knew to whom they belonged.

Five minutes' walk and up at the camp they were hot again. Dusty, the smell of cow shit; and the rubbish trapped against the wire fences, blowing across the land, spilling from the bins. Jasmine agreed to come over for a drink with Billy and Liz later in the day. And, perhaps, dinner also.

In the office later that afternoon, after Jasmine had returned to work, Samson came in and sat on her desk. 'We go swimming some time, eh? I take you to a waterfall I know. Beautiful. Everyone that see it want to take photo. You wear your bathers that you do, with your cheeky bum, eh?'

At High Diving the river beneath the tree is calm again. The tree is still wet. The water still flows toward the rapids, and leaves fall and drift away, and bubbles break the surface now and then. Bubbles from the mud, or turtles, or little crocodiles maybe.

Some Get Together

Gerrard said, to the other boss ones, 'Better have a meeting soon.' Just them mob but, eh? He say, very calm and clever, 'So we can work things out. Talk about the problems here, and how we can work together best. In other places, communities like this, I've done it. It helps.'

So they sitting there in Alex and Annette's house, drinking coffee, hiding faces behind cups, eyes looking round quick like they nervous animals; looking here, there, this way, that way. Sip the coffee; slurp, slurp. Who we got here? Gerrard, Father Paul, Alex, Annette, Murray, Liz. Ah yes, we not there maybe, but we know that mob, we hear things.

Gerrard makes his chair look too little. He too big that one. Long legs up next to his ears like a grasshopper maybe perched there, ready to hop in. Father Paul, sleeves rolled up over his strong arms. He gripping his cigarette tight, laughing loudest. He gunna work with all these new ones, he gunna be patient this time. Murray fidgeting, he move little bit this way, little bit 'nother way. Then he find a nice comfortable place, and he sit still with his legs apart and his beer belly resting good there. He looking at his scrubbed red fingers, eating his fingernails. Alex and Annette sitting together; they glad they all in their house. Alex's legs crossed. One foot swinging swinging, fingers tapping. He a clock, you know, trying to make time his way;

this second begins ... Now! Another one ... Now! Little round Annette sitting right closest next to him, sideways, hands in her lap. Liz writing their words down in a little book.

So. They having a hard time here in Karnama. Maybe this is not the place for them.

Gerrard would have shifted in his chair. 'Well, let's make a start then. I've run these sorts of meetings before, where the senior personnel get together. Perhaps we could take turns chairing them from here. I'll start, today. The idea is just to throw things around; talk about what's bothering you, problems, who's causing trouble, what's not getting done. That sort of thing.'

'Where to start, eh?' said Father Paul, sympathetically. Laughter. Alex and Annette held one another's gaze for a moment.

Gerrard made a suggestion, and they all said 'Aye', and put their hands up in the air.

Gerrard talked. He named some people. He said he was having trouble getting people to work punctually, or arriving at all. Getting them to finish jobs, even halfway properly, was impossible.

Annette elbowed Alex. 'Exactly,' he said, slapping the back of one hand in the palm of the other. 'Exactly. Our cleaners, our gardener, our AEW ...'

'Using the terms loosely,' interrupted Annette.

'The problem,' continued Alex, 'is to get them to work on time, turning up regularly enough to learn how to do a decent job.' He sighed.

'And, the kids. Half the time — no, more than that — they haven't been fed or cleaned, and they fall asleep in class. What are their parents doing? Playing cards? Drinking?'

Father Paul dragged hard on his cigarette. He pulled it from his lips like it was a bullet caught there, and crushed it in the aluminium ashtray. Annette wrinkled her nose. Father Paul leaned forward.

'Before, ten years ago, the way we used to do it was with vouchers. That way you made sure there's enough for food, for the kids, clothes … Then what's left over, the cash, they can use for cards, or whatever. But we can't now. The church is out of it. It's self-determination now.' And he shook his head.

Murray shifted his buttocks on the vinyl chair. Gerrard turned to him, but he dropped his head.

Alex, wrinkling his brow and turning his hands palms up, said, 'Why not? Why can't we do it that way now?' He suddenly put his forefingers together and pointed forward. 'That's the way to go, surely? Gerrard, you could give each of us the wages for our workers, and we pay them. We could pay them, or not pay them, daily. Immediate positive reinforcement. They'd see the consequences, immediately, of not turning up. We could dock their pays.'

Gerrard squeezed his nose between thumb and forefinger, and his face showed pain. 'Can't do it. Ab Affairs, DAA — whatever they're called this week — fly money out once a month. We're accountable, and it's for the previous month. Anyway, we can't.'

Father Paul snorted, and, leaning forward so that his elbows were supported by his knees, contemplated his cigarette.

Annette looked at Alex, who drew himself up straight in his chair and said, 'But you, or your girls, are always getting the timesheets mixed up anyway. Can't we just fiddle it somehow?'

Gerrard ticked something on the list before him. 'We're not getting anywhere here. Alex, Annette,' he gave her a smile, 'what other things do you want to say? This is the place to get it off your chest.'

Annette decided this was her chance. 'It's just not good enough, that's all. We work like slaves for their kids, and they're just leaving it all up to us. They don't care. And what about the power? The powerhouse breaks down — every second day or whatever it is — and there's no air-conditioning. It's hell in those rooms then. Talk about hot. And the smell! And the school seems to be the first to lose power as well, and last to get it back. How come? It's all wrong.'

Murray spoke. All eyes turned to him. 'Actually, we gotta turn the power off at the moment because number three engine is the only one working well. The SEC are coming out next week to upgrade the lot. But, the school, and your houses … It's a big drain on power. All those air-conditioners. If you could turn them off when they're not necessary.'

Annette could not be stopped. Her cheeks were flushed. 'But the kids must be most important! What are our priorities? And what about the water then? What about that? I've gone over to the store when the school has no water, and seen taps just running, wasting water, and we're over here, with little kids, and we can't even use the toilets. Now, is that right? Is it fair? I tell you, we're getting sick of it. What we should do is shut the school every time the power goes off, or the water.'

Alex seemed about to deny that they would do this, but Murray got in first. He spoke softly, but his voice was tight. 'Try to understand. I've tried to explain about the power, and the water … The river — that's where we get our water from — the river is a long way from the school. You're last in line. Because you have the newest buildings and homes, and there's nearly always work to do on the pump, like everything here.

When I turn it off, to fix it, or just run it down if I can, then it might be that some taps are left on somewhere, and no water reaches the school. They're very thin pipes. I can't be going spying, turning off taps everywhere. You can't blame me.'

'But Murray,' Alex was trying on authority, 'surely the school is most important, we'd all agree on that.' No one said anything. 'Can't there be a diversion across, so that the school is not last. Or so you can cut the water off to the camp only.'

Murray's chin was up. 'You do it then. You're an expert? How are we gunna do that? Who? You know all the other jobs that need doing around here? You gunna help me train people?'

Annette seemed swollen with anger, and choking. 'And the power! We've been sitting here at night, sweating in the dark, and there's been lights on at the mission. So how come? Tell me that.' Tears welled in her eyes.

'Maybe once,' said Murray. 'Only once. The mission is on a different line. But what are you saying? Just say it. Do I tell you how to do your job? Do I tell you how to teach? There's plenty of things going wrong on that score, that I keep hearing about.'

Ah, yes. So they have this big meeting so they can get things off their chest? They gunna have big chests then. And that Annette, she have biggest milk. Big ones out here, eh? She look like little tank with big guns right out front then.

Loose Tongues

Jasmine came with a bottle of whisky and a puppy. She held the bottle firmly by the neck, but the puppy was unrestrained. It bounced around, almost tripping her, and ran, slipping and sliding on the linoleum, into the kitchen as soon as the door was opened.

'Shit, an invasion!' The puppy cannoned into walls, ran under the table, and slipped and scampered away from their attempts to get it back out the door. Eventually they succeeded.

They sat at the kitchen table with glasses of whisky before them. 'Ah. Like Somerset Maugham or something isn't it? Living in the tropics, living in more privileged circumstances than the locals, sweating and drinking whisky.'

'Wasn't it gin?'

'Hardly appropriate here.'

'I'm going to get myself a pith helmet, and a monocle,' said Liz. 'Perhaps a whip even.'

'For Bill? Kinky.' Jasmine wiggled her eyebrows suggestively. They had more whisky. 'I think I'd get myself a houseboy,' Jasmine continued after a time.

'For your housework? Or to cool your passions. You want your desires slaked, woman?' asked Liz. Then, seriously, 'How come you came to a place like this anyway Jasmine? Unusual for a single woman, isn't it? I think so anyway. I wouldn't be able to do it, not on my own.'

'I was unhappy. I'd split up with my man, I wanted a baby. I thought I wanted a baby. I think maybe I'm running out of time. I'm thirty now.' She laughed at herself. 'Oh, and the CES just said the job was available. This was in Perth. And I'd been up here before, in Broome and Derby anyway.'

They mouthed little words then, for a time. Jasmine was probably relieved when she thought of something with which to change the subject. 'You know old Walanguh is sick? So they say, very sick apparently.'

'Is he one of them that stays down under the mango trees, near those old tiny huts? Fatima's husband?'

'Yeah, I think so. With all the dogs. And naked most of the time, so the Sisters are always saying.'

'Yeah, I was over there the other week. I was walking back from the river and Sebastian yelled out to me. He was talking to the old bloke. So I went over there. He was hard to understand. I could hardly understand what he was saying. He looked all right though, not sick or anything.'

'They reckon he's been sick off and on for a long time. But now it looks like he'll probably die even. They flew him into hospital, which shows he's sick, otherwise he wouldn't let them send him in there. So everyone is saying.'

'Sebastian told me that he's a "powerful one", or was anyway. I s'pose that means they have a lot of respect for him.'

'The mission reckon he killed a lot of men when he was younger, so the Sisters and Brother Tom say, and they've been here longest. They say he was a great storyteller, and singer and that. And, the Sisters say, a womaniser.'

'Maybe they like to think about that, the details.' They laughed, an easy joke.

More whisky. Billy noticed that Jasmine's throat was flushed. Suddenly the pup barked and leapt from the verandah. The three at the kitchen table turned their heads and saw Murray appear in the frame of the door with the pup leaping up at him, its tongue and tail waving. This time they managed to keep the dog out.

They pulled the curtain across the sliding door. 'In case someone comes it wouldn't look too good if we're all here getting pissy.'

The rain began. 'First afternoon rain for a while, eh?

'Yes it's starting to dry up now. Tourists'll be in in a couple of months, or less. And the locals'll be going out for, in with, grog. You hear they wanted to fly old Walanguh out, to hospital? He wouldn't go.'

'Yeah, we were just talking about that.'

'There'll be a big funeral if he dies, just about everyone here's related to him one way or another. He's Fatima's husband, did you know? The mission married them, but I don't think there's any kids, they certainly don't seem to have much to do with one another these days.'

More little talk, more small whiskies. Their words not finding targets, not so well aimed, but more abundant, and criss-crossing, colliding in space between them.

'Look at that pup.'

'We should be getting our vehicle in soon.'

'He was the last of the litter, the runt. From Samson, you know, the dancer, the family that look after Deslie.'

'I get so tired here, in the heat.'

'No one wanted him.'

'They'll be able to get grog in soon, in the dry.'

'No one was looking after him. He's a petrol sniffer. And

there are, or were, very few petrol vehicles here. Samson's his cousin, or uncle …'

Too many words. They said many things. Murray said, 'I'm glad to get away from the mission a bit. Everyone's bitching about Father Paul, and then practically cheering, secretly, that he's leaving.'

'Leaving? Really? When?'

'On sabbatical, I think it's sabbatical. Soon. Maybe a few, or several, months' time. I think. Something like that.'

Murray's boots rocked onto their toes, and onto their heels. Then one leapt over the other as he crossed his legs, and stretched them out. His foot bumped Jasmine's.

'Sorry,' he blushed.

'S'alright.' Did she notice the blush? She spoke to Billy. 'How's the taping going?'

'What?' Murray's question.

Liz explained. Murray raised his eyebrows. 'Why bother? You want to encourage them? They'll lie to you you know. Still, I guess you could fix up their English when you write it up for the kids or whatever.'

'Not necessarily, not just that. Look … I'm not finding time to write them up anyway.'

'No one'll thank you for it.'

'Ha! Ah well. What else can I do? I like that sort of thing. And I'm Aboriginal, of Aboriginal descent. A bit of tarbrush in me.' Oops. He gave a derisive snort of laughter. Too many whiskies for Billy maybe. 'So I'm interested. That must be part of the reason I asked to come here. Most chalkies only come here if they've got no choice. I dunno. Maybe it's stupid any of us being here, if we look at it.'

'Why are you here then, Murray?' Liz focused on Murray.

All the eyes turned on him. She continued, perhaps protecting her husband from criticism that may have been about to come. 'You're not a lay missionary, are you? You get paid?' Murray was spotlit. Everyone else around the table sat in a dimmed, shadowless light.

'No, no.' He was quick to deny the occupation. He was looking at Jasmine. 'I'd been labouring, plasterer's assistant, for years. Lifetimes.'

'How old are you?' interrupted Liz.

'Twenty-nine,' he said promptly.

'Sorry,' said Liz. The spotlight was off. 'We're all doing our ages. It's dark in here, isn't it?' She turned on the room light. Thin shadows returned.

Murray continued, 'So I came here, voluntary, when I saw it advertised in a local church bulletin. After three months Father Paul asked me to stay, for wages.'

'You are a Christian, committed then?'

The spotlight flickered.

'My family are. I go to church, here, once a week at least. Father Paul explained that that would be required.'

'So, you're not a Christian?' Liz was raised as a Catholic, lapsed in her early twenties.

'Yes, but … this mate of mine, he was at uni, he sends me reading. Kierkegaard … like Graham Greene, have you read …'

Talk, talk, and blue smoke drifting from Jasmine's cigarette. The smoke was the colour of the clouds outside. The room's light glowed yellow as the late afternoon light faded. The air-conditioner roared, as ever, unnoticed.

A figure, having materialised from the darkness, was knocking at the door. They feebly pushed at their whisky glasses, temporarily wanting to be rid of them. Billy went to the door, feeling tipsy.

'Milton, what's up mate?'

Milton was annoyed at feeling shy, awkward at the door of this new house, teacher's clean house, these gardiya all caught together with their glasses before them, and he alone.

'Come in, Milton.'

'No, I must go, supper now. Maybe we go fishing tomorrow, my car. You, me, Liz too, Alphonse.'

'Yes, great, yes.'

He left. They called their goodbyes as he closed the sliding door. Their eyes ricocheted as they returned to their drinks, and their laughter was tainted with guilt.

'He's a nice man, isn't he?' said Liz.

'Yes, very. And so good looking. Adorable.'

Murray looked at Jasmine as she said this, watched her soft throat as, dragging on her cigarette, she tilted her chin back. He pressed his fists between his thighs and stretched his legs.

'I'll have to leave. My turn to wash dishes tonight. Thanks for the drinks,' he said. 'Hey,' he addressed Jasmine. 'Seeing as how Bill and Liz are sorted out, what are you doing tomorrow? You could come with me and Father Paul if you want. We're going out to one of the creeks to fish, maybe a beer. Or if we don't go, I could help you make a fence for your pup.'

'Um, look, um, I'll come over early. You'll go early? I'll come over early if I want to come, otherwise it just means I need my sleep. All right?'

First Meeting

'Your net?' asked Billy as he and Alphonse climbed into the back of the Hilux.

'No. We got it from the mission, from Father Paul. Gun too.'

Milton drove, and Liz sat in the cab with him. Billy and Alphonse sat on the corners made by the upright sides and rear of the tray, gripped the uprights tightly, and planted their feet on the tray itself. Billy struggled to keep his balance and cushion himself against the shocks of the track. Sometimes they sped along. To Billy it seemed they went too fast for such a roadway. But, often, they remained in first gear as they crawled through washaways and rocks. Twice, Alphonse walked in front of the car through river crossings. There was one muddy patch in which the car sank. The mud was like porridge. Milton revved the motor and repeatedly changed between first and reverse, rocking the car. The wheels spun, mud spattered, the car stayed stuck. They had no tools, shovels or jacks with them. Billy thought of what the people at the mission would say when they heard about this, when they came to rescue them. How far was it back to the camp? Walkable? In this heat? Milton and Alphonse threw a dozen or more large rocks into the mud around the wheels. It seemed a miracle when they drove out.

Alphonse yelled out and pointed at a large goanna as it ran of into the scrub. Milton slowed and looked after it. They kept driving. 'When you see him,' Alphonse pointed after the reptile with his lips, 'you say "Maa", or some people whistle, and they don't run. You just walk up to him slowly, and grab 'im!'

The next time they saw one, and were driving slowly, Alphonse tried a whistle. The goanna didn't falter. 'You whistle one way, it doesn't work for me. Milton's father can do it. Walanguh, some others. The old people, they knew how.'

Billy moved so that he was sitting on top of the net with his back to the cab.

They stopped under a boab tree just before the slope of the beach began. There was very little wind. In the silence of the motor's absence they could hear the tiny waves lapping the beach. Liz twisted around to look at Billy. She was flushed and sweating in the heat.

Alphonse took the gun and Milton carried the net. They walked across the grey driftwood bundled at the high tide mark and down to where the mangroves began. The men were barefoot. Liz was pleased she'd worn light sandshoes because Billy found it uncomfortable walking in the shallows where the short mangrove roots stuck out of the sand.

Milton and Billy took an end of the net each. They dragged the net between them through the waist-deep water and Alphonse and Liz attempted to scare fish into the space between Milton and Billy. When one was trapped Milton pulled it to his mouth and, with his hands and teeth, broke its spine. He took it from the net and put it into a bag tucked into his waistband.

The shallows stretched a long way. They waded no deeper

than their waists. Sometimes they scared a small shark, or a stingray and it darted about at incredible speed, the stingray like an alien spacecraft in some sci-fi film. Often Liz was screaming and trying to get the net between her and the frantic fish, while Billy tried to hide his own anxiety, and Alphonse fired the small rifle at their prey. Once one of the larger sharks cannoned into the net, and there was a ferocity of splashing and screaming before it broke over, or through, the net.

'What about crocs?' Liz summoned up her courage to ask.

'Sometimes, maybe. This be clear water but. That's why we got this rifle from the mission.' Even to Liz's inexperienced eye the rifle seemed too small for such a task.

There had been a small box full of bullets which Alphonse carried in his pockets, but he was shooting so often that they were rapidly being depleted. His targets, however, were quite safe.

'Sight's buggered,' he said, squinting along the barrel.

It was tiring, walking through thigh-deep water, dragging the net, worrying about sharks, stingrays, the possibility of being shot. When they had maybe a dozen fish in the bag they headed back to the car, but first, on Milton's suggestion, they tied the net at the mouth of a creek.

'Fish swim in with the tide, we get them when the tide goes out again.'

They sat on the sand, in the shade cast by the car and the boab tree, and lit a small fire to cook the mullet.

'Don't take their gutses out, that's nice fat there. Nice fat one.' The mullet were thrown on the hot coals after the fire had died down. They ate the cooked fish gingerly because it burnt their fingers. The scales and skin came off with the ash.

Billy thought about a beer. They drank warm water from a plastic container Milton had brought. Liz thought about disease.

'AIDS? That kills you, eh? Them American people get it and die?'

'Like a horror film.'

'I used to fish, with my dad, with a net, when I was a kid.'

'You seen that video?'

'Some of the songs the band was doing I never heard before.'

They fished with lines down by the creek for a while. The heat, among the mangroves and out of the breeze, was intense. The sand radiated heat. Liz wondered when they would be returning.

'This be crocodile place.'

'Grab your bait and just pull you in slowly, boy.'

'Oh yeah, every afternoon nearly. Fatima likes to talk about the old days.'

'My little boy, you know Cecil? He plays with a ghost. My sister I think. She died. I see him looking up, you know, like at a grown-up girl. Sometimes he's frightened and he run to me and grab me and poke his tongue out back there. It's all right. If I not there I might worry.'

'Old people, they have black magic. They used to kill or destroy anybody. They send a shell through the ground, long way, and it come out and cut you. Or they fly like an eagle and just watch you watch you. Or they be a snake. Them old blokes here too, I mean Walanguh, them mob. But now they, they still have that magic but, they don't see anybody that's looking for trouble with them.'

It was late afternoon. The tide had not ebbed completely

and was still higher than it had been that morning. They would have to go and get the net. They couldn't just leave it. It was from the mission.

Liz stayed at the car. Alphonse took the rifle. There were two bullets left. They walked between a couple of thin mangrove trees and into the shallow water where the hard shoots stabbed at their feet, and headed for the creek mouth a couple of hundred metres away. When they were about halfway there they saw a frenzy of splashing at the net.

'Big fish now.' Alphonse and Billy talked excitedly. Milton was silent. The water was chest deep. They were about fifty metres from the shore, about twenty from the mangroves.

Suddenly Milton was shouting. 'Gun! Crocodile! Quick give me the gun! The gun! Gun!'

Adrenalin took over. Alphonse's eyes were big, his mouth open. Billy strained his eyes and saw a great crocodile, its head out of the water, swallowing. It looked jade-green in the rich light of the slanting sun, and the water on it sparkled. It was beside the net, facing out to sea. Billy looked at Milton. He was sighting the gun. He fired. With the echo of its report they saw the splash where the bullet struck the water beyond the crocodile. One bullet left. Milton looked at the gun as if he was going to throw it away. Alphonse was moving off toward the shore, walking as fast as he could in the deep water.

'The tree, climb the tree, there!'

They scrambled up one thin tree which stood, relatively tall, among the mangroves, Alphonse first. Milton stood at its base shaking the rifle at the others, wanting them to take it from him so he could climb the tree. They climbed as high as they were able, the tree swaying with their weight. They looked down to where the net was. 'Plenty fish anyway.'

Laughed in their excitement.

And waited for the tide to drop.

Milton saw Liz, back near the car, wading carefully into the shallow water. She looked pale and naked in the distance. Milton shouted a warning to her. She continued, staring straight at them. They waved and shouted together.

Liz entered the water. The mangrove shoots were difficult to walk among. Where were they? Where had they left the net? Was that shouting she could hear? Was that Billy in that tree? Where were the others? So hard to see them in the dark of the tree. She could see Billy, and, yes, the others now, waving at her. Puzzled, she waved back. She stopped. She understood, and turned and ran back to the shore.

They saw the tiny lacelets of water, the little splashes of water around her ankles as she high-stepped it out of the ocean.

In her mind Liz saw herself repeatedly running from the Hilux to the water's edge and back again. She stood, looked at the car, looked to where the others were. Turned a half circle. Would she be able to drive back and get help? Could she take a shovel and wade out with it as a weapon? There was no shovel. She waited. Billy would, Milton would know.

Cautiously, the men climbed down. There were only puddles left between them and Liz now. There were a few dozen fish in the net. They picked it up between them and, constantly glancing around and starting, walked back. It was sunset. The sand was patterned in ripples of gold and blue-black, the puddles shining liquid gold. A cool breeze and they were walking into the sun.

Liz told them what she had thought.

'Someone must be helping us.'

Chattering and laughing, they took fish after fish from the net, the threads of which dripped and sparkled with pearls.

Beneath the high stars, with a breeze and bright grins, they bounced home through creeks and moonlight. Big glassy-eyed fish surrounded them. The trees waved them past.

We Drink

'The builders are here, got in this morning,' Gerrard told Billy when they met between the office and the store. 'Their vehicle's knocked around a bit. The road's still pretty bad they say.'

'They starting Monday then?' Billy asked. Gerrard nodded. Billy continued, 'Any of our mob working with them?'

Gerrard leaned forward. 'You're joking,' he said. 'And whaddya mean, "our mob"? No, this lot don't know how to work.' He leaned back again and looked around. 'Anyway, one of the builders was here last year apparently. He knows them. There's grog around so someone must've got him to bring some in for them.'

Alphonse, Raphael, some other young ones, they down near Running Creek opposite the old people's camp. They had flagons with them, passing them 'round. They sitting there in the shade, on the rocks, just talking and drinking but when they got a bit drunk and started up they got noisier. Deslie was down there with them. He didn't drink but. They didn't let him, yet. He come up to the store and get smokes for them when they run out.

Araselli of the growing belly went for a walk about sunset with Margaret. They were talking about what they did a long time ago and what it would be like now if all the old people were still alive. They talking about what you did when you went to school in Darwin, in Perth. They were talking about boys.

Araselli saw them first. Alphonse, Raphael, Milton, Bruno, and that young one, Deslie. They were sitting in that long grass on those little river rocks at Running Creek. Them boys yelled out to those girls. 'Hey you girls. Hey Margaret, Araselli, what you doing. Hey, spunky girls.' Alphonse yelled out too. 'Araselli.' He young that fella. He shouldn't drink with them older boys, them men. He shouldn't say Araselli's name, or look at her. They rumbud, see. They looked at one another, again, all right. Done more than that, Alphonse, Araselli, and their growing belly.

Araselli said, 'Those boys are drunk.' Those girls bent their heads and looked at each other and laughed. They turned around and ran away laughing, and looking back at those boys. The boys called out, but didn't run after them. Too drunk even then. Too lazy too, probably. But Alphonse must have felt a hunger and ache inside him, looking after her like that, the way he did.

Later they came up to the camp here and were shouting and making noise. Alphonse did fight with one of Araselli's brothers. Raphael was yelling yelling yelling all the time and acting like a crazy man. He pushed Sebastian even, a little bit, and Sebastian's boys came in and they took him away and pushed him, shoved him. He's crazy that Raphael. We should do something. They was making noise all night. And Raphael even had a mission vehicle next morning and he was driving crazy in it. He could kill someone that one. I don't know how he got it, maybe stole it from that Murray. Father Paul was away that weekend. If he was here this wouldn't happen. When we were on the council and Father Pujol was here this didn't happen. We should do something. But they don't listen this mob.

Murray was over at the mission workshop early in the morning. Raphael came and asked for a Toyota. Murray said no. A mission vehicle didn't go anywhere unless someone from the mission went in it.

Murray and Raphael were standing on opposite sides of the utility tray. Murray realised that Raphael was drunk.

'I know you don't trust me ...'

'Sorry Raphael, that's the way it is. We don't lend them to anybody.'

'Steve said yes. I asked him just now. He said take one.' Steve was a lay missionary who had been there a month.

'Maybe he got mixed up. He can't say yes or no about the vehicles.'

'He did. Brother Tom, he there too.'

'Sorry Raphael. No can do.'

Raphael was edging around the tray.

'You white hole. Fuck you gardiya prick. Why not? Why not you tell me why, eh?'

Murray moved around the utility tray to keep opposite Raphael. Murray had heard of Raphael's capacity for violence, and he was worried. He realised that some of the other young men were standing about fifty metres away on the edge of the workshop yard.

'You gardiya hole. You don't trust us Aborigine? You don't wanna help black people? One day I make you sting, I lift you proper.'

Murray had the utility between himself and Raphael. The

workshop was behind him. This was ridiculous. This bastard was mad, and there was no sense arguing with him. He began moving toward the workshop with his back half turned to Raphael. He had his head down but was watching Raphael on the edge of his vision.

Raphael stomped off to where the others were, but kept yelling at Murray. 'Fuck off. Look, crawl off like a dog.'

Murray was angry and humiliated. Raphael and the others were walking away. Murray turned into the workshop and busied himself.

He heard a vehicle roaring from the mission grounds a couple of hundred metres away and immediately walked over there. Brother Tom was standing at the mission gates looking up where the road led through coconut palms.

'You give him it?'

'No. He called out as he drove past, said he'd seen you. Did he? Had you seen him?'

'Yeah. He abused me. I said no. I thought he was going to fight me.'

They could see the Toyota speeding recklessly and sliding around the corners of the small tracks leading around the edge of the camp.

Murray turned to Brother Tom. 'What do we do? What do you do to protect yourself if they do want to fight?'

'Don't let it happen in the first place. Use a shotgun. Shoot them below the knees.' He gave a snort of resignation. 'Only joking.' They inhaled and sighed. 'It is no good. You can't talk with a drunken Aborigine.' He smiled ruefully. 'That Toyota will run out of fuel very soon. I used it yesterday. As long as no one is killed first.'

'So when it stops we go and get it?' asked Murray.

'Yes, when it stops we will go up there. Many of them will be angry with the young men. They do not like Raphael. The way he bashes his two wives, Stella and Gloria, anyone. We will go up there and see.'

Billy and Liz were over at the school on Sunday. From there they watched a fight take place among the houses near the school gate. Two women were pushing and sparring at one another like buck kangaroos. A group of men and women jeered and cheered them, and swore and cursed one another. The distance and the window glass meant that the shouts carried thinly to Billy and Liz, and the dominating silence made it strangely theatrical. It was pathetic of course, but also, somehow, brave, to be making an effort of any sort in all this vastness. They stood at the edge of the window, so that they would not be seen watching, and the frame made the scene seem almost as if staged. They were intrigued.

Next day at school the senior students were sullen and subdued. One girl wrote this in her journal:

> Someone bought grog to Karama and all the people get drunk and they start having fights with one other that drinking business makes the older people like Fatima Walanguh Sebastian Samson very upset so when all the people are better next day the old people talk out loud to all the people who was drunk and tell them what they think of them when they are drunk and of course they feel shame.

Francis sat on his own and worked quietly all morning. He wrote little, but drew a careful and detailed picture of a muscular and bare-chested Aboriginal man careering through the mission grounds in a Toyota. White people fled in all directions. Young black families gathered in bunches and laughed and cheered, some older ones sat under the trees watching glumly. Deslie, who couldn't write even his own name with confidence, wanted to colour it in.

At recess and lunchtime all the kids were talking about how Raphael was driving like he was in a race and how he pinched a car from the mission. They were excited and impressed with his daring.

Is This Hunting?

Murray drove fast. He drove like one of the young blokes, like Raphael, like a hot-rodder. His car bounced and bucked over the rocks and lumps and corrugations, its suspension yelping and moaning. Milton was with him. They were going out to get oysters because low tide was at sunset and it was already getting late.

Jasmine heard them approaching. She was walking along the track between the airport and the tip. They stopped and offered her a lift, and she leapt in as the red dust passed them and swirled back and around the vehicle.

Murray drove even more ferociously, keen to impress, and on a rocky curve the car teetered, for a moment, on two wheels. Milton raised his eyebrows. Jasmine nudged him. Murray whooped and laughed. 'Scare you Jasmine? These women can't take it. What do you reckon Milton?' But he drove a little slower.

'Good car this,' said Milton, 'I'd like one like this.'

At the beach they picked their way among the slippery rocks and prised off large oysters. The sun was almost setting and they slapped at the midgies and mosquitoes. Jasmine and Milton worked together, putting oysters into the tin Milton carried. Milton turned to Jasmine as they crouched together among the black rocks. 'Hear? Listen.'

From the mangroves came small noises. Popping, clicking, sucking. Milton was solemn. 'Djilina. In the mangroves. We're all right, they're shy. You be here on your own but, sittin', sittin' lookin' at the sun with the mangroves behind you, one of the men ones might get you, take you away. They tall, long beards and hair; sweep behind 'em, cover their footprints. The women are good, just cheeky sometimes, but they don't take people. Old Walanguh, you know, Walanguh? He was taken by them when he was little, and they grow him up. And he has power, you know? Like magic.'

The longer they listened, the more they heard them. Regular sounds, like careful footsteps, hesitating and creeping. Milton whispered, 'My father was out here last week, just sittin', just sittin' watchin' the sun. He turned and he saw one. Him disappear again.'

Murray called out to them, his voice thin, struggling feebly to reach them through the thick light. 'Enough?' He held up a full bucket.

It was dusk, and, as they drove back, it was darkness. The headlights picked out the tree trunks beside the track. Among them were tall, thin, stooped beings. They were watching. The wind brushed at their long beards and hair as the car hurtled past.

Murray drove across the airstrip on the way back. 'Shortcut,' he said. He sped up. The headlights picked out two pairs of eyes. 'Kangaroos,' exclaimed Milton. 'I had a gun, I'd get 'em!'

Murray accelerated toward them. 'Tucker!' he whooped. 'Tucker time.'

They hit one on the passenger side of the 'roo bar, and Jasmine saw it large and pale in the lights, heard the thud, saw it shrinking in the darkness as it was hurled past her door window.

'One!' Murray the cowboy.

His mouth was a tight line, his face hard in the refection of the dashboard lights. He swung the car around, the rear drifting out in the graded gravel of the airstrip.

The other 'roo was bobbing fur, bleached in the lights, becoming larger and growing legs tail head as they sped toward it, caught it, hit it with the brakes locked up and the gravel sliding around them. It cartwheeled forward onto its small arms and the front tyre went over it.

'Got 'em. Done.' Murray gripped the steering wheel hard and pushed it. 'Better than a gun,' Milton was laughing. Jasmine held her bottom lip in her teeth. They sat in silence for a moment. A moment of a motor purring, an indicator light flashing ridiculously. A full moon and hearts beating.

Milton and Murray slung the corpses over the 'roo bar.

Next day, Milton told Liz and Annette that Murray had given the camp a feed.

'Shit, what is he? Great white hunter?'

'But someone's got to look after them. The kids'll be well fed for once anyway,' said Annette.

Billy flew out one Friday afternoon, and arrived back on the Sunday night driving the Toyota utility he'd bought in Derby. The tray was heavily laden, and a small aluminium dinghy was strapped on top.

Some days later Billy heard a voice calling his name.

'Hey!' Sebastian was waving from across the school fence and walking toward him. Billy hesitated, then walked across to the fence. 'You got outboard motor?'

Billy nodded.

'You might say no, but can I use it, this weekend, me and

my boys? We look after it, bring it back straight away, same day.'

'Sorry Sebastian. I have to say no. Otherwise I might end up hating you if something went wrong. You understand?'

This time Sebastian nodded, but he was disappointed. Billy didn't believe that Sebastian could guarantee who would use the motor and how they would treat it. Billy couldn't bring himself to trust Sebastian or his boys to look after his motor.

'You come. Your motor, my boat. We look for some turtle together, eh?'

'Yes.'

'Yes.' Sebastian nodded vigorously. 'Tomorrow, you pick me up at my place. I'll wait on the road, you know, up from my place?'

Liz came with them. Sebastian's wife, Victoria, came also. Sebastian had his harpoon, knife, a plastic container of water. Then Milton climbed in the back of the utility, and then Beatrice, and Jimmy ...

'Shit,' said Liz, 'how many more?'

'Eh, Sebastian, that's it then?'

Sebastian, Billy, Liz and Milton went in the dinghy. Victoria, Beatrice, and a disappointed Jimmy stayed on the beach.

They followed the coast, the small outboard motor working hard to push the aluminium dinghy with four adults aboard.

Milton looked at his father, then stood at the bow. He stood on the front thwart with his harpoon in hand. The harpoon was a long thin piece of wood, like a spear. It had a metal tip to which was tied a long length of strong rope.

Milton moved so that he had one foot each side of the point

of the vee formed by the bow and was standing on the gunnels. His weight forced the bow down. He stood tall and surveyed the ocean around him, adjusting the balance of the harpoon in his hand as he did so.

'Go slow, just creep.' Sebastian repeated his statement with a gesture of his shaking hand. Billy decided to watch the hand, which also indicated the direction they were to go in. Sebastian was concentrating on the surface of the ocean around him now that he had, by reference to the ocean floor and to landmarks, found the point from which they started the hunt in earnest.

'This bottom, see? Turtle like near this rock, crabs too, big ones, for tucker.'

They followed the coast, the great rocks standing in the deep blue sea, and the red beaches, white beaches, between them. The motor droned, the ocean lapped at the aluminium hull. The sea shifted, glinted, winked in the powerful sunlight.

'There! See him?' Sebastian whispered tightly. 'That way.'

Billy steered the boat in the direction indicated by Sebastian's pointing hand. Milton's toes gripped the gunnels. 'Shh. Slow.' Billy and Liz hadn't seen anything. There was a shape, like coral moving, a few metres before them to port. Milton went up on his toes and launched himself with the harpoon. Almost as he hit the water Sebastian sat back with a grunt. Milton surfaced, spluttering. An embarrassed grin twisted his face as he pulled himself in over the bow, almost nosediving the craft as he did so. 'Missed him,' said Billy, pointlessly.

They retrieved the harpoon. The tip was bent and they spent some time on the shore hammering it back into shape with a small boulder.

They continued. It was warm even on the ocean, and with

the steady rhythm of the motor, soporific. Milton remained precariously balanced at the bow, and Sebastian sat in his slouched way, as if folding in on himself, but with his eyes alert and shifting. He was not shaking. He was … was it him, humming? Billy kept an eye on the two of them for a sign, and Liz gazed into the deep, changing blues of the ocean. Here and there birds gathered where stricken bait fish were herded to the surface. The birds squawked, and fell, picking off the small fish.

Milton dived a second time and Billy saw the harpoon, saw the harpoon accelerating away from them at an angle to the surface of the water. The rope was uncoiling and springing out of the boat. Sebastian clutched at the rope, and Milton, having leapt from the water like a dolphin and become man again once in the dinghy, held it firmly, and went to haul it in. The rope went limp.

The next time Billy saw the turtle first. Its head popped from the surface, suddenly, not twenty metres to their right. Billy hissed and swung the boat slowly that way. Its face seemed to register surprise. Liz said afterwards, 'Like ET, or an old man.' Milton dived, and they saw the rope snaking out as if it wanted to escape them. Billy cut the motor on Sebastian's command and watched as Milton and Sebastian held the rope, and strained. The bow swung around and pointed along the rope to the turtle. They began hauling it in.

The turtle was alongside. Billy helped, but it was too heavy to get aboard. The boat would capsize. Sebastian and Milton held it and Billy steered for a nearby beach. They went very slowly, for the dinghy was leaning heavily to the turtle's side where the two men held it, and the gunnel was only centimetres from the water. It was difficult to retain a grip on the turtle.

With the boat supported by the sand the three men managed to haul the turtle on board. It was heavy, and its skin had an almost human texture; thicker, and more leathery to be sure, but still it felt like an old person's skin. Billy thought he would like to taste its flesh.

Billy stuck his knife into it once or twice, around its throat, and it waved its head and legs about. 'Kill it! Kill it properly, don't be cruel.' Liz yelled at them and pushed Billy. Milton and Sebastian looked bemused. Billy sawed his blunt knife across the animal's throat a few times. Dark blood spurted, and thick tendons and veins were exposed. 'Yes, that it, kill it,' said Sebastian, and he rubbed his hands together.

They motored back to the beach where they had left the others. They sat very low in the water. The wind was up now, and the small wind waves broke around the bow and splashed them. Once or twice the dinghy, with so much weight at the bow, wallowed, and seemed about to dive into the depths. Milton moved as far back as he was able and they continued even more slowly.

Billy was unsure of which beach they had departed from, but he saw the black shapes of the children by the water's edge, and then the vehicle. It took forever to reach them.

Jimmy and Beatrice ran into the shallows and grabbed the bow as they beached. Victoria ambled down from the shade of the trees behind the dunes. Billy and Sebastian dragged the turtle up the beach on its back. Its limbs continued to twitch. The children poked at it, and kicked it. Victoria smiled. 'Big one, eh? Good one.'

'What do you want, eat it here, on this beach, or go back to camp? You tell us, it might be too hot for you maybe. We want you to be happy.' Sebastian asked them. They hesitated.

Everyone packed up the gear. They left the dinghy upside down in the dunes.

Crossing a creek on the way back they saw a large goanna. It raised itself and raced from the creek bed. In the rear-vision mirror Billy saw Sebastian mouth one word. The goanna stopped. All those in the back of the utility began laughing and, as Billy accelerated out of the creek bed, the goanna was released into motion.

Sebastian asked them to drop him off a few kilometres before the camp. 'We not get enough for us ourselves if we eat this one back there,' he said. They rolled the turtle off the back of the ute and it fell where the fire would be. Milton pursed his lips and held two fingers out to his father. Sebastian put a cigarette between them. The two younger children stayed with Sebastian and Victoria, but Milton came back into the camp with them to tell some of the others to come out for a feed. They dropped him outside one of the huts, and he waved goodbye over his shoulder as he walked in the front entrance.

'Could've said thanks, don't you think? It wouldn't have put him out or anything,' said Liz. 'Sebastian did, that's the difference between the old ones and the young. They just take you for granted.'

'Yeah. Shall we go back out there in a while, see how it's going?'

'What!'

'Have a taste.'

'Yuk. No! You go if you want.'

Her skin burnt, her flaming hair dry and crackling, and turtle blood spattered all over her.

They Drink

Sister Therese she run the health clinic. She the young one from Spain, or Philippines, maybe. Nice little lady, bit hard to understand but. You see? There's all sorts of language spoken in Karnama. Spanish, Spanish English, Philippine Spanish, Philippine English, Aboriginal languages, Aboriginal English, Australian English, Government English, Politician English. And more. Got them all nearly.

Sister used to stay over there all the time then, at that health clinic, maybe because it was air-conditioned, and all with new sinks and toilets and fridges and taps and that. Close for emergencies also.

One night Sister rang the mission. We only had phones in Karnama a little time then. She was frightened. Murray he could hear it in her voice as soon as she spoke.

'Murray, please can you come? There's drunken men outside the clinic. Shouting out and calling my name. They cannot even hardly stand up.'

Murray tell her: 'You'll be right Sister, they won't come in, you've got good locks. Anyway, I make it policy to have nothing to do with drunken Aborigines.'

But Sister Therese was frightened. 'It's not Aborigines. It's the builders.'

They were too drunk. This was not work day, see, and they been drinking long time. All the people were watching them, laughing. It was funny really. Kids copied them, staggering and talking lazy like. Father Paul and Murray went over there pretending they was just driving. They joked with the drunk men and got them over to mission with them.

It's no good having people like that in Karnama. They stay over behind mission workshop away from the people. They came to build houses but don't let the young men work with them. They look at the women, part laughing and part hungry. They bring too much beer with them.

Every night they drink until have to fall asleep. We know. Some of the women go over there. They say to them, 'Hey, come over to our camp. We can play cards too. Have some tucker, maybe a little drink.' Eva went over there, Araselli too, even with the baby in her. Milton's wife, Annie, she went there too. And even some of the women who have lots of kids. We know, and people talked about it.

Everyone know they had drinks there. They sell beer to some of the men. Too much money. And then we had drunken people shouting and fighting and too much noise at night.

And two times some of the people — it was Raphael — sneak over there in the daytime when they were working and empty their freezers. Took all their beer, everything. They came back and opened the fridge, and saw nothing. Nothing. Just emptiness.

They got wild. They told Gerrard about it, and they tell Father Paul too. We were wild too, but not because they were. They shouldn't have grog here, not if we don't want them to. The council made a letter like this:

From now on
No grog in Karnama
By Plane by overland By any whatever
The Karnama Aboriginal Corporation Land
is now a dry area
ANYONE breaking this council rule
Will be Punished
Mission or other workers found Drinking
on Aboriginal land will also be Punished
No vehicles car ETC will move
Around Karnama after sundown
Unless for emergencies

Chairman and council

But who took any notice? Moses and some other councillors, they drink themselves. But they don't go silly like these young blokes.

We don't like the grog, really. It's no good for us. We don't like it. Them young ones, they get drunk, they want to fight. They get a car and think they're like in a video. One day someone get killed, a kid maybe. They drunk they hit wives, fight with other blokes, go after their rumbud. They don't listen.

One young bloke grab Fatima, he's supposed to be her rumbud and not look at her even. He grabbed her and push her away when she tried to stop them fighting. One day maybe someone just lay her out, rumbud or no rumbud.

Some of the young ones, still at school even, some of them like that too. Drinking and that. Young Deslie, he was standing in the road turning around and around and yelling out. Sebastian sang out to him from down near the school. He didn't hear, he didn't listen. And Franny, that dreamy one, drunk and fall asleep, sleeping in his own vomit.

When Father Pujol was here it was better. We didn't have so many Toyotas maybe, but now only chairman's mob get them anyway. No one fight then, no drink anyway. He warned you once, twice, then he made you leave, throw you out of the place. Especially if it was a white bloke causing trouble. But there wasn't so many white blokes then either. Just mission and couple of teachers.

Tell us, we learned anything from white man yet? Nowadays people make a mistake. Maybe tired. Little by little Aborigine going down. Drinking and dying. Making circles, littler and more little. We don't like looking, and seeing it that way. We want to fly up again.

They can't forget about our roots, they can't leave behind and go to the whiteman roots. That no good.

Our time, we never see all these things. When early people was alive, in their own land, we never see such things. When we were little children, when we grow big, all our life we see things get all mixed. We see wrong things for our people, so far for the Aborigine the gardiya make trouble. Grog, money, everything.

So. What we gunna do? We can only do, we can only say. They can listen to us. They can believe us, what we say and what we tell them.

That's all we say. That's what we ask.

That's what Billy should write down and show those kids.

Fun and Games

Gerrard moved into the clinic accommodation when Sister Therese moved back to the convent with the other Sisters. She didn't like being on her own and so close to all the drunks. Gerrard set up his exercise bicycle in front of his video recorder and pedalled away in the morning before he went to the office and in the afternoon before he had dinner. The house was the only one in Karnama with ducted air-conditioning, so he didn't get too hot and he sweated less doing his exercise than he did just sitting in the corrugated iron office during the day.

One evening he invited Billy and Liz over for a meal. He liked food and he liked cooking. They took beer with them, and he opened a bottle of wine. He had wine flown in by the crate. Billy, Liz, and the wine breathed, and Gerrard spoke rapidly over his shoulder as he stir-fried.

He hoped his wife would be able to join him within a couple of weeks, now that he had this place. He didn't think she'd be able to take the heat and, well, the environment generally.

After the meal they played Scrabble. Gerrard told them of the plans he had for getting the community to begin operating small enterprises, so they wouldn't be relying on hand-outs. And they'd come to understand things like reward for effort. 'But the problem is they get good money for doing nothing, so, you know, why bother?'

Gerrard started the game. He told them he didn't play much, but that his wife liked to when they lived in places like this. His first word: BLACK.

'Topical, Gerrard, but not a big scorer. Eighteen.'

The next word. MAGIC. Gerrard roared with laughter.

'Still relevant! Twenty. You been earbashed yet about the blackmagic?' He made one word of two, said it slowly, staring at them dramatically. Then he rolled his eyes. 'Amazing. They're even frightened of the dark. They've concocted some superstitious mix of primitive church; you know, devils, the angel Gabriel's feathers, fire and brimstone; and bits of their own old voodoo stuff.'

BEGIN. 'Ten.'

'I haven't played this much,' said Billy. 'I don't play much, not, like, games I mean.'

Gerrard snorted. 'C'mon, you're a teacher aren't you? Hey, aren't you a bit of a writer? So I hear. You should be a whiz!' But he wasn't. Gerrard played well, using the board like a map to collect the treasures of triple scores. Liz was competitive. Billy lagged behind. And he was drinking too much, the wine confused him.

'Nice wine? I like this drop,' said Gerrard. 'Half a bottle a night with dinner. A little more allowed on weekends. Disciplined drinking is vital to good digestion. One of life's pleasures. Moderate drinking, everything in moderation … Hey what about this?'

VIVANT.

'Piss off, Gerrard. English only.'

'Okay then.'

VELVET.

Gerrard smirked. 'Look at these words. BLACK, VELVET. Billy had GIN in BEGIN. What are we thinking of?' And he studied his new letters carefully. Liz showed annoyance in her glance at Billy.

The door slid open. The dark, warm air rushed in. It was Moses. He stood at the door, one bare foot inside the room, the other out. They could smell him.

'You got something to mix? Ginger ale, Coke, something like that?'

Gerrard laughed and gave him half a large bottle of lemonade. 'Don't drink too much Moses, you need to be on deck in the morning.'

Gerrard told them that Moses and a couple of the other council members drank pretty well every night. 'They do it properly though. You know, quiet. Just with the family. Don't bother anyone. They know how to drink.

'You know I've bought a bus?' He suddenly changed the topic. 'For the community to use.

'The kids, the old people, hardly ever get to go out. It's mostly just Moses and those with him; his sons, his family.

'Some of Samson's mob, of course, once he gets that new vehicle for the ranger's job. You seen it? Lovely. Air-conditioning. Wonder how long before that's wrecked. But the others, specially the old ones and the little kids, they hardly ever get to go out to the beach on the weekends, or anywhere, and they love that, you know.'

'Yeah,' said Liz, 'don't we know it. It's hard enough to get past them when we go out ourselves. You could end up with everyone with you if you didn't say no.'

'Can't a roster be worked out for the community vehicles?' asked Billy.

'Not easily. Use of the vehicles seems to be a perk of being chairman, or a council member. I'm not gunna rock the boat on that one.'

'That's what they've learnt quickest, from us,' said Liz. 'Perks, privilege …'

'Corruption?'

'Well, maybe,' Gerrard was reluctant. 'This is the real world, you know. Anyway, I thought I could pay one of the young blokes to drive the bus, out of funds, to the beach and back on Sundays. Even for bringing tourists in when the boat comes in. They could do corroborees in here even, and the community could hire the bus.'

They had taken a break from the game. Gerrard got out of his seat. 'More wine?'

Well, all right then. If you insist.

As he went over to the refrigerator he demonstrated his exercise bike to them. His torso rocked, his long heavy legs pushed and pushed, and the pedals whirred. They cheered him drunkenly. Going nowhere, and red in the face, he looked at the meter before him which told his speed. He stopped pedalling, and held his hands clasped over his head as if coasting over a finishing line. He had to slide from the saddle suddenly, and put a foot to the floor to stop the bike toppling. 'Oops.'

He brought the opened bottle of wine back to the table. 'Not as good, this one. But still, we won't notice now, eh?' And they continued the game.

'You hire the bus out, Gerrard?' asked Liz. 'Since you bought it privately and all?'

'Oh yeah,' Gerrard shook his head. 'Otherwise it wouldn't last. There wasn't enough community money to buy one, believe it or not. I thought they might buy it from me later. It's for the community, it's for them.'

'And pocket money for you,' said Liz, with a smile.

'Of course,' agreed Gerrard, unabashed. 'For the community's benefit. Alex and I've agreed, it'd be good for the school, the school could hire it too. The real world, Liz. Economics, exchange. What've you got to offer, Billy?' He laughed, and said again, 'The real world.'

Nearing the end of the game. Gerrard in front, Liz a close second, Billy a distant last. The second bottle of wine gone, and they'd drunk the beer as well.

'C'mon Billy, what've you got?'

'Doubt,' said Billy.

'Doubt?'

'Yes, doubt.'

'About what?' laughed Gerrard.

'About me, the past, what I'm doing, where I belong, the future, um …'

'You sound like the mob here,' slurred Gerrard.

'You're drunk Billy,' said Liz. 'Anyway, you can't have doubt. Both B's are on the board and it wouldn't fit in.'

'Oh.' His eyes were bloodshot, and he looked tired and pale, a creamy, jaundiced colour.

Gerrard and Liz, magnanimous in their victory over him, looked at his letters.

'D, T, Y.'

'Look. Here, with OUGHT.'

'DOUGHTY.'

'Don't have doubt, but be doughty,' Gerrard and Liz seemed to be laughing at him.

Gardiya. Whities.

'A good score to end with Billy.'

'Look at the board. What did we start with?'

BLACK MAGIC BEGIN.

'Wooo. Gotta black magic woman,' Gerrard was laughing and singing, badly, as he let them out of the door. It was late, dark, and quiet.

'Remember Billy, not doubt but doughty.' Gerrard yawned, said good night again, and closed the door. The light went out. Billy and his wife yawned their silent way home. Home? To their house.

Billy, all a totter, was remembering a story Milton had told him, about a visit to Derby. Admittedly Milton was drunk at the time, but he'd seen a snake. But it was not a normal snake.

Milton Sees

Now that he was proper sparked up, a bit drunk, Milton wanted to be where it was quieter. Maybe with his brothers and that, playing cards. He stepped out of the bright whirl of laughter and shouts, eyes and teeth, sweaty bodies cold glass beer smells. He stepped out of the Spinifex Hotel and into a dark shower of gravel as a car, wheels spinning and motor snarling, was launched from the car park.

Not far to walk. With his tax cheque this year he might buy a car, maybe that one from Alex. Maybe a bigger one. Drive around Karnama, in the bush, pushing trees over. Get those girls looking at him. Those schoolgirls, those cheeky ones.

He jumped a small fence and walked toward the goal posts gleaming in the moonlight on the far side of the oval. It quiet now. Night-time. This was not his country. Maybe he'd go back and sit with those others under that tree opposite the Spinny. Mad bastards them though. Be fighting soon enough, and that Veronica make a man walk like a duck. True.

Could be ghosts here, on this oval. Quiet night like this. The hiss of cars on bitumen came to him from the far side of the oval. He headed for where the headlights probed under the streetlights there, and felt much relieved to climb the fence onto the path. Safer.

He saw the snake in front of him. King Brown, at night

even, just up a bit and looking right at him. His heart loud and fast and he meant to take a stick and kill it there. But it waited. It waited. It watched him. He knew it. This is not a snake this is a man. He could see it, you know. It was waiting for someone and it had a man's eyes. Just quiet and proper deadly.

Milton stepped sideways onto the road and walked wide around it.

He walked on the side of the road for a long time, looking back where the snake was still waiting, still watching. A car came along and he stepped back onto the path. He was near the Boab Inn now, and he saw some people drinking in that little quiet park opposite. He told them what had happened and they all shot off to his cousin's house down past the army place.

Milton fell asleep inside the house later that night and when he awoke it was light. People sitting on the steps drinking from cans. No one fighting. They was just happy. Someone had a ute, and Milton drove to visit another mob with some cartons and some people in the back.

They just did some drinking, talking, some watched a video.

Milton sat outside, resting his back against the wall. An old man walked over and sat down next to him.

He said sideways to Milton, 'Thanks for not killin' me.' Milton nearly laughed. He didn't know what he was saying. Maybe he was joking. But then he saw the man's eyes. They were like the snake.

Stingray

Billy, Liz, and their students took the bus to the beach. The school could hire the bus cheaply, partly because of the agreement between Gerrard and Alex, but also because of a subsidy from community funds. The trip was in many ways, perhaps, a form of trade-off. Later the students would write about it. So, there they were — Scrap Metal music blasting on the stereo, eskies of food and cool drinks, fishing lines — all chattering and laughing. The new, and somehow soft, bus seemed incongruous with the hard light, the dust, the shimmering trees and bush, and a track that always jostled and shook you up.

They stop just once, for a tree that had late bush apples. Something like a radish, but injected with air. Like a Chinese Apple, like a red heavy tough bubble, stick-bashed out of a scrubby tree. Billy enjoys the collecting. A kid in the bus shouts out. The bus stops and whoosh! everyone's off to get bush apple. Figures all through the bush. Appearing, disappearing. A shadow in coloured shirt fits from trunk to trunk; a flurry of them become the kids throwing sticks up into a tree and, in virtually the same motion, plucking the bush apples from the air as they fall, and briefly bounce.

In the bus, shimmy-shammying through sand and rustling

leaves, the kids check each tree is where it should be, and read the tyre prints to see which cars have been where, and name sites. There's rock paintings in there, I think. They stop for a bit to look.

We climbed and climbed and we went right up to the top of the rock. From there you look out to the sea and you can see all the beaches and feel the wind. It is a lovely view. We told Sir and Miss if they wanted to see some better rock paintings so we took them right around the rock. They liked them. Then Jimmy went into a cave and we saw paintings of people, animals, tools, and Wandjinas. We also saw some bones of long time ago. But then we thought it might be a Law cave and we were frightened. So we got out, and we did want to go to the beach anyway.

At the beach everyone dispersed along the shoreline in small groups. Except Francis of course. And he's not right, you know. He's been a little bit sick ever since he was a baby. And maybe he's a bit spoilt. He's different; big thick glasses, little bit deaf. He sat on the beach in the shade of the bus and listened to AC/DC on the Walkman that Moses bought for him.

Billy and Deslie went together. Billy was hoping to learn something about fishing. Walking calf-deep in the tepid water near some mangroves Deslie grabbed Billy's arm. 'See, Sir? See? See. Stingray. Good eating sometimes, them ones.'

Eventually Billy did see. A stingray, some fifty centimetres across, was motionless between where they stood and some rocks before them. 'You watch it, Sir. I get stick.'

Deslie crept back from the mangrove's edge with a thick stick the length of his forearm. Billy pointed unnecessarily to where the stingray remained. Deslie slowly raised the arm holding the stick. He threw it, moving rapidly toward the stingray as he did so. Billy saw the stingray as if flying on the surface of the water, splashing, straining, racing toward open sea. Deslie snatched up the stick from where it was bobbing in the water. He ran through the deepening water in the direction of the stingray's retreat, the stick above his head. He threw it again, picked it from the water and, running and splashing hard in the thigh-deep water, he threw it a third time. He stopped where the stick had landed, looking around him. He bent over and, with his back arched awkwardly to keep his head above water, began feeling around in the sand. 'Here somewhere, Sir.'

Billy looked away, a little embarrassed for Deslie's sake. It had escaped. His eyes followed the shoreline a few hundred metres to where the others had gathered on the rocks not far from the bus. They were fishing there, and some gathered oysters before the rising tide made it impossible to do so. Billy turned around and Deslie was walking toward him. He held the tail of the stingray in his teeth and his left hand gripped its jaw. His right hand broke off the barbs at the base of its tail.

'Deslie, you're fantastic.'

'Good eating, Sir, these, when they're fat.' He held the stingray flat and belly up on a rock, and cut a small opening with one of the barbs he'd saved. The skin opened as if from a scalpel, showing white flesh. Deslie poked it with his finger. 'This one no good.' He dropped the stingray back into the water and kicked at it. Sluggishly, it swam away.

They walked further around the coast. Deslie asked Billy to work out compass directions using the sun and his watch, the way he'd shown them at school.

Billy hesitated, 'It's only approximate Deslie, and I need a protractor to reckon it accurately.'

Deslie laughed. 'I don't need to do that, eh? Do I, Sir? I don't need to make those reckonings. I know this country, I'm here, I'm Deslie.' He pointed to the ground beneath him and rapidly stomped his feet, and they laughed and stomped together, as if dancing in their joy.

Billy maybe felt a little bit silly then. He was meant to be the teacher. And walking back, under Deslie's direction, through the twists and curves of the mangroves and the tide rushing in again, he thought of how Deslie no longer used his childhood name because someone of that same name had died in the recent past, and of how Deslie was not of this country, really, any more than Billy himself was. Yet Deslie seemed so confident of who he was. At least, more so than Billy; take away his job at the school and what's left?

They all crouched in the shade of the bus and lunched on fish, oysters, sandwiches from school, cordial. 'You ever hear them spirits, them devils in the mangroves, Miss? You know 'bout them?' asked Margaret. 'They got long long hair, and the men, long beards. You hear them, when it's quiet, if you careful. 'Bout sunset time. Little sounds you know. Them men ones sneak up behind you and steal you away. The women try to whistle, warn you. You know Walanguh, old Walanguh? They took him when he a baby and he did stay with them. That be why his hair all white.'

They were all watching Billy and Liz, hands frozen in the act of delivering food to their mouths.

'True? Is that true?'

'Yes, that what they say. It true I think, you hear them. My daddy he saw one, one time, at Murugudda.' They all quietly agreed.

They were in the bus, with its motor idling, when Deslie remembered he'd left his fishing line on the rocks near the mangroves. He ran to collect it. They watched him running back to the bus through the soft white sand, grinning at them. Behind him the rich blue sea suddenly erupted. A huge manta ray burst into the air close to the shore, and they could see the ocean cascading from its back and beneath it the torn and foaming whorl it had left. For a moment it hung, impossibly, in the air, then fell with a great splash. They could breathe again. Liz felt the bus should have burst into cheering. Deslie looked at them, behind him, at them, and ran faster, not laughing now.

Visitors in Great White Boats

Milton and Billy went fishing in Billy's dinghy. 'This way.' Milton's arm pointed across the smooth ocean toward some land, vague in the distance. He sat at the bow, his shape dark against the milky turquoise sea and the traces of mist which remained above it, as yet untouched by this day's breeze.

They skimmed across the ocean. The outboard's roar was left behind them, and the aluminium hull amplified the skip and tap of the sea. A lone dolphin flashed across their bow, dark and swift, and flew, once, for a blinking time only, clear of the water, splashing them, before looping away into its own blue silence.

Milton knew a place around the headland. He was returning there, to that place, the one quite close to the rocks and red beach, but where the water is very deep. The old people used to walk there. Milton and Billy motored slowly to and fro across it, dragging silver lures. Occasionally the lures broke the surface. Great fish sprang from the deep, and silver arcs flashed past the boat. Sometimes a lure was hit clear of the water.

The sudden singing of a line as it tautened. The queenfish Milton brought in; it shot into the air shaking itself to free the lure from its mouth. Milton kept the line taut. The line cut the water as the fish swam deep, and it burned in his hand. Billy had silenced the motor. A tension, a singing line. The fish leapt again, it seemed in slow motion, and hung in the air for a moment, a template held against the blue hues of sea and sky with a crowd of silver droplets feeing it.

Milton hauled it in, and the gaff pierced its armour of scales. Red blood spurted over the floor of the dinghy, and over their bare feet as the big fish thrashed among the stiff corpses of its fellows. They cursed each fish with joy, and with a tiny whispering fear as they saw the sun fade in each great, glassy, dying eye.

There were little suns all around them. They bounced from the knife blade, the aluminium of the dinghy, the ocean's surface as the sea exhaled. Little suns sparkling thorns. The sea breeze began.

Returning around the headland they saw the catamaran which brought the rich tourists. It was moored out from where they'd left the car. They circled it in the dinghy, not having seen it up close before. The few staff remaining on board came out and called down to them as they tossed around in the echo of their motor and the chop bouncing off the large hull.

Someone invited them aboard, so they tied the dinghy to the catamaran and were led through small upholstered rooms, treading the carpets in their blood-caked feet. They sat at the bar with the crew and shared a beer with them, and spoke in embarrassed belches. It was small and muffled after being in the spread of the sea, under the roofless sky, in their tiny resonating dinghy, yet they spoke beneath those low ceilings as if across a great distance. The tourists and some of the crew had gone into the village to have a look. There was a corroboree tonight, for the tourists. Milton had forgotten, Billy hadn't heard.

It's a good idea, that crew said, having the bus take the

tourists into the settlement itself. Must be rough on the bus though.

They took the dinghy ashore, waving their thanks to the crew gathered at the top of the ladder. The catamaran looked more impressive from the shore with its white paint sparkling as it slowly turned on its mooring, its shape and size so novel along this coast. It looked so out of place, so pristine, and so, well, advanced that it could have been a spaceship.

Halfway back to the camp they came across the bus. The chassis at the rear rested on the ground, and the vehicle sat at an uncomfortable angle. It had become bogged, and Raphael, revving the motor and spinning the wheels, had broken the rear axle. The tourists sat huddled under the trees, like exotic and very ripe fruit, unable to survive the heat and about to suddenly decompose into this foreign soil. Only fading pastel clothing, a sandal or two, and their rusting cameras would remain to show they ever existed here. Their hands waved the flies away from their flushed faces, and their breathing was rapid and light.

Some of the tourists accepted Billy's offer and crammed themselves into the back of his vehicle and under the dinghy which, roped to a high rack level with the top of the cab, provided some shifting shade. Billy drove as carefully as he could, suddenly mindful of the frailty of the pale people behind him. The hot metal stung their thin skin, their soft flesh bruised, their eyes wept with the wind and dust. It seemed their brittle bones would break, their very skeletons fall apart within them as the Toyota lurched along.

Usually Billy and Milton distributed their catch as they came back among the houses. As they drove back through the camp Milton would tell Billy where to stop, and to whom they should give fish. It made them feel strong and generous. 'Proper hunters, eh?' one or the other of them would say.

They did the same today, otherwise the fish would be wasted. But they did it hurriedly, because of their cargo of fail humanity, but also because that cargo revived itself. They remembered they were paying passengers, and they transformed themselves from cargo to consumers. They cooed at the babies, wrinkled their noses at the smells, stared into the grimy gloom within doorways and shook their heads at the rubbish and the signs of neglect. Their cameras whirred clicked flashed in accompaniment. Such black skins, such bright sun; this would mean problems with film exposure for sure. The people receiving fish kept their heads bowed, and showed no pleasure in the gifts. They mumbled and turned away. The tourists wanted to be friendly, and shouted at them, apparently hoping that they could communicate with the aliens by doing so.

So everyone was pleased when they saw Jasmine. A white girl. A young white girl. Oh, all alone here. How does she do it? And Milton, awkward and grinning, gave a large fish to Jasmine. She was just outside her place. But he saw her standing, blank faced, with the heavy fish in her arms and changed his mind.

'I'll fillet it, clean it, bring it back to you.' The passengers, standing on the tray, looking down on Milton and Jasmine, nodded approvingly among themselves. Milton leapt back into the cab and, even from the driver's side, Billy felt himself wrapped in the curves of Jasmine's smile and cleavage as she leaned in the passenger window. She gave Milton a quick kiss on the cheek. 'For the audience,' she winked.

The tourists disembarked, slowly and stiffy, at the community office. They felt better now, having reasserted themselves. 'What an experience.'

Gerrard organised vehicles to ferry the others in and tried to arrange to get the bus fixed, somehow. He opened the artefacts store and invited the tourists to look through what was there. 'Feel free to have a look around,' he said, and some of the tourists continued to circle within the small store. The rest of them moved to just outside the doorway, and stood there, turning their heads from side to side, squinting and grinning. Then they headed for the community store which stood on the fringe of the housing and by one of the school's gates. One person detoured toward the stone buildings and green lawns of the mission grounds, and a couple walked over to the school and peered in the windows of a classroom, before Alex, putting in some more weekend work, and always guarding his territory, came out to investigate them.

The corroboree that night, the first held for tourists at the camp rather than one of the beaches, was not a success. Too many of the men were late getting back from helping Raphael with the bus, and his bad mood had tainted them all. Samson didn't turn up. It was a half-hearted affair, which didn't start until after dark, and even then the fires did not glow, but weakly flickered and sputtered because they were lit too late and no one cared to stoke them. The performance finished early. Many reasons.

Gerrard said afterward that he wasn't going to pay them, but he did when Samson started talking about the people getting together and sacking him. He was not a project officer's arsehole. They didn't want the bloody tourists here anyway.

Perhaps the tourists enjoyed the argument more than the dance.

Milton came over to visit Billy later in the evening. Billy had kept out of the way, not wanting to be asked to transport tourists back out to their catamaran. He was filleting fish, and putting them into small freezer bags when Milton arrived.

They filleted and packed the remaining fish together. It was a plan they had worked out this morning. Like most people in the camp Milton didn't have a refrigerator, let alone a freezer. Now he could come over during the week and get tucker for just him and his family. They kept the packs stacked separately.

When they had finished they sat under the air-conditioner in the lounge room and drank tea. Milton looked around the room and admired the house again. 'Maybe I'll get one like this next time, one of these new ones,' he said.

Billy looked at him across his cup. 'Who? How do you decide who gets the new ones?' he asked.

Milton shrugged. 'It just happens. We all talk about it. Chairman, them on the council, their mob first.'

He picked up an old newspaper from under the chair and found the motoring section of the classified advertisements. 'I want a Toyota like your one, strong one. My father can have my little old one then.' He pointed at the small photographs. Billy read out the advertisements and prices, and they speculated on whether it was best to go all the way to Perth or Darwin and drive one back. Billy calculated how much Milton would need to save from each pay, and for how long. The result was depressing, so they ignored it.

'I could leave it here, with you, in your yard then, maybe, when I wasn't using it? Hey, I can leave my car here now, when I want to?'

'Sure Milton, but why would you want to do that?'

'All right for you, you haven't got everyone, like family, cousin-brothers, everybody, using your stuff all the time. I need a box with a lock to keep everything in.

'Then I could maybe get rich, go on holidays like these tourists that come here, if I wanted to. But I wouldn't expect the people, where I went, to put on shows for me like in a zoo or something. And I wouldn't complain to their boss and say I won't pay, for seein' nothin' but a lot of old men and kids kickin' dust and drunk men yelling.'

But many times the tourists come to the camp here, to look at the real Aborigine people. Them tourists from the *Kimberley Cruiser* boat, but them terrorists (tourists, yes?) always here in the dry time with their shiny four-wheel drives.

That *Kimberley Cruiser* is one big boat. Carpet all through it, little swimming pool on it, little pub there. Everybody has their own room, for himself and his wife or husband. Them people proper old but, most of them. Moses been on that boat. He went with Gerrard one time to have a look. He told us about it. Gerrard took a trip from here to Wyndham, or Darwin. He told us how food is cooked for you and is like on videos. He had a good time, and it cost him nothing. It was free for him. This last year that boat started coming in here for us to dance for them, because Karnama has the best dancers. Or pretty close to best anyway.

Most times we all go out to the beach and dance at about sunset. Fire dance. We have a fish, get oysters, maybe camp out. But sometimes now we get Gerrard's bus and we bring them in here, if they come early in the day.

They drive in and their heads all turn around and around and they wave back like they are toys. They get of the bus slowly, because they all so old. They look mostly the same. White, big hats, clothes so clean. Pink spots, little pink bits around their nails and eyes. And they all smell sweet like soap, and powder. People here thought they came in to see the river, and they didn't know why they just stayed around our store, and kept taking photographs. One man might take a photo of his old wife holding up one of our kids. Or a photo of her standing in the shop with all us mob, buying things. They think we monkeys maybe. Or sitting on the ground outside, in the shade, with us. We laughed when their clothes got dirty but.

Some of the people here say we should stop letting tourists in. They just treat us as we in a zoo, or something. Even government ones, not all of them. Talk to us like they can't talk proper English.

Those boat people, we can laugh at them, even though we get sick of their cameras. We can get away from them. But the tourists that drive in, ha! You go to a beach and you can't be alone with your own. We tell you, it's not so good if there's strangers on the beach with you. One mob stole an outboard from a big boat the government gave us. That was the only outboard we had then. They take all our oysters. Sometimes they make more rubbish than us, and some of our mob bad enough, for sure. They shit everywhere. You go to some of the beaches and there be toilet paper everywhere through the bush behind the beach.

People everywhere in dry time. If you stay at the office, the basketball court you can see them coming in. School holidays time especially. One, two, three, more. Dust with them, but sun still shining of them. Stuff packed everywhere; on top, on trailers, crammed against windows. And they look look look. Stop outside the shop, come in and stand around with us.

We can make money from them. Gerrard says that, lots of people say that to us. What for? What we want their money for? What can they give us for what we have? More grog? More card games? We must be mad bastards. That's what some other people think. Father Pujol's time, no tourists here.

Not even museum people come in then. Plenty now. And too many people want to go with them, show them things. Drive around in a big four-wheel drive, just like tourists themselves. They say they will help us to look after our sites, and guard the old things. But, how come?

In the old days we did look after our sacred sites ourselves, without letting white people, white men, women, take care of them. We know what to do. These others shouldn't interfere with our sacred things. Kiddies of ours, young men even, they not allowed to go near our sacred sites, trees even, that was anywhere in the bush. We didn't let them know because they wasn't men. They had to be initiated before they could go to these things and they sacred to us. They are very sacred things. We didn't say nothing to nobody, we just look after these things ourselves. That's why we don't like white women or white men coming to ask different things about our things, or saying we should do this, and why don't we ... That's our sacred things. What they want them for, too. It's not right for so many people to show them things. And what are we? They studying us too? Like animals? Or maybe they want to steal our secrets, and when even the black man has lost his special things and his magic, then — hey, here it is! — the whitefellas have it and they use it on us.

Maybe we will have to change. Maybe make more things sacred, not just places, and keep them just for us. But then, we already sell some things to tourists.

Maybe we make a little building like a church, ourselves.

You know, you can't act the fool with our Law. It'll kill you.

True. Like when a young man, uninitiated man, eats food that he shouldn't. Maybe he eats bush turkey. Well, you see. He get feathers and bones growing out of his knees. I hear one man got cancer from showing and working on sacred sites that were too powerful for him. That might happen you know.

But it is maybe true we have had tourists for a long time. Old Dr Oliver, he been coming up here every year since he was a young fella. He stays with Fatima, in her hut, on the little verandah there. He brings up a big Toyota and takes her and some of the other old people out to show him things. He takes photos and videos of old camps, and ovens. Indonesian ones. So those Indonesians, they tourists too, long time ago. White people also. But they stay.

There's another story, very good story, about early days and tourists, about this place. It was somewhere about Long Reef, somewhere about there. This bloke, Indonesian bloke, came in with a lugger, and he saw this girl. Young girl, and pretty. He made love with her, and he tell her, 'Come on, we can go on this lugger. We'll take you.'

But the girl wanted her husband too. Silly girl, she did jump on the lugger, with her husband. Her husband Walanguh, or the one who father for Walanguh, I forget. Walanguh told this story.

They sailing sailing sailing. This white bloke told him, told the husband, this Aborigine man, 'Climb up there and take rope to tie it with.' The Aborigine man climbed up to the top of the sails on the rope.

And this man cut that rope! This white bloke cut that rope. And he fell, that Walanguh one, he fell into the sea. They left him, swimming, swimming right out there in the ocean.

But this Aborigine man, he's a magic man and he was swimming across and he sing for that whale. He sing song for that whale, and that whale was way out swimming in deepest ocean. The whale went in close to the man, and the man get on top of his back next to his head.

He sat there above the water, in the sun and the spray, and he patted the whale, and he told him, 'We go for that lugger and we smash that lugger!'

The whale swam fast with that Walanguh man up on its back. They went straight for that lugger, and smashed it. Smashed it to pieces!

The man got his Aborigine girl, put her on the whale, and away they went to their home, to their island. When they got to that special island the whale came into the shallow water. They gave it fish, all kinds of fish. They patted him, and they let it go.

And this is a true story this one, this is a true story again. This mob here can tell you. Same words again.

And where is that island? You thinking that, eh? You want to know? But it might not be there, where it was, that land. Maybe just bones, nothing.

Listen, we tell no lies to you. Not ever. But we could help you there, maybe.

An Ending

Walanguh moved himself into one of the tiny old huts down behind the mission. The Sisters tried to dissuade him, but they failed. The huts were each not much larger than an outside lavatory, and were scattered among large mango trees. Loose sheets of iron flapped in the wind. In flood time the river rose up the slope to lap at the lowest huts.

Walanguh slept outside, under a tree, on some blankets slung over an old wire-framed bed. His dogs kept unwanted people away. If a child ventured too close they would have brought it down, possibly torn it apart. The dogs barked at anyone who approached, and Walanguh would either silence them and welcome the visitor, or let them bark and snarl and keep the intruder at bay. And Walanguh would not even look up, not until that person had gone away.

He called Billy over to him one afternoon as the teacher was returning from a swimming session at High Diving with his students.

'You bin tellim them kids story?'

Walanguh was smiling hugely, with his face half averted. He punctuated his sentences with laughter, and kept winking as if he and Billy shared some joke. His dark face was etched with wrinkles, and white whiskers stabbed from his leathery skin. He held a fleshy bone in one hand, and gnawed at it between words.

Billy kept a watchful eye on the dogs. He hadn't thought Walanguh knew about the taping sessions. He attempted to explain that he hadn't found time to transcribe many of them, but he had done so with one or two, and the students seemed to appreciate it, liked hearing familiar words and stories in the classroom. But no, he really hadn't done it much.

'Your pudda — grandmother — my sister, she die, eh?'

Billy could not understand what Walanguh was saying. He thought it was something about the river, about Walanguh's sister or grandmother, about crossing the river. Walanguh was grinning and chuckling the whole time, pleased with himself. But Billy could not understand.

Walanguh grunted and threw the bone to the dogs. Billy, a little relieved, left.

'Any smoke?' Walanguh called after him, rubbing his thumb and forefinger together, and casting his smile.

Within twenty-four hours Billy saw Walanguh again. He saw the old man's face, very close to his own, and he saw the sleep in the corner of the eyes as the old man winked at him. The face began drifting away, and skilfully spat a wad of tobacco from one side of its mouth, without ceasing its cackle.

Billy saw the old man, fat like a balloon, drifting along in the sunlight, way up above the mango trees and coconut palms. He was silent now. There was no sound but the rustle of leaves in one breath of wind. A thin trail of smoke went straight up into the sky from a campfire below, and Walanguh drifted through it, drifted through it, and the smoke was barely disturbed.

Billy stood among all the people of Karnama, all of them silent and in awe, but many of them not looking up at

Walanguh drifting through the blue. Many were transfixed by the shadow, Walanguh's shadow, which, solid black, skimmed and rippled along the ground while the old man, naked and shameless, his penis shrivelled below his swollen belly, grinned and waved at those few who turned their eyes up to him. He drifted away and up, going up and up and away.

And the noise returned to the people, who, with a cough and a sniff, turned to their other tasks. Except Fatima, who began wailing grief and beating her skull with her fists. And the dogs howled.

Billy and Liz woke to the wailing early in the morning. They could hear it even from their bedroom.

So Walanguh died. But still, he had been sick for a long time. He was very old. The Sisters at the mission used to bring food to him every day, even when he moved back to one of the little huts with all his wild dogs. Not many people visited him, only some of the other old ones, and Fatima of course, who trusted and loved him the more now that he was growing old, weak, away. He spent his day in feeble dreaming. The night he died some people did dream of him, so they said. He was in their dreams the way each of them remembered and knew him best.

People were upset, but it was no surprise.

But one thing began from his death. Beatrice's young parents did not make sure that Beatrice, a growing girl, was smoked properly at the funeral. She did come to wail with them, and she looked sorry. She, smart little girl so clever at school and who the gardiya really liked, did not take trouble to walk through smoke as the Law says. Her parents didn't trouble to make her.

Some noticed it, but so what? It was not a tragic death. We

living in the twentieth century now you know. Only a little girl.

Look at it. A clever little girl doesn't even bother. Alphonse and Araselli not bothering with things. People not believing, people not trusting, people not caring. All falling down, all asking to fall down. That's all we need to say for now.

Beatrice, she knew nothing. Raphael, her silly bugger father, was one of those whose eyes saw the shadow but didn't know. That man is empty and has nothing inside him, except when he drinks from a bottle or spurts into a woman or has money in his hand. So. A modern man maybe. That's all we say for now.

Breakin'

Liz walked into her house and out of the green heat. She could hear music above the roar of the air-conditioner. And the soft clicking of the typewriter. She followed the sound to the spare room. Beatrice was hammering away at the typewriter. Two other small girls were dancing to the music which trickled thinly from the cassette player.

'What are you girls doing here!' It did not sound like a question.

The two dancing stopped, and bowed their heads. Beatrice turned around laughing, half singing to the music she heard. Her large eyes reflected Liz's red temper for a moment, then she looked away and resumed punching the keyboard.

Liz grabbed her by the arm. 'Out! Get out this minute!'

The two girls ran before her, and Beatrice walked by her side. Liz wanted Beatrice to struggle so that she could restrain her, use some sort of force. 'I'll be seeing Uncle Moses about this, you'll see. You can't just go into people's houses like this you know!'

'We always do, with our houses.'

'Other kids in here too, Miss.'

'What? What other kids? In here?'

'Yes, Miss. All 'em. Beatrice first. We just followed her, Miss.'

Beatrice smiled up at Liz. She still had not spoken. Liz shook her. She remained silent. Her smile stayed.

'They took stuff, Miss. Your clothes, Miss.'

'You tell all them kids to get that stuff back. Go! I'm seeing Uncle Moses and anything missing will come from your parents' pays. You three, Beatrice, Isobel, Rosenda, make sure you tell the others.'

Isobel and Rosenda ran off. Beatrice jogged behind them, then ran to catch them up and tried to push them over. Liz felt like crying. She went into their bedroom. Clothing was strewn across the room and the drawers and wardrobe doors were open. Her make-up had been used, the bedclothes were rumpled. She got out a pen and paper and began making a list of what was missing.

Liz and Billy went over to the office to report what had happened. Some of the small children on the basketball court were running around, laughing, with Billy and Liz's underwear pulled over their heads.

Moses was surprised at what had happened. 'It's no good. These parents are not looking after their kids. Some people are too soft with them too.' He looked at them a moment longer than necessary, and asked if they knew the kids. They told him. They told him what was missing. They gave him the list.

Gerrard was not surprised. 'Little sods. This used to happen all the time when I was in Warburton. What are you going to do?'

When they were walking home they saw Beatrice walking toward them. She had on one of Liz's jackets. She was beaming. They stopped her. She smiled at them. Liz grabbed her arm and started taking the jacket off her. Beatrice made no protest.

'Beatrice, what are you doing? You can't do this.'

Liz released her grip on the child, and Beatrice simply continued walking.

'Bye Miss.' It was already a surprise to hear her speak.

Stella was at their gate with her daughter, Beatrice, at about sunset that day. She gripped the girl's arm severely.

'This girl in your house today?' Stella shook Beatrice like a doll. 'She using your things? I'm sorry, I don't know why …' Stella was upset. She shook that girl again. 'Say sorry.' Beatrice mumbled something. Her face all puffy from crying. 'Now I show you, I'll whip her here. You'll see.' Beatrice cried out to her mother for pity, and Billy and Liz watched as Stella began hitting Beatrice across the buttocks with a stick taken from a tree. Beatrice's cries tore at them all and made Stella more angry, more confused.

Liz muttered, 'Stop, oh …' and said, 'Stella, thanks for your concern. We don't know why, we don't understand. Beatrice is such a good girl, usually. One of the best.' She said this for Beatrice, believing it.

Stella still clutched Beatrice's arm. 'I wanted to show that my kids don't get away with, don't break into teachers' houses, don't steal things. They make me wild. This one, she givin' trouble all the time now.' She hauled Beatrice roughly away, the child sobbing and stumbling to keep up with her mother.

'Bye Stella.' Billy and Liz looked at one another, turned for their door, went inside.

Aliens

Children: elbows splayed, tongues protruding, heads close to desktops; their calloused bare toes gripping the desk rails, their weeping boils forgotten for the moment. The children at their schoolwork.

Beatrice slid out of her seat. She walked behind Cyril and punched him on the back of the head. Liz's searching gaze swung up as Cyril yelped. Her eyes settled on Beatrice, and warned of trouble.

Beatrice, on a sea of her own, drifted toward Liz, drawn by that stare, and halted, abruptly, at the edge of the teacher's desk.

The small girl rocked gently on her feet as she suffered a reprimand. Suffered? She tilted her head from side to side as if listening to an internal clock tick-tocking. Her eyes were wide and unblinking, a small smile touched her lips. She did not respond to Liz's questions. She seemed like in a dream.

'You can't go around just hitting people like that! Not in my class you don't!' Liz spoke sternly, growing angrier at the child's indifference. The last sentence was a shout.

A shout that jerked Beatrice's head back stiffly. Her cheeks sucked in, and released with an expulsion of air. A glob of spittle sailed proudly through the air toward Liz, and landed on the desk before her startled face.

Beatrice pirouetted to face the class, all of whom sat

dropjawed and goggle-eyed at the spectacle. Beatrice, tiny sweet Beatrice, raised her right fist in triumph.

'Yaah!' she screamed, laughed, and the children giggled their embarrassment.

At first people thought, Raphael! It must be him. He maybe bashed Beatrice for stealing into Billy and Liz's house. But after a time they knew the truth. There really was something wrong with Beatrice.

At school she listened to no one, see, and would simply get up and walk out of the room, or hit the other children, or throw things. Whatever came into her head. You cross her and she scream, spit, bite, kick, punch. And Billy or Alex would come running to carry her away in a bear hug.

Yes, the teachers spoke to Moses, the chairman, and to her parents. They didn't know what.

Beatrice stole things from the store. Everyone looking at her. She fought with the other children, and adults even.

In the store Beatrice attacked Francis. She grabbed his spectacles and threw them away, giggling. He clumsily struck out at her, and she felt the blow and came at him with her limbs spinning like a cartoon fighter in a cloud of dust and swearing.

She walked into him, a kicking, punching, screaming, swearing devil, and poor Franny; sixteen years old, a big boy, he broke before her madness. He rushed for the door sending cans of food and shopping tumbling into his path, jostling and pushing at people to get past. Beatrice ran after him. Everybody was laughing, 'Aiee! Wild one! Look! Look at that devil girl.'

But they stopped. They had to. They had to grab her. Franny fallen over, and Beatrice standing over him kicking and throwing cans of food and stuff at him, screaming screamingscreaming screaming.

Milton grabbed her, he gathered her up in his arms and carried her off, still struggling and shrieking, to Raphael.

He might have belted her then. We heard her screaming, and Raphael, and Stella. Gloria too. He always bash his women, maybe his daughter.

No one knew what to do.

She was crazy.

She got crazier. Sometimes she just sat down, for a long time, rocking herself, or crying, or with her face vacant and responding to no one. There was no one home there.

The doctor flew in. Lights flashed down long tunnels at her. Her chest was tapped. She giggled at pale fingers and tongues of cold metal.

They took her to Wyndham for tests, and Stella went with her. She was pregnant again. Crazy Beatrice and her swollen mother flew in a little plane to Wyndham and Raphael stayed behind.

Samson arranged to bring in some beer and flagons on the plane that came for them. So, for a couple of days while crazy Beatrice sat wide-eyed with nurses, crispsheets, antiseptic fumes curling around her, we also had crazy people around us here, shouting and fighting one another and haunted by their own alcoholic ghosts.

But at Wyndham they didn't know. They could find no bruises or breaks to support the idea — the hospital people said things at coffee and biscuits — that she'd been treated bad by her parents or relations. Bashed, or worse. They poked her with their dry pink fingers, but found no evidence of sexual abuse.

The doctors thought it might be meningitis from the water. We drink it straight from the river.

Beatrice and her swelling mother went to Darwin Hospital for tests. Beatrice was mostly quiet now, sitting rocking rocking, and humming, her eyes unblinking.

Her mother sat with her, swelling all the time. Stella's ankles were all soft and spongy, and in the mornings she vomited. Beatrice didn't seem to recognise her.

Stella wasn't happy. Her daughter being like that. And she was lonely, and perhaps she or her new baby might catch the craziness from Beatrice.

But then, everyone here seemed mad. They gave her and Beatrice a room of their own. Stella sat in a corner, she pushed herself into a corner by the window and looked out through the gaps in the venetian blinds, down on the car park below. Both Stella and Beatrice wore ill-fitting hospital gowns. Sometimes they just stared at one another. Like standing in front of one of them funny mirrors, thought Stella.

Pale people spoke to them, but didn't listen, or couldn't understand. Stella heard their stabbing heels and laughter ricocheting down corridors, fading away, returning louder from another direction.

Sometimes it got so that they had to strap Beatrice down on her bed, she was so wild and violent. The first time this happened Stella stood shocked, for a moment. Then she attacked the attendants, her thick voice, usually so soft, tensing up into shrieks and curses. They had to grab her. White soapy scented people ran at her and pulled her away with their soft hands, but the bones so hard beneath the flesh.

So was she going crazy too?

They explained things to her. She didn't want to stay. The air was bad, there was the food and the cold hard toilets. The humming silence, the echoes, the crisp sheets and stainless steel.

But she had to stay with her daughter. Even if she went crazy with her, or locked the door and swelled herself up enough to fill the room and crush the both of them. Three of them.

She rang Raphael. He'd have to come and rescue them, or help somehow.

A Journey

The high school mob went to Darwin. After two days on the rough track the bus rolled onto the bitumen rattling like a money box, and with lengths of rope and towing cable holding up the fuel tank.

On the first night that they camped Fatima, Liz and the girls went down to a creek to wash the hot dusty day from them. They waded in. Liz threw off her clothes and immersed herself in the flow, the bubbles tickling along her belly and the rocks smooth and cool on her flanks. Her pale skin glowed in this landscape and light. Some of the girls joined her, bodies glistening in the fading sun, small flecks of foam fleeing from them in the darkening water, their voices teasing Fatima who squatted in her wet clothes, frowning. But she had to laugh too, couldn't help herself it seemed.

They came back to the fire, the colours of the tents draining away with the light, and they were like a tribe approaching the flames.

In the tents that night. 'Just like us, the same, but red hair there, too.'

'Hey Raphael, Raphael!' Deslie called out. And there was Raphael, in a taxi, in the middle of Darwin, just like that. They ran over to the taxi as it waited at the traffic lights, and Raphael told them he was going to the hospital to see Stella and Beatrice, and they told him where they were staying. Then, green light, traffic moving, he was swept away just as if he was in the river at home.

'No door handle,' said keen-eyed Deslie, puzzled, as they walked toward the glass front of the hospital reception.

'Automatic door.' Sylvester read it.

'Aiee! Like videos, you know. You stand, it opens for you, eh Sir?' said Franny, peering at Billy with his head thrown back and those thick glasses of his balancing on his nose.

Young Jimmy and Deslie ran to the door, and stopped hesitantly before it. The door yawned, they leapt through.

A nurse led them into the elevator. They all crammed in together quietly enough but, squeezed together, the screams of 'Oh, my guts!' as the elevator rocketed them upwards, and the giggles, vibrated through them all as one mass.

They followed the nurse's stiff white dress and rapid pattering shoes through narrow sharp corridors and among hard glossy surfaces.

There was a small room. There, huddled in a dark corner and away from the dim window, was a figure. There, in a creased nightgown was Stella. Her face opened like a surprise, they saw something like fear, and she burst into tears. She held the older girls, and she held Fatima, and she wept, laughing. Smiling once, twice at Billy and Liz through blinking eyelids and tears.

They ate on the lawn by the car park, far below the shrinking room, and breathed properly once more. They moved in close together, and touching now and then, watched the people walking to and from the reception area; watched for anyone who hesitated before the automatic door.

Beatrice hugged her knees. She let no one in. 'She's better, she knows you.' The girl rocked herself gently, her blank face occasionally manifesting a glorious smile, a smile so powerful that it would animate everyone for a time.

'I ... I dunno if ...'

It was getting too much for Stella. The hospital wanted her to remain, for the child's sake. And she was able to control Beatrice when she went wild, better than anyone else anyway.

Like we said, they had to strap her down, tie her up, stab her with big needles, fill her with drugs. Maybe that helped make her like she was now.

Stella needed a break. Raphael had come but he'd gone again. He was like a child himself and no help.

They took her with them for the couple of days they were in Darwin, driving around in their grubby bus, with the kids ogling the shiny cars, and racing one another to be first to shout 'My car' and thus gain imaginary possession of it. And fighting about this. She was with them when they surreptitiously grabbed at the fish the tourists fed at Doctor's Gully, teased the caged crocodiles at the crocodile farm and stroked the stuffed one in the museum. They went roller skating one evening but only Deslie, Billy and Liz got onto skates. The others were too shy. Too many gardiya. And the girls they saw smoking in the toilets, why they thought they were too good. There were some in there, half-castes, they thought they was film stars themselves.

The hostel where they stayed had a swimming pool. Most of the other residents, mostly young international backpackers, lay around it, working on their suntans. Billy and Liz commented on two of the schoolgirls, Stacie and Rita, talking to a young

Swedish girl in the pool. The three of them breast deep in water against the side of the pool, in intimate conversation, and Rita, quite unselfconsciously, stroking the girl's blonde hair as she spoke to her.

The school kids took over the pool. They played chasey in and around it. Leaping in and out like amphibians, noisily, innocent of pretension. Only once was there trouble. Some young European men, perhaps German, began playing a casual game of water volleyball across the heads of the black teenagers. One aimed at Deslie's head, and guffawed as he bounced the ball from it. Deslie smiled sheepishly, and made apologetic words as he swam away. The Germans laughed more, and another pretended to take aim. Maybe tears of confusion came to Deslie's eyes.

Then hot-headed Liz's voice cut through the braying, and she stormed over and snatched the ball from the young man. The dark youths gathered around their teacher as she marched off to give the ball to the receptionist.

Fatima spent time at the hospital with Stella, but she didn't like it. They didn't like you chewing tobacco. There was nothing to do, except wonder at Beatrice, and talk — enough to frighten one another — about why she was like she was.

It was a comfort to look down at the car park. The coloured cars silently going in and out, patiently waiting for their drivers, the little people fast-stepping about.

The doctors didn't know what was wrong with Beatrice. They were sending her to Perth now, for tests, and for other doctors to look at and poke.

Raphael arrived at the hostel on their last night there. His voice echoed in the dimly lit and late night corridor, 'Jimmy, Jimmy, you here?' A hoarse, slurred whisper. Everyone had gone to bed. Billy recognised the voice and went out into the corridor. Raphael was drunk and his breath was tainted with stale beer, cigarettes, and vomit.

'Hey Billy, sorry. I come see my little cousin-brother, Jimmy, eh? He here, Sir?' His voice wheedled a little.

They spoke softly together. Raphael seemed a happy, quiet drunk here in Darwin. He faced the stairwell. Behind his back one of the bedroom doors opened. The head of one of the older girls appeared around the corner of it. Her eyes were wide, to see as much and as quickly as possible. Her glance met Billy's gaze. She raised her eyebrows in a query, grinned. Her head withdrew. The door closed softly.

'But, they're asleep, mate. You've had a few drinks, eh? You might go silly. Kids, you know. They might get stupid.'

Raphael put his arm around Billy. They were walking down the stairs. 'It's good to see you, you know. I miss my home, you know. You?'

There was someone waiting for them downstairs. Looking furtive, and trapped, Bruno waited for them in the shadows by a public telephone. 'Hey.' He swaggered over to them. A couple of the young men from the swimming pool stared and smirked.

'Hey, you got ten bucks for me? Pay you back, true god.'

They went down the street and had a beer. Bruno put his arm around Billy. 'I respect you, Sir, you know, I respect you.' He was tapping his own chest. He was hitting his chest, hard. 'I respect you, true.'

Raphael pushed him away. 'Leave him you, let him be.' He put his back to Bruno and faced Billy. Bruno pushed his way back in.

'We had a fight, Raphael and me. See?' He pointed to his swollen lip. 'Raphael, he hit me. He put me down. Boom. On me bum.' He laughed.

'He's drunk, don't worry,' said Raphael, slurring his words, and pushing Bruno away again. The barman was keeping an eye on them.

'Hey, you got ten bucks, for me?' said Raphael. 'Don't give him nothin'.' One of Raphael's front teeth was missing.

Billy didn't want to give them money, because, because … He gave them an equal amount each, and couldn't but feel patronising, and condescending, whatever he did. He felt shame for them.

The taxi driver didn't want to let them in, but Billy persuaded him they were all right.

I am a white boy, I am a good white boy, safe. But this hurts.

'See you at home, in our country,' said Billy. Did he really say that? Bruno, smilingweeping from the drink and homesickness, waved frantically. Raphael looked at Billy impassively. His face was swept away into the hot night, the exhaust fumes, headlights, snarling motors.

The kids were all for driving straight home, non-stop, like a bullet. So they said.

They wanted to stay in the bus as they drove through Katherine. Black people were drunk, and sitting on the ground outside the pubs, or at the back of car parks, or on the grass near public toilets. People looked at our people, too, as if they were drunks, or not good enough. Think they were savages, or monkeys or something? For all these reasons, and more, our young people felt shame.

They all wanted to get home. The bus was hot and smelled of unwashed bodies and clothes. Sun streaming through the windows, hum of tyres, roar of the motor and the wind. Nerves stretching like drumskins.

The kids started to bicker among themselves, and even the adults; Fatima, Liz, Billy were short-tempered. Nearing the end of the trip, Stacie suddenly burst into an explosion of obscenities. They stopped the bus, and Stacie accused Deslie, and he her. They were told to get off the bus until they could behave.

Deslie went meekly. Stacie stayed.

'Fuckin' gardiya pricks, fuckin' Deslie.'

She raved. Liz tried shouting. So did Fatima. Nothing.

'Leave her, Fatima.' Fatima wanted to hit some sense into the girl.

'If I was not so old.'

They were not going to continue on until they had resolved the problem. Billy let the other kids of the bus, if they wanted to. Stacie had to stay. Most of the girls stayed with her, grouped around her seat.

Billy and Liz tried shouting at her. They tried just letting her curses wash over them, trying to shame and silence her by just looking at her quietly.

'Don't you look at me. What you lookin' at? Not a monkey, am I?'

In the rear-vision mirror Billy could see the boys milling around, throwing stones. Sitting in the shade together. There they were, hundreds of kilometres from the nearest station even. A two-wheeled track, red dust and rocks, disappearing into the distance. Heat, and a grimy, clicking, buzzing quiet.

Stacie's mutterings dying away.

It was not going to be resolved, not here.

They spent their last night camping. Stacie and four of her friends retired into one tent as soon as they had eaten. The atmosphere was quiet. In a moment aside Liz wept, briefly, in Billy's arms.

Franny said, 'Fatima, tell us some stories, eh? Ghost stories. By the fire, and we'll sit up late.' They did, that last night, and all the tents had to be moved so that their openings faced into the fire. All except for that of Liz and Billy. There was a circle of tents looking into a fire which was kept blazing, and there was one tent outside of that circle, in the darkness.

All night, noises and screams. Billy and Liz tried to quieten them, but could not because they were so excitable, and getting close to home. They didn't want to be controlled by Billy and Liz. Stacie was quiet still. Fatima, out of sympathy for the teachers, yelled at them to be quiet and good, because it was not yet their country to do what they wanted. But then her own words frightened her, too.

The weather was unseasonal, and the heat an oppressive, even intimidatory presence. There were dark clouds low in the sky, crowding in fatly, and glowering. It seemed there had been rain, because once or twice they had to stop the bus, and wade through a creek to check its depth. Their voices sounded thin and feeble in the large space.

And, as they entered the comfort of their home country and there were only a couple of hours or so to go before they were among the buildings of their village, Jimmy said — Billy heard him — Jimmy hit his fist on the seat with excitement and said, 'I wish I could go back drunk.' The boys all agreed with him, laughing at the spectacle, the heroes they'd make.

And, closer still to home, Sylvester said to Billy, 'Know what? I look forward to just eating tea and bread again.' After all the regular and heavy meals.

Raphael was back, still weak after being drunk for so long. Hating himself again.

In a hospital, in Perth now, Beatrice clicked her tongue and rocked herself to and fro. Her mother filled a space and a nightgown beside her, and the papers documenting Beatrice's condition grew larger.

Fatima visited some of the other older ones: Sebastian, Samson, Moses too. They talked about her trip to Darwin, Walanguh, and Beatrice.

Liz rang her brother, who was a doctor. He checked on Beatrice's condition, and what the filing cabinets and computers held on her.

They didn't know, not really. Maybe some sort of meningitis, or a brain inflammation.

Billy told Fatima what information they had, proving his access to the big automatic-doored labyrinths. Fatima listened, and thanked him.

Franny Sees

Deslie went with Billy to Franny's house. Franny hadn't been to school and everyone said that it was because he'd broken his glasses.

They went in cautiously, wary of dogs. It seemed too quiet for there to be anybody home. In the doorway of one of the rooms there was a pile of dog shit.

Franny sat on a single bed, and didn't notice them at first because he was concentrating on something he held low in his hands. He looked different without his spectacles.

Billy and Deslie sat on the bed beside him and looked at the object of his attention. He held a cigarette lighter in his hand, and his spectacles in the other. At the edge of one lens, where its frame met the spectacle arm, the plastic was black and misshapen where it had been melted.

Franny was upset. 'I can't wear these, Sir. I try to fix them this way, but …'

They went over to the workshop at the school.

'Miss Storey, she from where, Sir?' asked Franny, as they attended to the spectacles held in the small vice. 'And you, where you from? Who? Your mother? Father? Grandmother? Your grandmother, she from here?'

And when our Billy came back from far away, searching, he saw

Franny peering at him through the repaired spectacles, his eyes swimming behind the thick lenses. 'You, Sir, people say you is like us. True?'

Well, not black. Or dark brown, or purple-black, or coffee coloured, or black-brown. Maybe tan. But what is this? We are all different. I am not the same.

Some Explanation

Gabriella came back. Another school holiday. She saw her home, the camp. The river. Ocean. It was the same. Oh, maybe a couple of new houses being built, some new white faces; the builders settling into the community and elbowing a place for themselves. Their white faces, those elbows, various white appendages; like ephemeral bush flowers.

'I see now. I see it's a funny place. It's how people would like to think of Aboriginal people. Still some hunting, still bush tucker, some dancing, some art. Even a mission, a mission still with power. Clout.

'And then there's this gambling, and drinking, and fighting. Kids running wild, and sleeping with dogs. The huts, and the campfires in the yard.

'I reckon the people, the government and the bureaucrats, the white mums and dads battling with their mortgages, the sports coaches and the teachers, all the wide world want to see the Aboriginal people like this. But wanting to be helped, wanting to better themselves. Able to be helped even.

'I'm thinking. People been talking to me. There's Aboriginal people everywhere you know. Even like you, paler. We are all different, but the same. Something the same in us all, that's what they say. Not many Aboriginal people live like this here. Only couple hundred here, little places like this. But in

Melbourne, Sydney, Perth, you know, there's many. Not maybe like us here, but started off in this way, sometime. We like the forgotten tribe of chosen ones, eh?

'Trouble is, even if I want it, I don't feel like all them others, not just because we're Aboriginal …'

'No. What about feeling, "kin", identifying with a subset … like some people you click with? But what do we share, or have in common? Is it a something, a spirituality or a creativity, a propensity to …'

'But then there's not just Aboriginal people in there …'

'Yeah. I know, but I mean, maybe it's been kept alive more …'

But. But maybe we gotta be the same so's we can make people remember that we belong here. And we got something to tell. Here first. For a long time. This whole big Australia land binds us. And we fragments of a great …

A Dreamt time. A maybe rented time. A time the fabric of which is tom and rent and now not holding together, like a torn flag fluttering.

Like a magic carpet falling.

But we never had.

'It's like political, isn't it? Make people remember, face up, know …'

Remember? Billy does. Father and uncles and all coming home happy drunk one 1967 day, laughing and singing in the backyard and they burnt all the fence pickets on the fire and the fames leapt danced flickered across the neighbour's face which was like a pale moon rising, frowning, over the skeleton fence. Next day Billy's father, giving him boxing lessons so he could fight back anybody, told Billy he was Aboriginal. That's why Nana looked different like that and you could see it and she was taken away from her home a place a special land somewhere up north and he should be proud of this part of us that makes him what he is.

And he was. He was proud. That little Billy was proud at home and he told himself it was like being an American Indian on the movies. Part Cheyenne, or Sioux. But he went quiet with this information like a Featherfoot scouting because too much noise may bring trouble and you never can trust.

He has been quiet.

Gabriella has been looking at him. Her face is very serious and gentle, and Billy feels grateful, even before she speaks.

'You writing up the old people stories yet? You're the man for that all right. Billy, you're the man for that.'

The Man for That

But Billy was not sure he was the man for that. Oh, he wanted to be. He wanted to be some sort of seer, a teller of tales, the one who gives meaning, and weaves the unravelling and trailing threads of the lives and histories here together so that people can be held up and together by the integrity and sense of the patterns. He who sings the world anew so that you know where you are.

It might not be true to do that, if it could be done.

And, in truth, he had barely started even transcribing the words of his sources. Oh, he had read one or two anecdotes to the students. They had looked at the words on the page and recognised the syntax of the voice that Billy read. They were surprised at it, and laughed. Sebastian, too, had come to the class to listen and elaborate if necessary. He had wondered at the rendition Billy gave, the rhythms of his speech altered a little, and the different timbre of his voice.

Billy thought it may be like magic. He thought his audience realised the power of literacy. This man can tell the same stories, use the same voice almost. Better maybe. Billy wanted to have power and magic like that. Like they said some people used to have, in the old times, when people believed.

When Gabriella said, 'You're the man for that,' did she mean, 'You're no good for anything else'? That's what the gardiya thought. It was a waste of time. Although Alex was interested. 'You mean they listen when you read?' But the others? Nope. And Liz, she had trust, this one from another old land. But maybe that was just her love for Billy.

Sebastian, Fatima, Samson, even the kids; they seemed happy that he wanted to do their stories. They wanted these things written down: that they worked hard to help build up the mission, that they were clever and proud, that they still knew some of the old ways, and the old ways were good. The old people wanted to make it happen that the young ones got power in the white man's way also, and did not drink or fight so much, and could be proud.

Did they think there was still magic in story words?

And Billy saw the drunkenness. It was real. And the wife bashing. The rubbish. He saw people manipulating the young government workers who visited, and then afterwards bragging; Samson, Moses, sometimes younger-but-learning-fast Raphael, bragging about getting a flight out and coming back with beer and wine, or about the new Toyota they were getting … He saw the things Gabriella was now seeing too well.

Samson, since Gabriella's last visit, had been officially appointed the community ranger. A man had visited the community for a couple of days, and Samson had been the first to speak to him. Samson had so impressed and charmed the man, the more so when he knew there was a vehicle involved, that he got the job.

The missionaries tried to dissuade the government agent from his choice, but they failed.

So it was not long before Samson and his boys were sitting proud in the cab of their new Toyota, their women and kids in the back. Samson had also been given a khaki uniform. He pulled the wide brimmed hat down tight on his head, and carried a notebook in his shirt pocket which he pulled out and scribbled in regularly. Could he write? He lost the pen, and that was the end of that.

See? He was like a clown really, acting out, and some white people laughed at him. And that Toyota, his boys or someone rolled it and nearly killed some kids who was in there, and other childrens scratched their names in the paint so that before long the inside of the doors under the windows was bare metal.

The old people, would they like all these things written down too? You need history to understand all this, don't you? But you can get and guess that elsewhere.

In Karnama Billy would like to have been a mechanic. Then it could have been he that people came to be nice to, and to flatter, so that he would fix their car. Or a builder. A good welder. A pilot, to cheaply fly the people out, and not permit them to bring crates of alcohol back in, and to be respected for that.

Like Father Pujol, he always go to the airport when people flew in. He welcome them, and help them with their things. Then he drop their bags, like accident, their bags fall on the ground and he listen for the sound of breaking glass. Then just look at the person. 'Oh, sorry. Maybe it's good that broke, eh?'

But Billy was the man to write the stories, stories in which he didn't belong. The old people told them better. Even the young kids. No one here read books, except at school. And except the gardiya, who read stories of sophisticated and ruthless people, or histories peopled by heroes.

The people who belonged here liked to talk and listen

around a campfire. Yes, they liked to listen. And now they watch videos all through the night, and recite lines of dialogue, role-playing with one another.

Here, then, was Billy. The man to write up stories.

It surprised him in class, how Deslie, especially, took to listening to him reading. Even before school. Billy sat in a beanbag, and Deslie beside him, and they read. It was as if it was parent and very young child.

It was funny, really, how they got on so well. He who couldn't read or write, and he who wanted to read and write everything too much and maybe too hard.

Bornfree

'Deslie's on the roof,' said a figure at the doorway, silhouetted against the night.

Billy and some of the kids, watching a video in the classroom, had heard nothing. Deslie was on the roof. Why? They couldn't hear him still.

And then it was like in a video itself when Billy went out with a torch and climbed up and shone it onto Deslie. He lay flat on his back, his eyes showing the high black sky and its stars. The torch a yellow comet rocketing forwards, taking up the sky.

They helped him down gently. He was not like a person, more like the outside part only and hollowed out. He bumped against the wall and he resonated slightly, like a drum.

He is killing his insides with that petrol, sniffing it.

There are some things to tell about Deslie, because he is a different one. He is not from here. He comes from Beagle Bay, and we call him Bornfree. He got that name when he was a little one, because he just ran wild and no one looked for him.

He nearly never went to school. His mother and his father, they drank all the time and they just left him, let him go. His mother killed someone one time, in a fight, with a bottle. She went wild, and broke, and they took her away, to Fremantle or somewhere.

Deslie grew, and filled himself with the bush. Like the other kids say, like Sylvester said to Billy, 'He a proper well-trained blackfella that one.' He catches fish like the best men here, and many times he goes out fishing or hunting on his own. He dances. Our other kids are too lazy.

Billy liked to hear Deslie talk about when he was a little boy. The teachers, or other bosses, would try to get Deslie to school, but he would run away from them. He saw them coming; he inside in the shadows, looking at them through a doorway or window, they pale and shimmering in the bright sunlight as if over-exposed and their colour gone. Their hands jerking, heads turning toward him as he moved. He's off. Gone! Whoosh! Thunder in his ears.

Sometimes he'd flee on a horse, little bloke like a flea on a horse, eh? Bareback, no saddle, nothing; bare legs gripping, bare feet flapping, fingers in that old horse's mane. They might shout at him, but after a time they didn't really want to get him.

Lots of times he met up with the old people in the bush and helped them. He liked that.

But then his cousin brought him here to live with him and his family. People worried about him, he was sniffing petrol, going too wild all round. He went to school all the time here, because they made him. But he was not clever at school. Couldn't read or write, not even his own name, but he was clever enough to trick the other kids, and teachers, too, most of the time.

Like when the class played Hang the Man, that spelling game. Deslie, he copied a word from a book and showed it to

Billy. Billy sat at the back of the class when they played this game. Someone might guess a letter and Deslie would just look around the class like he was teasing. When he glanced past Billy, Billy would nod either yes or no, and hold up his fingers to indicate whether the letter was the first, second, third, or whatever. Deslie then checked the word, and copied the letter onto the board in big letters.

At church, when they put the words to hymns up on the wall, Deslie looked at the words as he sang, just like he was reading them for the first time.

He was a funny boy, that Deslie. Make you laugh. Make you cranky too. He fought with the other kids a lot, and sometimes he was a bit sneaky. But they teased him because he was not from their country, because his parents didn't want him, because he was dumb at school.

Deslie remembered one good thing about his school at Beagle Bay. He did go to school every now and then, and each time it was more awkward for the teachers to know what to do with him. So one time they gave him a book with a cassette tape. The book was not much good to him, except for some little pictures in it, but he listened to the tape. He remembered it. Billy was surprised when Deslie talked to him about it, and he asked Billy to read it to everyone in the class.

Deslie and Billy went fishing down in the gorge. They were walking back, Deslie carrying a barramundi almost as big as himself. See? Told you he was a good fisherman. Billy had caught nothing.

The fish was heavy and they took turns carrying it as they picked their way over the red rocks, gleaming from countless polishings by sand and wet season rapids. Really, they needed a canoe or a raft. And Deslie said yes. This is like … I could be Huck, and you Tom, he said. Billy wondered about that.

And Billy did read Tom Sawyer to the class; he skipped bits when his listeners started to wilt at the onslaught of verbosity, just bits here and there.

The younger boys made a raft and took it out at High Diving, and pushed one another of it, and sank it, and swam back and made another.

But they drifted away from the book, it on one current and they another, because there could be no white man running away from the law here. And why was that Negro like that?

It's like in Australia, maybe, when you go to Derby or Wyndham. Or, yes, the people in Darwin and in Katherine did look at you, sometimes, as if they think we are like that Negro.

Early in the year Deslie used to come over to Billy and Liz's place to visit. He shared meals with them several times. They heard him telling the other kids. 'We had supper, didn't we?' and he'd list the food to the other kids. They realised he was bragging to the others and suggesting he was a favourite.

Sylvester said once, 'I don't like to go to other places, people that I don't know.' And, after persuasion, 'Shy, maybe, or something like that.'

They started to dissuade him from coming because of this, and because they started to feel exploited, almost, with Deslie turning up at meal times, and leaving soon after unless they were watching a video or television. At school, also, he took up all their time, wanting their attention, and they had to write down what he said so that he could copy it into his journal. But even then he couldn't read it back.

A film was shown, most weeks, at the basketball court and most of the indigenous community would be there to view it. The audience was, of course, small. As was the screen, which perched just off the edge of the basketball court facing the office.

One time, when a film was showing for the third consecutive night, Billy and Liz went along in response to the rave reviews issuing from their students. They sat on the ground, their backs against the office shack, just to one side of where the projector threw its beam from the doorway.

A full moon rose and shamed the flickering images on the shabby screen. The globe in the projector failed, and while it was being fixed and cursed, the children skipped around, and nimbly through, the adults sitting on the dirt.

The film voices were thin and brittle in the night, in contrast to the voices of the watchers, which sounded thick and warm, imbued with the darkness. The scents of sweating bodies, of rubbish and decay, of the bush and the river nearby prevented them losing themselves in the film. But the security of friends and family, the easy reach to home, the very clashes between this world and that of the film added to the experience and significance of watching it.

Deslie found Billy and Liz in the dark as children sank into sleep around them. Small bodies lay huddled and scattered on the ground. Deslie sat next to Billy, their shoulders firm together. 'You treat me like I was maybe your own son.' And he fell asleep, his head on Billy's shoulder.

But it was not so, it became less so. He came for no more meals alone. Liz was not sure that she trusted him, and didn't like it that he would come so early in the morning. He called to her as she left the house one morning. She heard, and looked, but could not see him. Eventually his voice led her to him. He was under the house, face down in the soil, and giggling at her confusion. Another time he told her how he had looked in the window and seen her walking around in her dressing-gown, still stumbling with sleep.

Deslie called out to Billy also, and Billy found Deslie snaking along in the darkness under one of the classrooms, his grinning teeth spitting laughter, his eyes sparkling with excitement.

Someone, at the mission, said they remembered Deslie when he was a small boy, at Beagle Bay, and when he was called Derek. He had to change his name when someone in the community, who had the same name, died. That wouldn't have helped him at school, having to work out how to read and write a new name.

They remembered, or someone they remembered had told them, that Deslie always had a small can tied around his neck, and petrol in that can. Well, yes, that's partly why he came here, because his cousin was worried about him and the vehicles in here are nearly all diesels. But his cousin had kids growing up, and a son just a little bit younger than Deslie himself.

Deslie was better now. But every now and then, no! He dipped a rag in the lawnmower tank maybe. Petrol ate up his insides, his brain, everything. Burned the nostrils, moved astringently, forcing into fissures and pushing hollows and enclosures within him that could never be filled. Next day at school he knew nothing, not even numbers, and was quiet. The others might whisper about him. His cousin gave him a proper hiding, too, after his sniffing.

So he might bump himself and you heard a sort of ringing sound. Emptiness within him, and his dark glazed eyes reflecting, especially, dark spaces, shadows, the night sky.

True. He was our youngest, our best trained blackfella. And not even in his own country. And he all the time dying away from the inside out.

Not Listening, but Learning

For a long time we knew about Araselli's growing belly, about the baby inside her. She stayed here, swelling and swelling, keeping inside and to herself for a long time. Then she went away to Wyndham to stay with her aunty.

She came back. In the old days people thought you got a baby from dreaming, from spirits coming into you. Now people know different, the young ones could even stop having babies and still have their fun if they wanted. Better not let Father Paul know but. Silly buggers. Maybe there is still some of the old way in it.

So whose baby was it? It was black, proper black. Everyone could see it was Alphonse's son. We knew for sure then. There you are. They had a baby together.

It was a pretty one. Everybody was happy to have a new baby. They could believe that they did not know, not for sure, where it came from.

And Araselli was proud and strong with everybody. Once, when all her friends were around her, she took the baby from Stacie's arms and quickly walked to Alphonse who stood with his back to her. She bumped him, he turned, she said his name and thrust the baby at him. He took the child, perhaps instinctively to save it from falling, and turned in a circle looking down, looking down at the grinning gurgling child in his arms. Alphonse and child. Alphonse himself grinning too big. The biggest smile.

He said nothing. He gave the child to someone so that they could return it to Araselli who had walked back to her friends and was laughing with them.

So. Araselli and Alphonse. They began to swagger around together, in front of everybody, talkingsmiling together. Nothing bad happened to them. They shouted back at the people who growled at them. Their parents gave up, because after all they had been arguing with them for too long and had not been able to change their minds. Brother Tom, the Sisters, they shrugged, they smiled, they held the baby, they drank cups of tea with those two and their baby. People gave up. They was young, good looking, happy.

But, they have promised ones. They rumbud. Before, Araselli and Alphonse only talked through certain other people. They were not allowed to look or talk to one another. But that's only the way it should be, the way it used to be. They used to do it like that, even Araselli and Alphonse. But now? Now they live in one room, have a baby together, don't hardly talk to anybody else, don't worry about nobody.

Things are all anykind and make no sense.

Alphonse is a strong young man, and clever too. When he was a boy, about Deslie's age, he went away to Melbourne with Father Paul. He went in a big sports day there. He came back with shining trophies which he gave to Father Paul to look after, and they put his photograph in the newspapers and wrote about him.

Father Paul let Alphonse go and use a room in the mission to do exercises. He made him lift weights, and he timed his running with his watch.

But Alphonse lost interest, being busy with Father Paul all the time after work, and working with Brother Tom all day in the garden. He got too tired, and he didn't really want to go away running against white fellas anyway. What for? Not for himself.

They trusted him at the mission. He used to drive all the machines, and they knew he could be left to do jobs on his own.

He was always the one who drove out to the airstrip and loaded and unloaded supplies. When they put the telephones in, Alphonse would ring the orders through for the mission. Then, without the mission knowing, he arranged for them to bring beer in. For himself alone.

Now? Alphonse and Araselli, with their baby child, stay in one small room, and they keep it for themselves. They have a video player. The room is dark because they have a heavy blanket across the window. When the air-conditioner used to work it was cold too, and they would stay under a blanket. It was different then but, because that was before the baby. Now they lay there in the dark, and it's hot, and the video screen flickers colours across their faces, and their eyes reflect the screen, and they look at their child and see the two screens in his face, and they look at one another and see them there too.

Deslie tells Billy that they just lay there all day and don't let others in. Have some grog, too. The other girls, and Stacie tells Liz this, reckon that Araselli's just bossy, and is scared of the other girls taking Alphonse away from her. She used to be good fun, but now! Not any more. She gets cranky.

Some of those girls, and women, been going over to that builders' camp, and drinking beer. It's not good you see. They get a little bit drunk, and friendly because they like it, you know, and they do silly things gunna cause trouble. They not ask the men, not ever. Those white blokes shouldn't ask 'em over to have a drink. They sneak over there you know, don't tell anybody where or when or whatever, but we know. Believe us, we know.

We told council, 'No grog.' But, no one listens.

That Araselli. What's with her? She want trouble? Plenty of it already anyway, with her going with Alphonse when they're rumbud and they have that baby. We talk about this and talk about it and we have to do something, or there be all sorts of things going on make Karnama go down get worse too quick. But who listens? We got no stories, we got no punishments. We losing it. We losing that power.

In the evenings the builders make a campfire by the shed where they sleep and store their gear. They sit around, eat, and drink. They drink until they are sleepy or until they know if they have more they cannot work tomorrow. Experienced drinkers.

All the school teachers went there one evening. They were asked for a meal. They walked into the light, and sat with those men. Billy smiling, quiet joking, but not able to say much and often not being heard. Annette left early because of young Alan. The big heavy flanked men conscious of that woman who remained among them.

As the night aged Liz got angry with the talk of the people who lived here, with the men's muted braying about women, their own appetites. She stood up, said some angry things, and the men said they were sorry, and not used to a lady in their camp. She got angrier, blazed there in the light, and left. Alex tried to explain it away. At the school, he said, it's very trying, we're all tired. And Billy said I think she is right, quietly, I agree with her, it seems there is nothing to say. And he disappeared.

Some mutterings. Then, like testing, like reassuring itself, a louder voice. Haw.

Each night the laughter and the voices carry from behind the mission workshop where they are camped. Haw haw haw from the flickering firelight and the bright neon torches. The pop and fizz of cans being opened, and the jokes about the women and who they fancied.

Eh Barry, that Sharon fancies you mate. You gunna try her, or what?

I'm a married man, mate.

She's all right. Put a bit of weight in her legs. Big tits.

Shit, I wonder if you grabbed 'em young and tied their fuckin' feet up like the chinks do, eh? Stop 'em gettin' such big hoofers. Squeeze some meat back into their fuckin' legs.

Fuckin' legs.

What's her name? Araselli? You get her up the duff? That baby yours?

Nah, too black for you.

She'd be all right, I reckon.

Geez you're a desperate bastard.

Haw. Haw, haw. Cans popping, meat sizzling on their fires.

People have seen some of the women over there. On the edge of the light. Shadows were there, different voices. Just for a laugh and a drink they say.

Raphael and one or two other men went over to the camp one Friday, night-time, evening, to talk, have a drink. But they were not wanted there. It was polite. They had a drink or two, but knew they had to go. When they left it started again.

Haw haw.

A Saturday morning, very early, and Milton was knocking at Billy's door. He came in and sat down.

'Oh no, what I gunna do?' He laughed ruefully and pushed himself back into the armchair. 'Mr Seddum sack me I reckon. Alex gunna sack his gardener.'

Billy was puzzled. He studied Milton closely. 'Milton you're pissed. You been drinking, haven't you?'

'No. Not just now. Last night, yeah. I didn't know, see.' His head was bowed. He straightened and relaxed his arms, pushing himself to and fro in the cushions of the armchair. He looked up, gave an unreliable smile. There was something shameful in his pleading, bloodshot eyes. 'I had just two maybe three cans so I was little bit drunk and I had the taste of it. Someone gave me little glass one, you know bottle, and I had that. I didn't know.'

'What are you talking about?'

'If I go and tell them now … They forgive you. It better to confess and say you did do wrong. They forgive you like Christ, eh? Oh, but that Father Paul, he frighten me. He must forgive me, eh?'

'Forgive you for what?'

Milton pushed himself back into the chair again, then drummed his fingers on its arms. He pivoted both bare feet on their heels and moved them in little arcs.

'I didn't take 'em. I only drank some. I knew, and I wasn't gunna drink any then. But they was already stolen.'

Billy laughed shortly, and leaned toward Milton. 'You

buggers pinched Brother Tom's home-brew and now you're feelin' guilty.'

'Not me, that other mob. I should tell them now, eh? That best. My father said I should 'cos they know.'

Milton felt guilty, but he was also frightened of what might happen if he told them. Especially of what Father Paul might do.

He kept shaking his head, talking of confession and forgiveness, his head down and his forearms resting on his knees. Billy and Liz looked at one another.

Eventually Billy walked over to the mission with Milton. They passed within twenty metres of Sebastian, who sat in the shade of a tree outside one of the houses. He appeared not to look at them.

Billy left Milton standing by the outer wall and large gate of the monastery courtyard and continued looking for Father Paul. He found him at the other end of the monastery building examining the door of the old kindergarten. Billy realised why Milton had not been keen to look for Father Paul over this way. This must be where they kept the home-brew.

'G'day Paul. Bit of strife last night I hear. I had a visit from someone who knew about it, and's now wracked with guilt. He's waiting over at the monastery there. Okay?'

Father Paul hesitated a moment. Looked at Billy a second time. 'Right. I'll see him later. Thanks.'

Much later that same day two cans of beer sweat on a laminate table in the monastery courtyard. Two cans of beer are lifted to two mouths. Father Paul's fingertips are nicotine stained, and his thick fingers sprout tufts of fair hair. Like the hand of God, it is large, and mottled, and the fingernails are bitten down to the quick.

'I always sleep with my door open. Anyway, during the night I woke up. I was lying on my side facing the wall, but I knew there was someone inside my room. So I turned, as if in my sleep, and I could tell who it was. Raphael and Alphonse. They came only a few steps in before one of them grabbed the other's arm and beckoned towards the door with his head. I heard Raphael whisper, "Not here."

'They were drunk, I could smell it. Raphael's a dangerous bastard. I couldn't see any point getting up then. But I was angry. So when I found out they'd broken in and pinched the beer, I knew who it was.

'So I went over, early in the morning, and walked into where they were sleeping. I knew they'd be crook as dogs. It was all bluff. I was shouting, "Let's fight, come on! You break in and steal from the mission, you're looking for trouble." I walked in rolling my shirt sleeves up and just stood over them.

'They were crook, they just looked at me. Just lying there, looking at me. The family was there of course. They apologised and promised they'd pay for the beer and the lock, bring Brother Tom's bottles back, and donate a week's pay to the mission.'

Billy just nods, keeps nodding. He has no voice here.

'I went with Moses and old Sebastian straight over to Gerrard's place and sorted it out so that we can get the money taken straight out of their wages, before they get it. They'll be in church now for a week or two.

'What can you do? Call the police? Again? For what? They didn't say who else was in with them. Milton we know. Most of them, probably. Bloody Alphonse.'

Billy sips his beer. 'Alphonse?'

'He's a disappointment to me, that one,' says Father Paul. He looks at his fingers tapping the can. 'The trouble with Alphonse, with a lot of the people here, is that he doesn't want to push himself. It's no good for him here, it's too easy to just slip back. No, not back. That seems impossible. But it's too easy to, to fall. Maybe one day he'll get on the council, and get the pick of the vehicles and charter fights out when he wants ... He'll get lazy, a worse worker. I wanted him to go away, but ... And now, look at him shacked up with Araselli. And her. She's one of the ones the builders have had over there.'

'Araselli?'

'Yeah. But see, I'm being paternalistic again. I'll be glad to go on sabbatical ... Look what we wanted to give these people, and now ... What can you do, eh? I don't like what I do, have to do. We have just taken things away.'

The empty can is crushed in a powerful hand.

Billy saw Milton at school next day. Milton was relaxed. He had helped collect up the bottles for Brother Tom and he was going to church every morning and evening. Father Paul had heard confession from him.

Not Just Madness

And Beatrice? What was the world like now, for her? Most of the time she seemed as if in a trance. Eyes large, rocking rocking herself, and her ears filled with her own sounds. A roaring in her head, torrents of blood rushing like the river at home; eddies and whirlpools of thick blood; blood spilling over bone seeping into sandy flesh. And a thudding, like footsteps of giants pursuing her endlessly. Great hairy beings, their feet pounding, worst at night and early morning.

It might be that sometimes she felt squashed flat and fat like the plasticine puppets you sometimes see on television, and unable then to correctly move even a finger, or lift a heavy foot from the ground so much did it weigh. Her facial features were disappearing into a swelling face, flesh closing over her eyes, over her nostrils. While the black sky grew higher she was crushed beneath it like a figure in a comic strip, the ink running from the top of the frame.

Another time she became pale and thin. A grey mist hazy world. She felt pain when a breeze brushed her thin brittle limbs, when her clothes touched her skin, and she made the tiniest careful movements lest she snap something with the mere leverage of feeble straining muscles.

Voices rushed around her, a cassette tape speeding up and about to break, spinning tighter, screeching at her, voices of enraged cartoon chipmunks and ducks, but grown large and shouting spittle into her face. People rushed toward her in a video fast forward, and then went past, or away, and rapidly became tiny figures shooting away down long corridors. Nurses' uniforms walked to and away from her, the fabric noisily scratching and grinding. Doors slammed and echoed as if the room was a steel drum. But then in all this frenzied din a door would suddenly slam, silently. Silence would begin ...

She found that by concentrating she could change her perception from fast to slow, and vice versa. But she then went from one extreme to another, and could not halt as she went desperately past the correctly paced world. So she went from gross to brittleslender. And from a frenzied rushing world to one in slow motion where speech became a succession of spastic groans and she helplessly watched events occur. Watching waiting for a cup to fall, watching it fall slowly unable to move to catch it, watching it fall waiting for it to hurry up and reach the floor, watching it break into pieces, counting the pieces as they bounced, waiting for them to reach the floor again, again.

Sharp things moved inside her body, through her blood, stabbing inside her foot, shoulder, stomach, head.

Snakes winked at her, tongues flickering before slipping behind doors, into briefcases and boxes.

Faces changed as she spoke to them. She couldn't trust. Faces even changed from human to animal. Limbs grew out of walls, pockets, clipboards. Smiles held knives in their teeth. An offered hand became a fist or boot which struck. Eyes detached from faces and became glaring groups, satellites spinning around her head and flashing blue bolts of hatred.

She watched the sun fall from the sky each day, and catch in the fork of a tree away past the car park. It stuck there, bleeding its colours until dark.

One night she saw the moon tumble across a cloud torn sky. It fell and spilled over two figures lying on the grass far below her. In the morning she saw that sculpture there.

Stella returned to Karnama. She thought she was going mad, and would, for sure, if she stayed with Beatrice in that hospital with all them strangers.

She had got fat, and couldn't smile any more.

And, at last, people told her that someone did sing her daughter, because she did not do the proper thing after Walanguh's death. Fatima should have told her.

Amazing?

Them doctors should have been able to tell about Beatrice, them with all their brains and soft hands and smells.

They called us. We fixed it. Good for them that they asked us, and let us. Some of the old people went down to that hospital; Samson, Fatima, Moses …

The doctors let them stay in the room with Beatrice. They slept on mattresses on the floor, and nurses brought food to them.

They fixed her up. So, there are other ways, and other brains too, even if they may be going away, dying, these days.

Billy got hold of a newspaper, and they read it at the school. Some of the kids read it aloud to the old people:

GIRL SAVED BY BLACK RITUALS

An amazing series of rituals to rid a dying black girl of a tribal curse was carried out in one of Perth's major hospitals.

The girl was believed to have been cursed by Aboriginal elders.

A clinical psychologist became concerned that the child had been 'sung' and arranged for the Aboriginal tribal elders to perform an exorcism on the comatose child in Sir Charles Gairdner Hospital.

Being 'sung' is a ritual similar to the so-called pointing of a bone.

The elders, from the Kimberley, visited the child three times. The child has returned to her community and is fit and well.

The old people laughed, and told them there were many things they knew and understood that other ones did not. But Stella, she was not laughing. She got her daughter back all right, but that little spirit inside her, it pass away. Finish. People could see. She was small now.

Break In and Out

Franny has a new cassette. Moses has been out to a conference in Derby and has brought it, and a new Walkman, back for him.

He sits alone in a room, unseeing, the music swirling in his head, raising his spirits through some strange capillary action. Absorbed, looking in, he could be a mad zombie boy, with one lens of his spectacles smeared with glue and melted plastic and masking tape.

Elsewhere, kids throw stones and break the windows of the houses under construction, a basketball beats against a backboard, bodies spear into the water at High Diving, and eyeballs at the card game shift.

Those eyeballs and cards shift, and there is the sound of voices running like a river, then louder with excitement and rapid laughter, soft again. Dark hands quick, grubby cards rested on thighs, hairy bellies splitting shirts, scratchings and shiftings for comfort. Time drifting slowly with them. Who's there? Milton and his missus Annie, Moses too. Stella, happy with these moments, and the new one growing inside her. Raphael, Samson, Gloria, lots of people.

They're all playing under the big tree among the huts. It's Friday afternoon, and everyone's got their money and work's stopped. The children have also been paid for their work at the mission garden. They run around with lollies and cool drinks and, despite their sticky fingers, leave wrapping paper, money, coins and bottle tops trailing behind them. Not hands enough to hold such wealth. The video games out on the dusty cement have bodies clustered before them like fruit; limbs, heads, eyeballs, and fingers bunching coins blossom from the screens.

Gerrard and Jasmine are slung out in their office chairs, their paleness glimmering in the dark room. There is sweat on their grimy skin, and the whirring electric fan bullies the hot air and swirls the aromas of absent bodies around them.

Knock on Alex's door and see him in his office with his boy, constructing models for the boy's projects which they send off to his correspondence teacher in Perth. Alex cursing the crackling two-way radio and the people here, and dreaming of when the telephones will be properly installed and he can communicate with his world.

Liz and Annette similarly sit in separate houses, before separate televisions, linked up to a common satellite dish in their shared backyard. Thundering air-conditioners mean their televisions must be turned up loud, and the pink heads bare their teeth and shout at them from cosy metropolitan studios.

Deslie and Billy walk along the hot red rocks beside the river, near the upper tidal limit, hoping the gorge will give them some of its barramundi, out of season and all. Billy feeling his schoolteacher authority slip away.

At the card game Annie is winning. Money is gathering up in her lap, money piling up in the centre of the card players.

The little kids are using coins instead of marbles for a game. They attempt to lob coins into a small hole they've dug a couple of metres away.

Alphonse and his mother are screaming at one another. He's bringing shame, what he's doing, he can't live with his rumbud, not here, doesn't he care about anything or anybody, just acting anykind? Things are flying through the air at him, his mother's hands slapping him, tears flooding. He grasps his mother's shoulders. His father wades into the hot tears of the scream-flooded kitchen and fills it further with threats and fists. Alphonse blunders, then, out the door, shouting, voices and tears tumbling through the open door behind him, making him stumble. He kicks at the dogs, their yelps arc up into the sun, its light all spears and diamonds to Alphonse's eyes, sharp and glittering. He's running down to the river. The sun is plummeting.

Deslie and Billy see a figure running hard across the rocky fat, a spindly black figure against a vast blood-spattered eggshell sky. They drive silently back through the dust, a great silver fish changing colour on the tray behind them.

Night-time.

Moses sits on a narrow bed, drinking with his older sons. He's a quiet drinker, maybe he's teaching them. Some of them don't drink. Franny there too, music still in his head.

At the card game the firelight flickers on the mound of money tucked up in Annie's skirt. A serious game, silent and quick. Bodies around fires, bodies sprawled before video screens, bodies coupling. Alphonse, who knows where? Out on the edge of the dark, tight with anger, clenching and clenching his fists, grinding his teeth. Araselli laughs about it when she hears he's argued with his family. She's a young woman, she don't care any more.

Stella lying in a room listening to Beatrice sleeping.

Gerrard dining with Alex and his family, all wrestling with one another to show who has the most trouble working with the blacks.

The builders haw-hawing, fizz-popping, slipping away and linking with the shadowy figures outside of the firelight.

Late in the night Annie is rich. Araselli, wondering about Alphonse, returns with some of her friends from the builders' camp. Later still, deep in night-time, Alphonse, all hollowed by his rage, numbed from the tense screaming of his muscles and sinews, approaches the community office. He crosses the basketball court, and the moonlight is strong enough to throw a shadow of the axe in his hand.

So, there was big news the next day. Alphonse had smashed up the office, wrecked it; axed the doors, walls and desks; flung chairs and books, papers around the room. He threw artefacts onto the floor and trampled them.

Billy saw Gerrard walking rapidly past the basketball court with muttered curses popping around him. Too busy to talk, his lips curled in a snarl, his belief in the ingratitude and dubious worth of the lazy bastards that live here now vindicated. Maybe he felt proud of his importance and the wise resignation in his voice when he spoke to the police.

The police took shame-faced Alphonse away. Now he and Araselli must forget. The request for the police was, this time, so quick, that they had no time to gather together all the summonses for our young bucks here.

Forms of Retreat

Remembering this bad time, thinking back, we see that it started with everyone leaving here. No, not everyone. But many.

Alphonse of course. The police took him away. He was with his family. They flew in, got him, he was gone.

Annie and Milton chartered a plane, quietly, just for themselves, with all that money Annie won at cards. They went to Broome.

Moses was driving out to Broome also. He had a big meeting to go to. He was taking Francis with him. That Franny, he was a spoilt one. It may be that Moses felt guilt for the bad way Franny was brought into the world.

Moses didn't leave until night-time. He didn't want to take lots of people with him. He knew some would go and get drunk, run out of money, get homesick, fight or make some other trouble, and eventually ring the community here and ask for money to get a plane so they could come back to their home.

So they — Moses and Franny — were driving through the coconut trees and on their way. But just then a big mob came running up between the houses where the big casino tree is. They were running pretty hard, some of them. Grim and quiet, some looking behind, the fastest ones slowing down and laughing nervously as they got to the vehicle. They said there was a devil-devil, maybe two even, hiding behind the casino tree, someone saw it. Who? Dunno. Maybe from that crazy woman's house, the one she keeps in there. But they didn't talk too much; just jumped in the back of the ute and said, 'Drive.' Their eyes had gone big and round.

The people that got up early next day — it was young ones, the children — found money and cards all scattered in a trail going away from the tree and up to the coconut road. Some said that yeah, they saw the devil footprints near the tree. Yep, like a bullock's foot, and there was also footprints with heel, toe, no instep; but it was all messed up pretty soon and no one could really tell.

Anyway, the scared ones had a cold trip out, all huddled together on the back of that Toyota, with just one blanket between them. Raphael, Bruno, Paulie, Gemma, Scholastica and some others. But things got worse. Very bad.

And Milton, who few out with his missus Annie, he was not really ready for holidays. But probably, because Alex was also going out, Milton was worried about having that woman — Annette, Mrs the Great — as boss. What about her? Dalek Woman. She like a robot in one of those films. Short, built, walking with little quick steps. Could be on wheels. Her arms straight in front of her pushing, pushing.

She was boss of the school, once, for a couple of days when Alex had to go away to a meeting. Hard woman. She trundled into the community office, yelling at giant Gerrard that he was not to pay the school cleaners. She'd take their pay, she said, her voice angry but cold like a recording, because she did their work for them. No, really, she would give them their pay only when they worked. She told them not to bring their children when they were meant to be cleaning because they just made more mess than there was to start with. Her face went red like her lipstick and she was short-circuiting when she saw Annie bring her dogs into the room with the vacuum cleaner.

When she was very angry her voice went loud and sharp like a saw or a rattle in a car, and she made people want to sneak away, pull their heads down into shoulders and creep away. People took off their heads and hid them in their pockets so that they didn't see or hear her, and so she couldn't tell who they were.

She thought people were her slaves. She told Milton to do too much weeding and to mow the lawn right to the edge of the fence. It was hot, man, you know. He didn't come back to the school while she was boss.

At school assemblies she looked more alive; smiled like a snake or a crocodile. Lots of teeth. She did have a friendly smile, when she gave the little kids the pretty bits of paper which had her writing and a little picture on them. The kids got one if they came to school clean, with combed hair and good clothes, and on time. Then, at the assembly, they stood next to her, with her hand clamped on their shoulders, and she told everyone who the good mums were too.

Sometimes people watched her, crossing the grass of the schoolyard, coming to the shop in the late afternoon. She came in a dead straight line, lookingstraightahead, following the track from her house door to the store, holding money bunched in one upheld fist.

'Shoo! Shoo! Off you go, you know you're not allowed here now.' She frightened the little kids away from the swings and they took off, running and tumbling before her as if she was pushing a minefield before her somehow.

She got to the shop and most of us looked away, or maybe smiled shyly at her. Maybe get behind her and stick your elbow in someone so they laugh, or yelp, and she might turn and look at you along her sights.

Gabriella called her Dalek Woman.

Anyway, it was true, true for sure, that Milton did not like having her for his boss. So he and his missus, Annie, and the money, went away for a little holiday.

So. People were heading out for Broome. And Alex took Stella with him to Broome, too. He needed contact with his kind. There was a teachers' meeting; it was a Principals' Conference and an Aboriginal Education Workers' Conference held together. Maybe Stella was not so happy to go, but she'd see other people from other Aboriginal communities there. She knew lots of people from those places.

Anyway, Alex had arranged for her to go. She did work at the school sometimes. He could not go if he didn't have an Aboriginal school worker with him. He didn't trust anyone else. He had also spoken to the hospital in Broome. One of the special doctors who had looked at Beatrice when she was sick, and who had been there when our old people fixed her, was visiting Broome. He wanted to see her. The hospital people would look after Beatrice during the day while Stella was at the meeting. They had a day care centre there. People were happy for that doctor to see Beatrice, and to wonder at how we were so clever.

You understand that Raphael was not very happy that Stella was going. But then, he finished going himself also. And in the true finish no one was happy. No one.

Alex, Stella, and Beatrice touched down in Broome just before the sun. It is a long fight in such a small plane. They were later than Alex had planned. Another principal, a man, drove them to their accommodation. Alex and that other man boomed cheerfully together in the front seat. Stella, in the back, held Beatrice under one wing and brooded over the plastic shopping bag full of clothing and toiletries which she clutched between her thin calves. Her ears still rang from the roaring plane, and she remained partially deafened by their unpressurised descent. She felt nervous, trapped between the pink necks of the men in front and Alex's big suitcase in the boot of the car. Sometimes the men turned and brayed, and their blue-green eyes bobbed and leapt all over her. The car was air-conditioned, the windows wound tightly up. A cold wind whistled within it. Stella eyed the streets, silently calling to the people she knew who walked them. Beatrice was silent also, but not sleepy. Silent and big-eyed, she rested her head against her mother's breast.

They were staying at a resort by the beach. It was a big, new place, like a village, with chalets spread around its grounds. There was a swimming pool, restaurant, crisp sheets, a television toilet shower in each room.

Alex went to eat with some of the others who were there for the conference. Stella, who had not yet seen anyone she recognised, did not want to go. She said she had a little headache. She and Beatrice wanted to stay in their chalet and rest. They walked to the beach and had fish and chips, just like a couple of tourists.

The AEW who was supposed to be sharing Stella's room did not turn up. So she and Beatrice had it to themselves. They sat in bed together in the darkened room, watching the bright, flickering television. Beatrice fell asleep, and late in the night Stella heard the voices of the others, loud and laughing, trailing away to the other chalets.

The dusty Toyota with its shivering passengers crowded on the tray rumbled into Derby that same evening. They stayed with relations to sleep, and Moses drove with some of them to Broome the next day.

When Alex knocked on Stella's door in the morning that mob in Derby were all still asleep. So was Stella. And Beatrice. They were snuggled up nice and warm and quiet. The knocking on the door hammered its way into their dreaming.

'Stella? Stella? Wakey-wakey. You're not at home now. Haven't got yourself a fella in there have you?' Haw haw.

Stella opened the door, smiling shyly. Her dressing-gown, bought for this trip, was tied tightly around her waist and held by her arm across her body, her hand gripping her shoulder in reassurance. Alex returned in a short while and took Beatrice to the day care centre at the hospital. There were tears in her eyes but she was quiet. Stella should have left her at home. Perhaps Stella should not have gone to this silly conference. Alex took Beatrice away by the hand. She looked back. Alex bent down to her as they walked, she leaning out from him and held by his hand. He spoke quietly. What did he say? It looked like deadly kind. She straightened her little self up, didn't look back.

To start the day some people — one of them was an Aborigine — spoke to all of the people at the conference. Later they sat around in small bunches. The room had lots of varnished pine and bits of bright colours and green pot plants. The bright sun fell in slices from the window blinds. It looked strange to see such a room with so many black people in it, arranged in clusters. Stella said that.

During that morning Raphael, Bruno, some other fella arrived at the conference. They just walked in. They looked shabby, silhouetted more grey than black as they hesitated in a triangular chunk of sunlight propped against the glass doors. They saw Stella, started toward her. Alex cut them off before they could reach her hearing or find her voice among the many. He told them everyone was very busy. See? They better come back later, in the afternoon, say three o'clock. They shuffled out, in single file until they passed through the doors.

They were back just after lunch. Again Alex spotted them and herded them out as if they were bullocks. He told them Beatrice was at the hospital day care centre.

They didn't come back. Before the meeting was closed for the day Stella asked Alex to ring the day care centre. But Beatrice, she wasn't there any more. Stella rang the woman at the day care centre, and that woman said Beatrice wasn't there.

When Alex and Stella arrived the woman smiled at them. It was a nervous smile. She was worried. A man had come in, she told them. He said he was Beatrice's father. She described Raphael. He didn't seem to have been drinking, she said. He said he was taking her home, she wasn't some animal for a zoo he said. He didn't want no gardiya looking at, no hospital using, his poor girl.

Well Stella was upset. Alex was cranky. He thought it was another typical cock-up. It was like handling kids constantly, dealing with these people.

He had to help. It was their conference. He drove Stella around and around in the hired car, around and around looking for Beatrice. He needed that air-conditioner. He had steam leaking out of his ears, a face that was all red, a mouth tight and skinny like a scar. They looked in town, they looked in parks, they looked at the football oval, they looked at the beach, they looked in the pub.

Eventually Alex left Stella at the house of someone she knew. She could keep looking, with their help. He had an appointment.

Halfway through his tennis game, just as he'd been serving aces to his colleague, Alex was called to the telephone.

The day care centre. 'Who's picking up the girl and her mum and dads?'

Her dads? Shit!

'I'll have to forfeit mate. Your game.' Alex reminded his rival of who was really winning. 'Bit of strife with my AEW. You know what they're like.' He regretted saying that. The other one just nodded, smiled. Smugly. They both knew it was not the right thing to say, not at a conference like this. Not to another principal of a tiny, isolated Aboriginal school who is vying with you for promotion. So Alex lost.

Alex was relieved to see only Stella, Beatrice, and Raphael at the centre. It could have been better though.

'G'day, Mr Seddum.' Raphael was ingratiating, a bit tipsy. Stella was quiet. It was difficult for her to smile.

Raphael and Stella asked for a lift to where the others, from home, were staying. When they got there the house was empty. Alex sat in the car, both hands clenching the steering wheel, and watched Raphael, Stella, and Beatrice knock, wait, look through the windows. They walked around the house, twice. At the completion of the second lap Stella slowly walked across to the car, and to Alex, dragging Beatrice. They talked through the driver's window. The motor was still running. Because of the air-conditioner.

Alex reminded Stella that she was in Broome for professional reasons. A lot of school money had been committed to her being at this conference.

Stella and Beatrice drove back to the resort with Alex, and Raphael continued circling the house. Dinner was booked for seven o'clock.

Alex sits at a table with the other headmasters. His gut contracts when he sees swaggering Raphael, bloody staggery Milton, shrinking skinny Bruno bastard entering the room. He didn't think they'd have the nerve. Cheeky. Bastards. Cheeky black bastards. That's what he thinks. All the efforts he's made. Must've been too soft with them. They're jacking up against him.

He watches them walk over to the table, on the far side of the room, where Stella sits. They stand around the other table, and seem to know the other people, Aboriginal people, who sit there. Alex watches them over the shoulder of a colleague sitting opposite him. It is hard for him to concentrate on what the man is saying. The room is noisy with conversation, with people eating, waiting for their food. The intruders sit at Stella's table. Did they know there'd be spare seats? They gunna bludge a meal? Oh, Alex must've been feeling pretty wild. His beer turns warm in his hand. He smiles quite politely and chats with his colleagues as he watches them laughing, eating, drinking at Stella's table. He cuts his steak so savagely that the fork bends. His colleagues are too polite to notice the intruders, even though the laughter from that table is loud. Hooting, voices competing for attention. But not Stella's.

After dinner Stella sidles over to Alex, who is drinking beer to calm and cool himself. The beer steams and hisses as it touches his angry red-hot lips. She asks Alex if he will ask the pilot if Raphael can return with them on the plane.

'Stella,' Alex's voice is too tight. It is like he is holding himself by the throat to restrain his anger, to keep himself seated. 'Stella, I think you should ask him yourself.' He makes a mental note to see the pilot as soon as he can and tell him no. 'Ask him yourself.' His grip loosens a bit and he nearly snarls, 'He'll have to pay you know.'

Stella returns to her table. Everyone in the restaurant is noisier. The talking is ferocious, particularly at the table of intruders. Look at them; dirty clothes, unshaven faces. Alex's shaven face is like stone. He is not talkative. The person opposite him is. Alex doesn't hear what he is saying, he just sees the mouth flapping. Raphael, behind the mouth flapper, beckons Alex. Alex doesn't move, but the words he might shout to Raphael fairly scream in his ears. Raphael comes over to his table. Those people with Alex wonder at the scruffy black man, but offer polite smiles and pretend to continue talking to one another.

'Oh yes ... Well, in my experience ... consequences ... what you must realise ... try to imagine ...'

'You might say no when I ask you this,' says Raphael.

'I probably will, but you won't know until you ask.' Grim Alex. This is better for him, eh?

Raphael wanted to borrow two hundred dollars for a taxi to Derby where he was going to buy a car he'd heard about. When Alex said no the other intruders came over. They waved their arms about, talked loud, complained that no one ever helped them out when they really needed it. A lot of people were looking.

Alex was angry and embarrassed. In his head he probably had images of himself failing about with a chair and chasing those black men away.

They left.

And the restaurant got noisy with talk again.

Alex and his fellows spoke earnestly about the difficulties of being a school principal in remote communities, and working with the community, with Aborigines.

At many other tables they said different things and tried not to laugh too much, too loud.

Raphael, Bruno, Milton walked back to the pub. They were sparked up. Maybe they'd get some beer, more money from Annie maybe, flagons; head back to the mangroves. Some house? The pub?

'Others be at the pub still, you reckon?'

What Hollow Ones See

Earlier that day they had all been there, in the mangroves between the main shops and the high tide mark. There were many people, a couple of flagons. Nearly always, it seems, there are some people there, drinking. Hiding away, trying to disappear from this world, make one where they fit better. That mangrove spot is not bad when the mozzies and midgies stay away. You can catch up with people, everyone will be there some time. Play cards, talk; not all people drink.

It is almost only Aboriginal people that go there. There must be some shame to it, then.

But on this day it was like a holiday for our mob. A time to see old friends and some family. For Franny it was his first time there as a nearly-man.

So. It was warm there, this day, in the dappled light and on the dry sand. It was pretty happy.

The time went quick. No one got drunk, some maybe just a bit sparked up. Franny had a drink and was tipsy, being young and not used to drinking. And he had a little puff of a joint that someone lit up.

People came and went. There was guitar music for a little time. Raphael, Milton, and Bruno wandered off for a while and you know something about what happened with them. They came back too late.

Then a bunch of people were moving off to the pub. Franny saw the world in such a different and new way. Never again would he see such a day. He would have been feeling good, then, like a hero and a warrior, walking the streets proud with the gardiya tourists and with his own people. A man of a tribe. The light was bright. Maybe this day had a special cruel light, but he wouldn't have seen it, would've hidden the word and the thought away. It might have been a warning, if he'd listened.

There were too many at the pub. All different peoples. Chinese ones, Aborigine, gardiya; old, young; men, women. There were singlets, jeans, long socks, white ankles under tanned legs, cracked bare feet. There was music, and roaring and shouting. Sometimes, in some places Franny stood, the music was so loud he listened to it with his chest. It was like he was hollow inside, and his chest vibrated like a drum. He smelled sweat, soap, perfume sharply sweet, stale beer, urine, tobacco and clove cigarettes. The interior bar was gloomy. There were strips and slices of light scattered around and over pool tables, and the old carpet was soggy and sprouting cigarette butts. Voices everywhere: taking off, screeching, snarling, flapping through the curling smoke and thin trunks of light like bats and birds. They alighted on shoulders and repeated repeated themselves, pecked and stabbed, or stroked with soft downy wings. Sometimes in a relative quiet, you could hear the click of ball and cue. Stabbing sounds of glass and stainless steel. But then the music would start again, a great blanket of it, angry and smothering.

Outside, in the yard where the band is playing, it is bright sun and people must squint. Their faces wrinkle up, their eyebrows come down. Sometimes, with beer in the belly, and a little craziness in the head, you might not know if it's noise hitting you or someone thumping bumping your back and chest. Out in the sun, the music noise is not like a great blanket, not even a bit soft. It is hard. The bass notes are maybe like bricks wrapped in hessian slamming into you. But it's all right. It's happy time. You shouting with the rest of them. Sing, dance, wriggle and stagger about. The white froth of the beer goes up into the hot and patient blue sky. The yellow liquid settles in scrawny guts and big hairy belly.

Franny is there. He too young, but he be there all right. Sitting hunched, then laughing and showing the cord of his throat as he lifts his head back. Others leave. Franny won't go with them.

Franny getting tired. Head on his arms on the table.

The day goes on. Much drinking, much noise. Some people get cranky and argue. Maybe if the people in this hot and sunny place stopped shouting touching dancing drinking for even just a little time then they feel unhappy, sad, angry. Hollow maybe. Maybe that helps explain why such bad things can sometimes happen.

This day goes on. The dark time comes. The sun falls below the noise and the floodlights of the concrete and fibro courtyard.

Franny lifts his head from the table when some people sit at it. He feels sick. His mouth is furry and his head aches. The faces of the people around him are those of strangers. They are caked with powder. Many are pale, stubbled, and streams of blood run through their eyes.

Out in the car park, in the comforting darkness again, Franny leans on a car. He vomits. With tears in his eyes he stumbles to the next car. Somehow, he opens the back door, and sways there, gripping the handle. The poor silly boy. He knows nothing, alone and sick.

It doesn't matter who the two men were that saw him. Their names don't matter. One was a bouncer, come up from Perth to work here. The other one worked on station, lived up this way long time. They been all day in a motel room, drinking and complaining and making themselves heavy, and only now come out.

Franny is about to fall onto the soft seat of the car.

Those two men stood at the edge of the car park and saw. They didn't shout. They ran over there, angry angry. Angry and wild. They pulled him out of the car, almost like he bounced up from the seat. Oh, he was black! Aborigine! They hit him, kicked him, punched him. He was like a bag, he didn't fight back. Groaned. Maybe they enjoyed feeling their fists and feet striking his flesh. They held him up to hit him. He slid to the ground; maybe yelled, sobbed, whimpered. Pick him up, hit him more. He fell again. Bang! Hit head on the bitumen. One of them killers hit him with a big brick. Oh, yes, they told us later. Oh, they jumped up and down on him. His heart went away.

One of them, proper thinking like, not like crazy, got his knife. They held his head back and sawed through his throat. Fish scales still on the knife. Cut his throat like he was bullock kangaroo turtle. Oh he was dead dead dead. Blood bits of meat on the ground. His heart floating around. Him, him no more.

How can this be? And those men? Well. They bayed at the moon maybe, savage dogs. Mad as mad. Very bad things. What did they do, those killers? They drink some more beer? Tell their mates they just stuck a boy, killed him? Wipe the blood and skin from that knife on the beer mat in the bar? Who can know the truth or their minds? They cannot be real people, these ones.

We thought, when we knew, that the law would get them. We stopped some of our people that wanted to kill them. We thought, you know, justice. White man's justice.

True. Silly buggers we be. We need a say.

Desire

Of course all the people were shocked at Franny's death. Word first came with the return of Raphael and the others. Billy saw their vehicle return: Raphael had acquired a new one, an old station wagon which looked like it had little time left to it after being bullied along the track all the way from Derby. Billy was standing out under the mango trees in front of his house which faced onto the main track to Derby. He saw them return. He waved, but they ignored him.

Moses stayed in Broome and Derby for a time with some of his family, for the trial.

Alex returned having heard nothing of the murder, and complaining only of his own problems with 'Stella's crew'. So the news made him quiet, anyway.

But the real shock was the verdict of the jury. Those that went to the court case returned in dribs and drabs. They were sullen and hurt. Moses tried to say how it was for him, and he spoke with the others, quietly. It was a disjointed thing, and hard to understand without anger and weakness and loss.

He had been in that court the whole time. Other people did march, protest. He been like a shadow in that court.

Yeah. It was in the news. On the television. Everything. And they let them killers go free. That shocked the whole Aboriginal people, the whole community, you know. Why, we, nowadays we follow the white law, you know.

They wanted us to follow the white law and we did that.

There was the rotting smell of unhappiness, defeat, and festering, helpless anger in the hot winds that slipped around the community and left the red dust in eyes ears between teeth.

It was not good. People carried bitterness, mistrust, defeat with them. In their pockets, purses, shoes; in their bowels and heads. It was always there, and now it was growing.

The students came to school late. Billy visited houses in the early morning. Everyone weary.

Billy walked to school early in the balmy mornings, and then home again in the bone-wilting heat. Liz and he, they slumped in the kitchen chairs and ate burnt mission-baked bread. They returned to school to do preparation until a couple of hours before sunset when Billy would go to the gorge and fish. The red rocks radiating heat, the sky bleeding, the river rushing with the tide. The sound of the water, all the time muttering, speaking, singing.

Moses, you know, he sat in that court, and sometimes Fatima was with him, and sometimes Sebastian. They sat there listening like big fools. Nobody telling them anything. Sitting. Looking at them talking twisting showing themselves off like big rich boss men. The boy dead.

After what happened you expect someone, the crown or someone, to do something. If we gotta follow the white law then we expect them to do the right thing by all Australians, by everybody.

We Aboriginal people. Look at us. We're low down, we

down there in the dark, and nobody. One time it was different, for us and this land. We had ones that could fix things, and could fly, disappear, punish.

We feel we must find our traditional homeland, go home, go back and try to forget. Or no? Maybe we should try to find answers to these problems. We are trying so hard for the past and our hopes to return. Maybe some of that past and our power.

Alphonse returned from prison. He was glad to be home, but he had like an adventure and holiday staying in prison for a short time.

Franny's murderers. What was their time in prison like? They looked unhappy at the trial. But not when it finished. They looked relieved and happy enough then as they skipped down the steps, into the embraces of their families. It was on the TV.

Yes, those murderers of Franny been clear off proper quick all right. They been run out of that court, into their cars, gone! Gone like a bullet. They frightened, see. Want to get back to Perth, Melbourne, and away. Away from us mob.

Oh, it be a long drive but. You drive all day all night day night day night, like that if you want to get there. No sleep, or only little bit. They not drive together. Not friends no more, you know.

One of them with his girlfriend. He make some stops on the way down, took it slowly slow.

Other one, him drive drive driving. One bit of road out there, long skinny lonely straight road out there in the dark time, something happened. Maybe he get out to check if he moving or not, because that road so long straight dark through the desert. Maybe a sharp shell from the ocean far away long ago come out of the ground and stab his tyre. Might be a kangaroo appear disappear in front of him and make him swerve, you know. And it could be that he see a fat belly black man flyin', swoop into the tunnel his headlights make.

Crash! He crash that car. Rolling and rolling over and over in his car, he so frightened even before that car start going arse over tit again and again and again.

He screaming out there in the cold cold dark time, no one to hear him, them black things in the sky between the sparkling stars looking down on him not caring. Him screaming, car upside down, wheels spinning motor hissing steaming. Blood all over him, arms and legs bent all wrong anykind, chest smashed, and heart still parked but going fast fast faster. Then stop. There. Dead dead proper dead bastard. Got him.

Other one? His mate? Death in our custody, eh? Can't make love, you know, can't make love with his girl no more. His dick shrivel up like a baby's, soft like a string. You put a special poison in his blood, make him go that way. Proper worried then. He have poison in his blood, have nightmares about us old people watching him. He see our eyes in dogs, in the kangaroos his car hits and hits. He see us watching him from the eagles high in the sky, from crows sitting on carcasses he passes. Even the seagulls back nearing Perth, they watch him with their all the time open eyes.

His girl goes. In his little place in Perth there he is like in a box. He start thinking about him being in a box, you know. Another box, small small one that fit him tight.

So we got him too. He makes a tube — he make it like a snake — that go from his exhaust pipe to the window of his car. He just sit in car then, start the motor, listen to radio.

Him dead. We got him. Just like old times. Still got power, see?

True. True story. Listen! We could do that. Could could could.

Dangers

Billy was buying beer from the mission. He would walk over there early in the evenings carrying an empty bag — an old superphosphate bag, or a large bin liner, anything like that — rolled up under his arm. A little time later you see him walking back with a carton of beer wrapped in that bag, and trying to make like he was just carrying something light and ordinary. But he tried not to stop or meet anyone. Father Paul had ample supplies, and sold it cheaply, but not to Aborigines.

Billy drank every evening, alone. Except sometimes, when the band was practising he'd take his own guitar with him and join in. He play pretty good, too. Then, at school he'd teach them kids some of the songs the band did.

But he was keeping away from people, and he was drinking too much, like some of our own younger ones did when they could.

He went fishing on his own on the weekends, very early. Liz stayed sleeping. He come home, and then start quiet drinking on his own. Why?

Maybe he was tired. Franny's death. Thinking about Beatrice. Walanguh in his dreams. Tired from the strain of teaching, and not being able to escape from the school and those other teachers. He was finding this place like an island, and in this community he was here as teacher, government teacher. Not happy being duty institution bound all round.

What he want? What about those stories? He should look there.

He returned each weekend, again and again, to those ocean places Milton and Sebastian had shown him. Some people would hear him, fewer see him, leaving just before sunrise. Often he'd be returning from the beach as others were driving out to it. Rattling and bashing across rocks and slewing through sand, the two vehicles approaching one another would have to slow and edge into the bush either side of the track. Billy, usually alone, but sometimes with Sebastian, in his Toyota ute with outboard motor, rods and tackle in the back and the dinghy loaded on top; the people in the other vehicle, also tipping on the other slope, with bodies and handlines and nets spilling out of the tray and laughing whooping waving at him. He should have been with them, they with him.

It was late in the dry season. Every day there were columns of smoke on the horizon. Father Paul told Billy they showed you where the people had been. A tradition of burning off the land combined with the mobility given by Toyotas resulted in numerous bush fires. The plains around our settlement were burnt and black.

For similar reasons he said, wildlife no longer existed close to the camp. After Father Pujol had been banished, there was no one to stop the people having and using guns. No reason except poverty. Only a few guns had been needed to slaughter anything within range of the huts and houses. This had occurred within ten years. No longer did 'roos and bush turkeys dot the plains. There were plenty of bullocks though. Half-wild cattle, bred from those not mustered by stations.

Oh, it was dry, and hot. The school and mission grounds

defiantly blazed green amid the black earth which surrounded them. The cattle moved closer to graze, even in daylight, and were occasionally chased by packs of dogs and children waving sticks.

Vehicles came, and went, often with dark bodies packed into the trays of the utilities. The red dust snaked behind the vehicles, and was spread by the wind. It was between Billy's teeth as he ground them in his sleep. The air grew dark with smoke and sulking clouds. Flies stuck in the corners of eyes and sucked at nostrils and lips. Burnt earth and stubble crunched under boots, and footprints were clear in the dust.

Billy still went to the river each afternoon. He fished, but rarely caught anything at that time. It was just quiet. The red rocks glowing in the shade, the river, glistening and dark, reflecting the afternoon clouds, and always moving one way or another with the powerful tides.

One afternoon Billy approached it from close to the camp, and walked downstream to locate the upper tidal limit. He found a large pool and settled down. He stood close to the water and at the base of a steep, rocky slope. Directly across the river from where he stood a small cliff face dropped sheer into the water. On this day the sky, and therefore the water, was blue. And, partly because of the size of the pool, and partly because it was between tides, the water was still.

Billy used a short rod and lures. A cast; a slow, jerky, retrieval. Cast, retrieval. Again and again.

Suddenly there was a strange noise. A loud scraping, dragging sound. Upriver, and diagonally across the pool, near where it narrowed, there was a ledge cut into the rock face. The sound Billy heard, magnified in the rock-surrounded stillness, was that of a large crocodile dragging itself on that ledge. He heard dragon scales scraping, and echoing down the gorge. The heavy reptile pushed, fell into the water with a great splash, and disappeared.

Billy was shaken, but it appeared to have been heading upriver, into the channel there. He decided there was no good reason to move or be frightened. He moved up the slope a few steps.

Cast, and retrieve. Cast. Retrieve. He kept one eye out for that crocodile. The water was so clear that he expected to see it swimming dimensions below, watching him.

People had warned him about fishing at the gorge. Take care we said. But he was wise not to fish with bait. A crocodile might wait below you, in the deep deep river, then swim up close and knock you with its swinging tail. You fall into the water, you crocodile meat.

He moved another couple of steps up the rocky slope, out of range of a lashing tail.

Suddenly, the crocodile returned. It came from upstream, moving into the pool at speed and pushing the water before it like a powerboat. Its head and back were proper clear of the water. The crocodile followed the other side of our pool, slowed, and stopped some forty metres across from him. It rested parallel, and close, to the bank where the cliff face changed to a slope of boulders. It submerged so that only its nostrils and eyes remained above the surface, but Billy could see the rest of its form in the clear water. Its short legs were relaxed and curled up slightly, and its tail rested on a rock just under the water.

It seemed to have barnacles growing on it, and was certainly very large. Billy knew it was the old one he'd heard of that had survived the times when its kind was trapped and shot for profit. A wise old crocodile.

It was surely watching him from the corner of its eye, although it faced downstream still, feigning indifference. Lazy, yet watchful, cunning with its dragon years.

Billy had stopped fishing and stood, also motionless. He studied the reptile as if enchanted. Awesome. After a time it turned, slow and silent, and with only its nostrils and eyes above the surface moved straight for him. It came slowly, millimetres per second. Slowly, making no sound, no ripples in the still water.

Billy stayed as he was, but thinking thinking I have misjudged the distance this thing is huge its eyes those lumps are the size of people's heads on the water it is so big and silent it is holding my gaze and why is it coming at me and when will it decide close enough a tail length or leap?

He broke, moved a few steps back and up, and the thing was gone. No ripple, no sound. The water just closed over it. The water, although clear, was dark in its depth and Billy saw nothing.

He left. Billy walked back along the river. It became a high cliff-sided gorge. In a place another few hundred metres up, where you could get to the water again, there was a gill net slung right across a narrow part of the river at the upper limit of a deep tidal pool. There were several small barramundi in it. It was sure death to whatever swam in that water. Billy thought about slicing the net. But didn't.

He walked back up the steep slope beside the river to return across ground to the community. At the top he looked back along the river into the setting sun and saw what appeared to be two birds swimming upriver together, each at the apex of a faint triangle behind it. But they remained perfectly equidistant from one another. They moved into a turn in the river, and in the shade there Billy saw that it was the crocodile. The birds were its lumpy eyes above the water. Its tail snaked slowly as it moved upstream, swimming like a big lazy goanna.

He fled. He felt silly, but that's what he did, thinking: no barramundi maybe, but I caught myself something. I know that crocodile now. He was excited and happy.

Kinds of Desire

It was to be the last tourist dance for the year. The weather was getting too unpleasant, the rains too close, for tourists to continue visiting.

All right. Friday afternoon. Jasmine and her bouncing pup visited Billy and Liz as they lunched. She told them the tourists were coming ashore and that the corroboree for them would take place at the camp.

'Gerrard's bus again?'

'Yeah.'

The three of them crammed into the front of the Toyota.

Jasmine kept twisting around and leaning out the window to speak to her pup, which leapt around on the tray like a mad thing. She worried it would fall out.

A group of small children stood up from their game and waved at them as they drove through the village. Suddenly, three dogs raced out barking ferociously, knocking aside the children as they did so. One of the children, sprawled on the ground, started bawling. Billy stopped the car, but he wasn't about to get out while those dogs leapt and snapped at Jasmine's pup in the back.

Milton hurried across and shouted at the dogs. They slunk away. Liz said, 'Come with us,' and he leapt into the back, and

Jasmine joined him there, relieved to be able to restrain her young dog.

They slid through soft sand, crept across dry creek beds, and rattled and bounced so noisily over corrugations that the cassette player, cranked up almost to full volume, spewed out distorted music. Billy looked in the rear-vision mirror and saw Jasmine and Milton bouncing around the tray like children, laughing, showing their teeth to the sky.

They first saw the catamaran from between the trees as they approached the dried marsh flats. It gleamed in the late sun, dreadfully white on the blue sea, and as incongruous as a spaceship as it turned very slowly around its anchor. Two yellow Zodiacs sped between it and the beach, ferrying the tourists in.

A number of men from the community sat in the grasses just above the rows of grey driftwood at the edge of the beach and watched the tourists disembark from the Zodiacs. Most of the tourists were aged and frail and, unwisely, had chosen to walk barefoot across the beach. They picked their way painfully over the shells which were exposed by the low tide. It was a long walk.

'M'walkin' like bird...'

'Lookin' for food.'

'Moses! Go carry 'em. You chairman or what?'

'They old eh?'

The men were silent as the first of the tourists arrived escorted by Gerrard, who held his hand under the elbow of one old lady. He chatted pattered charmingly and steadied her as she reached the soft grassy sand.

Samson got to his feet, wiping his hands over the baggy bum of his khaki trousers, to greet them. For a moment it seemed Gerrard was going to lead the tourists right past him.

The men were silent. Gerrard chatted on.

Samson swept off his old slouch hat and, clutching it in his left hand, he stepped at the party of tourists with his other hand stretched out before him.

'Welcome to our country ladies and gentlemen. Welcome. My name is Samson, like the strong fella. You see me dancing soon. This here some of the dancers and my boys.' Somehow Samson managed to show a sincere smiling face, yet also give his own mob a wink.

'How ya doing Samson?' An outstretched hand detached itself from the group. It was attached to just one large, soft, brightly garbed man. It clasped Samson's hand, and the two hands jerked stiffly up and down.

'This sure is a beautiful place you have here.' The American accent, so familiar from countless videos, resonated thinly for an instant before the bush drank it up.

Samson introduced Jasmine, Liz and Billy ('These are teachers of our children'), and a wall of clean linen and sweet perfumes moved upon them, firing questions. Liz accepted a role. Samson continued walking with the group, all heading for the shade. He winked and grinned at the others who drifted away as the camera filters came off.

On the edge of the flat, by the trees and vehicles, a bush lean-to had been erected. Artefacts and silk-screened T-shirts were scattered over some blankets spread on the ground.

As the tourists grazed across the blankets and artefacts, Gerrard was carefully arguing with Fatima and Sebastian. Despite Gerrard's care, bits of their shattered argument ricocheted through the other voices around them. Gerrard repeated his plan to take the tourists into the community for the dance, not to have it out at the beach. The council, he said, had already agreed to hire the bus! The dancing site, on the mission lawns, would be ready when they got there.

It was a short argument. Gerrard turned away; a frown went, a smile came. The blankets were sulkily rolled up.

The ship's captain turned. His sunglasses framed the refection of tiny black bodies collecting oysters among the mangroves. The sun glinted on the little pools left in the contours of the sand.

The pale hands of the tourists, like lilies waving the flies from their faces.

The bus wouldn't start. The starter motor clicked ineffectively. Gerrard sat in the driver's seat, hand on the key, staring nowhere, a silent sculpted anger. No one had a towrope, of course. No jumper leads, no offer of help.

He was a stubborn man, and it was decided, once again, to take the tourists in with the other vehicles. Billy made two trips, reluctantly volunteering out of some sense of obligation. Gerrard said they needed to stand together at such times. Billy did not argue with the phrasing of that, but ...

Many of the people from the community decided to stay out at the beach. They could camp overnight and return with the bus after Murray had been out and fixed it. Gerrard insisted that no one else try to do so.

The tourist 'corroboree' was a messy affair, and embarrassing for most. Several of the dancers had stayed at the beach with their families, and others just did not come. So, many of the dancers were not there. The tourists complained that the light was getting too dim for their cameras. Gerrard hassled Samson. Samson shouted, laughed, stormed and blustered about half naked, with his body painted, and leaves rustling about his knees. He became a sideshow, he was the show. He growled at the tourists, and posed shaking a spear at their cameras and appreciative laughter.

Many of the smallest boys were recruited for the dancing, which began in the rapidly fading light. The boys were sullen, and their painted faces smeared with tears. They watched the few older dancers and copied them, and so the dancers did not move together and it was all wrong. The families of the boys, perched on and draped over the vehicles parked on the edge of the area, whooped and jeered, and the dancers grinned or hung their heads. Some swore loudly and would have liked to fight. Samson yelled explanations to the audience. He alternated between playing the sergeant major and the jester; one moment authoritatively barking orders and cuffing the small boys, the next wheedling for the audience's sympathy.

Cameras slumped. Occasionally a flash went off, but less and less often. Some of the tourists were shaking their heads in anger and disappointment. Dust hung in the air, and the small smoking fires around the dancing area had sucked the hues from the setting sun. Headlights were turned onto the dancers as spotlights, and added a certain sad drama. It was like kangaroos caught in the shooter's light and staring, puzzled, at the source of their death. The enthusiastic and affectionate mockery which had come from the darkness behind the headlights dwindled away.

The performance finished early.

The mission offered two of its vehicles, one of which had interior seating for several, to help transport the audience back to the beach. But, even so, some of the tourists had to make the return trip huddled on the open backs of utes. They wrinkled their noses at the blankets offered to them as protection from the cold night air.

They were unhappy and, grumbling and shivering, followed the jumping torchlight across the dark and painful beach. The Zodiacs waited, bobbing on a rising tide. The water, at least, felt warm after the cold trip. The lights of the catamaran twinkled at sea.

Gerrard apologised abjectly to the captain of the catamaran, and as Billy returned to his car he saw him arguing with Moses and some of the others who usually danced but had stayed at the beach. A couple of campfires flickered in the darkness spread round them.

Billy turned on his headlights and there before him were Sebastian, Milton, and, just behind them, shielded from the light, Jasmine. They put their hands to their eyes and moved out of the beam. They'd stayed at the beach and now wanted a lift back to the camp. Sebastian sat in the front, and the other two hunched themselves behind the cab. Milton was shirtless and Billy teased him about getting in the back rather than squeezing in the front with him and Sebastian.

Sebastian said they'd had a few beers that some of the people from the boat had given them. He was silent. He turned around to glance at the two huddled behind as they drove of into the crepuscular tunnel before them. Billy glanced in the rearvision mirror.

There, their teeth bright in the moonlight, they laugh and sing. The leaves and the wind whip and roar right round them, whip and roar round that warm quiet place behind us. This car is sliding on silver sand, under a high black sparkling sky, and those two fall together, just touching. His black skin moves like an ocean in the moonlight, she pale as a spirit. Inside the roaring wind, that girl's hair is weaving, rippling. Lines, writhing desiring, moving between them. There's goosebumps in moonlight.

Milton bashed on the cab as soon as they reached camp, and leapt out before the car stopped. Sebastian shrugged at Billy, and got out of the car also. Jasmine declined Billy's offer to return to his place for drinks. Billy drove off, then back to return the scarf she'd left in the car, and saw her struggling to unlock the door of her caravan. She shouted, and kicked at it in a sudden burst of temper. They opened it together.

It was cramped in the van. Jasmine picked a carton of milk from the counter, and turned away from it holding her nose.

'Pooh … oh,' and she indicated a glass of whisky left exposed, 'I hid that there when some kids came knocking at the door. I never drink in the morning, but this time I was gunna …' As Billy left she called out, suddenly, after their goodbyes, 'Hey, we should have a party, eh, some time? Maybe invite Milton …'

Billy nodded yes, said maybe, drove away to sleep.

Something like Homesickness

Father Paul came to see Billy and Liz. He was leaving very soon, and the mission was letting him go, letting him know he was dispensable, even if only for a little time. But perhaps Father Paul was thinking he might not be able to find this place again. He might not come back. Did he know this already? He was, maybe nowtoolate, speaking to people and reaching out to listen and share. He wanted to speak, like when he was a younger man, about God. He was reluctant to, almost, with Billy. Billy was awkwardly reluctant, almost, to listen.

This Saturday morning they sat under a mango tree in Billy's front yard: Billy, Liz, Father Paul. They sat in the blue shade. Spots and strips of sunlight lay across the grass, creeping, growing, dying as the sun moved across the sky. They could see the steam rising from their tea, and when they first began to talk the sun sparkled white and hurt their eyes.

The teacups became dry, stained, lay in the grass like bones, and still they talked. The shade beneath that mango tree was narrower, and they sweated and breathed shallowly in the hot air.

Oh, they spoke of many things. Father Paul and Liz remembered when Liz had first gone to mass there. 'I wondered when you were going to turn up,' he said.

'How did you know?' she asked.

'You can always tell a Catholic,' he laughed, and turned to Billy.

'I'm nominally a Catholic. In name only. My father went to New Norcia actually,' said Billy.

'Oh,' Father Paul looked long at Billy. 'I wouldn't have thought that. I wondered … You know that we are, or were, of the same Order as New Norcia? Many part-Aboriginal children were sent there …'

'I know. He hated it.'

Lapsed Catholic Liz and Father Paul spoke of contraception, liberation theology, needless suffering, and Billy was mostly silent.

Father Paul said he was glad to be going on sabbatical. He was tired. He was tired of his role here. He was just running a business. He had expressed such doubts to the archbishop who had said that was where his talents lay; he served God in this way. Father said he wanted to be more of a priest, to be more personal, to do more counselling. But in a community like this, especially considering the history of the church and Aboriginal people, especially here … It was difficult. We must work to protect our vested interest, to preserve our institution, for our business, to preserve our God perhaps.

'I think God is changing. He must to stay alive in these people. Perhaps we need to think of Him as a great spirit, a creator spirit, an artist. A creative force behind the world, living in the world, and giving ceremony and the land. What am I saying?

'I don't know. See, even communion. It should be, ideally, more intimate. More even like what we're doing right now.'

'And this is such a small community,' said Billy.

'Yes …'

'But is it a community?'

'Perhaps not,' said Father Paul, 'without common beliefs …'

'You, at the mission, have,' said Liz. 'The people here have …'

'They have no real beliefs left, I think. Superstition perhaps. Still, you could say the same for most people. Maybe they, we, will end up with a new God here, some sort of major spirit from the Dreaming or whatever, who named everything and us — or should I say the Aborigines? — and created this special relationship. People, creation, the land.'

'Or just nothing. People shrivelling in this inhospitable land, within an inhospitable, wider society.' Billy had said little, and he mumbled this. Was ignored.

'And meanwhile, at the mission, we argue about logistics, detail, pragmatics — especially with lay missionaries who come here for a short time.'

'And this small community, like an island. Are there forces representative of a wider community, you think? Can we talk of it as if it was in a story? Is it a microcosm?'

Father Paul snorted. 'A microcosm of what? Our society? The whites here work hard. The Aborigines play cards, fight. What else? Incest, child molestation, violence, wife bashing. Alcoholism. Petrol sniffing. The church is dying.'

'Still, the church does exist here, after a fashion, which may be more than it does elsewhere.'

'Alex, you, Billy, battling to make your school work, and is your education relevant? The people here, sharp, learning to play government departments against one another; looking for handouts; out for what they can wheedle from the next crew of white do-gooders, government busybodies, investigators …'

'A microcosm …'

Father Paul sighed, and shook his head. 'I must be tired. I

need this sabbatical. Even the people here like to get out, for a break. It's a small community all right; intense, in a big land and space.'

'But the people come back again, they get homesick,' offered Liz.

'Is this place real? You wait and see. I've been away for a couple of years before. When you're away you wonder if this place is real.'

Oh, it need not be real. It is not this reality that we are homesick for.

But one time, not long before Father Paul left, he maybe sensed such a thing. Briefly. He and Billy were fishing, in Father Paul's big boat. They had come across a school of bait fish trapped on the surface and almost inert, perhaps in fear. The men tried dragging lures around the edge of the school, but nothing. In desperation they went right through the centre of the school. The small bait fish were packed solid. They parted before the boat, and reformed, solidly, behind it. They could see the sharks there, fins scything the surface; not in a frenzy, just regularly, back and forth. But still, nothing attacked their lures. There were few birds even. It was so still. It was a mystery to them, seemed somehow dangerous and deadly.

Suddenly one of their lines was hit. The bait fish started leaping. Sharks, speeding. Billy stood at the front of the boat, Father Paul struggled with his line, there were birds squawking diving from the low steel-grey sky, the water boiling and bloody, dark and silver flashes in the depths. God's grandeur! called Father Paul, God's grandeur. His rod bowed, reel screaming. The water dark and churning. Things thumped into the boat, leapt from the water. A shark attacked the spinning propeller.

Then it was as suddenly quiet again. The birds wheeling away in a group. The water brown and blood-red, but calm, in a pool around the boat. The birds gathering again in the distance. Father Paul reeled his line in easily now. Just a large silver gaping fish head at its end, the body bitten off.

And about this same time, Gerrard and the builders had some trouble out in their little boats also. They left soon after that. See? We made them.

They were fishing, plenty of them, in their dinghies, and drinking their beer.

Then came the whales, way up here in these warm waters. They were on their little boats and the whales came up beside them, very close.

This was exciting of course. But the whales came too close, like to bump them. Made big splashes. The men shouted, hit them with oars even. Those big whales did bump the boats, they made them rock and the men slipped, fell in their little boats, shouted at one another. Now they knew they were frightened. They thought the whales was going to smash them.

Start the motor, pull pull quickly, and go, get away.

Elsewhere, they laughed about it, and started fishing again. Then again it happened. The whales bumped them, and roared like monsters, pushed their little boats. Moving closer and closer, more and more, big and bigger.

They raced away.

They got back to their camp and talked about it, guffawing, privately wondering. Oh sure, it was an adventure. They filleted all their fish, and when Brother Tom visited they laughed about it with him. They said they were all half pissed, no worries.

They gave him all the fish skeletons to take away for the Sisters to cook up in a stew to feed the old people. Not the good meat, not the boned flesh. Just the skeletons.

But they were frightened all right. And so they, too, were going. And glad of it.

The builders had almost finished for the season, and would have left anyway. But Gerrard, he said he was also leaving this place, as soon as he could. He was meant to be here to help us, his wages come from us, from money the government gives us. But he was no good. He made money from us, and if we borrow some he would not give us our own money until he had been paid back. We pay him back all right.

Gerrard took some good fish to King Alex and his family. He told them about it, half joking, and a good story it was. They listened closely.

So they will go soon too. They too must go from this place because for sure they do not belong.

It is not reality we are homesick for. And not just us Aborigine ones either.

Exchanges

Jasmine borrowed the office utility one Sunday and took some of the women, and their children, with her. She regretted it.

They first hammered on the cab only a couple of kilometres from the community, shouting at her to stop. All of them, except for the children in the cab with her, yelling demanding. The children with her giggled and looked around. Ignoring Jasmine, her passengers wandered into the bush beside the track.

'Bush apple,' said the children beside her, and they got out too. They returned, Jasmine drove on, her passengers laughing and munching. One of the children offered a small piece of fruit to Jasmine. No one else did.

This happened several times on their way to the beach. Jasmine was offended. She told Billy and Liz about it afterward.

She thought it was bad mannered. She didn't know what she had done.

She is young, has no man or children, dresses like she does and all the young men looking at her. They see down her dress. Like Father Paul says, there should only be married people, white people, come in here.

When they got to the beach they yelled at Jasmine, telling her to drive over to the shade of a big tree there. She was nervous about going across the soft sand, because she hadn't driven four-wheel drives much before, and if she did get it bogged, well then what? Murray had laughed when she expressed such doubt to him as she left, and told her it was all right but still, she was not confident.

Some of the women seemed to expect Jasmine to have spare fishing lines for them. She didn't even have one for herself. She wasn't interested in that. She said later that she felt they just used her, as if she was only there just to drive them and be a slave. Bitches. And it was so hot. Jasmine sat by the car in the shade. A couple of the children stayed with her for a few minutes but then they too left, and ran to join the others dispersing around the beach, the mangroves, the rocks.

Jasmine wanted to go.

A car approached. She didn't move. It stopped, noisy rattling by her tree.

'Hey, lazy girl, why you not fishin'?'

Moses. Jasmine shook her head. 'I wish I'd never come.'

So, to her great relief, she drove off with Moses, Alphonse, and Milton in the old short-wheel-base Toyota. Kevin stayed behind with the office car to drive the women and kids back later. Moses had some beer in the car. Kevin didn't drink, and had merely come along for the ride when the others had left to find somewhere cool and private to drink their beer.

They drove back toward the community, because it seemed there were people at all the beaches today, and, quite close to the camp, turned off toward the river. They drove across a rocky part of the riverbed where the water, at this late time of the dry season, only trickled. The track became indistinct, appearing just before the wheels and disappearing behind them as the dry grass, surprisingly, sprang up again. They weaved around rocks and trees until they came to a distinct clearing surrounded by large rocks. Moses dragged a carton of beer out from under one of the seats where it had been covered by a couple of damp hessian bags.

The early beers were cool, and the clearing between the small cliff faces formed by the rocks was cool also, and in deep shade. The men told her that there were many rock paintings through here, but it too nice to sit here and drink so they would show them to her another time. In the wet season, they said, it was nice in this spot; you could shelter from the rain, there was always a breeze, and the water ran around this spot and made music from many little waterfalls playing. In old days, people came here always, Moses said.

What were they thinking, these people? That they were getting a bit drunk? How the breeze felt on their little-bit-numb cheeks. The light like diamonds winking in the leaves above. Of the voices just out of hearing in this place. Of their flesh, man and woman, dark and pale, alive.

Jasmine happy. She was definitely getting tipsy. This was a way to live. This morning was so awful, and now so good. This was real. This was Australia, she thought. I am living a unique existence, here, among these rocks and paintings, in this shade and breeze, beneath this sun, with these people. Aboriginal people. She hadn't really known Aboriginal people before she came here. Well, not real ones. Just some in towns mostly, down south, walking along the streets, sitting together in the distance, waiting at the end of queues. Oh, did she say this aloud? Her cheeks felt flushed.

They finished the beer. Well, there were more drinks at Jasmine's place. They could have a party. Quiet but. And it surprised Jasmine that they walked back, which Moses wanted to do, because it was a very short distance, and they wouldn't draw attention to themselves, and because Jasmine's place was right on the edge of the settlement closest to where they were now.

Jasmine lived in a small parked caravan. It was surrounded by a tall wire fence against which brushwood had been wired. But it was still possible to see into that yard, even from quite a distance, because of the gap that the gate made.

That night there was loud music playing there for a little while. And they were dancing, dancing like crazy people in the moonlight. Jasmine held her long skirt up around her thighs and danced like a forest queen in a gardiya's children's story. Alphonse danced with his feet motionless, like a drunk at a Sunday session. Even Moses danced for a minute. Milton copied Jasmine's dancing, to make fun of her, and she danced corroboree style, to make fun of him.

Then there was only the two of them. There had not been much to drink. The others had left. Billy, out walking, stopped near the gate and saw them. Milton and Jasmine slow dancing, close together, holding one another. The powerful moonlight made solid chunks of shadow, strong lines of silver. That light was so strong you could have climbed up it, toward the moon, and looked down on the two embracing within that tall fence, and Billy peeping from the side of the gate.

Jasmine moved herself out of the embrace. Milton held one end of her cotton scarf. They looked at one another from either end of that scarf, and Jasmine pulled Milton toward her by it, took his hand, led him into her caravan. For a moment they were seen in the door of the caravan as the electric light held them, their colours strong after the moonlight; purple-black, red, white, all in yellow light.

Further Evidence

You could see that Jasmine was hanging around Milton. She would happen to wander over to the school when he was gardening there, just to talk to him. The two of them sit down in the shade. She brought drinks over for him. He is a married man, you know that, and Annie is a good wife to him. Alex would have to come and join in the conversation so that Jasmine would leave and Milton could get to work again. Others just watched, noticed them there.

Milton's little sister wrote in her school journal:

One night my brother was drunk and he was making us laugh then he said to my mum I gotta nother wife here and we laughed again and then he told Ricky and Alan to ring up for her but Ricky and Alan told him that they have no silver left and what for anyway she got no phone there. Last night when I was trying to go to sleep I heard someone fighting and so I woke up and look who was that and went back to sleep then my mother came out and woke me up again and asked us who was that banging the house and we told mum that is Annie banging the wall and my mum asked us why she is banging the house and we said we don't know why she is banging the house and we went back to sleep again.

Misunderstandings Still

Liz and Billy were returning from a weekend of camping and fishing. They saw Milton, Alphonse and Araselli parked near the airstrip, but although they waved and slowed down to speak with them, they got no response. Alphonse drove away before Billy could stop his car; Milton may have moved one finger in a reluctant sort of wave as he drove off, but that was all. They looked angry and sullen.

'What this mission mob here for anyway? To help Aborigine, or what?' Milton's face worked as he spat the words out. 'It's not right they — they say they Christians?' He snorted. His fingers clawed with tension, then clasped one another, intertwining like a nest of snakes. 'Who say they can just shoot people's dogs like that, like murderers?'

He put his clasped hands to his forehead, and pushed his thumbs into his eyes. He sighed, dropped his hands to his thighs, pushed his shoulders back into the chair, and looked at Billy.

'Father Paul, this wouldn't happen if he was here. But they his horses, eh? They care more about them than us? They should be here to help us. They don't care, they just here to make money.

'I should get a gun, shoot those horses myself. Or tear down the fence, and let them go, free, run with the brumbies. That stallion be more happy then, anyway.'

Milton clenched one fist, and shook it as he spoke. The other hand gripped into his thigh. 'That mission better throw them out, get Murray right out of here. Sack Gerrard we will get him out.

'I see that Murray, catch him at the airstrip and I grab him, grab him by the back of the neck and rub his face in the dirt, how him just like a dog.' His bare feet drummed on the floor.

'And some people,' Milton paused. Billy had been disturbed to see Milton so transformed by his anger, and now he saw Milton soften for a moment as he said, 'Some people say maybe it is your wife's fault.'

They remembered. Liz had offered to look after Father Paul's horses when he went on sabbatical. Her house was between the camp and the paddock where they were kept, so it was convenient for her. Father Paul suggested people she could use to help prepare them to be ridden again. He said he had had a word with those people.

She did get people to help her, because the horses had not been ridden for such a long time. Moses came over once, first. He rasped down the hooves on the old gelding, the only one Liz had been able to catch. Hard work that. He held the horse's leg, he grunted and sweated as he rasped, and his bare toes gripped into the soil when the horse tried to kick him away. But he didn't swear, he didn't talk much, not to Liz.

Liz didn't try to ride the horses straight away, but tied them to a long lead and made them run around her in circles. Milton came to help her after that. It took him a long time, of walking and talking softly, to catch them. He rode each of the horses, within the paddock, and then rode with her the first time she rode the gelding out of the paddock and into the bush.

Sometimes the dogs from the camp got into the paddock and chased the horses. Sometimes the little children threw stones at them. Liz would get angry and shout, and she chased the dogs with a stockwhip.

One time she found cuts on the horses' chests and she spoke to Murray about it. He said the camp dogs had done it, probably by chasing them into the fence. She sought help from Moses, who laughed, and said that the mission used to shoot dogs for that. Liz walked straight away from him and brought Murray back with her. She was an angry woman that one.

So she, Murray, Moses, they stood in the hot dark office. Some other people, sitting outside near the basketball court and by the door, heard them talking, and maybe peeped in a couple of times.

Liz said, 'What can we do if people won't look after their dogs and keep them away?' She was talking most. She said she had chased them away and chased them away and chased them away. Maybe, if their owners can't keep them away, they should be shot.

Moses laughed. 'Too busy playing cards this mob.' Moses did not know what to do, really he didn't.

'You mean we should shoot them?'

Moses spoke to Murray. 'Mission used to, all the time. And now if they get with the ducks, chicken … Father Paul, he still shoot 'em, eh?'

What could Moses do, all on his own? Why did they want to make trouble for him? 'Maybe you have to shoot them still. Maybe they won't come back. We can hope, eh?' He laughed again and waved his hand. He was relieved when they left. He is a big man, but he sat down when they left and felt weak and bullied.

Murray was pleased because the dogs could cause a lot of trouble with the stock and poultry, and in the gardens. When Father Paul was here the dogs never went into the mission grounds because everyone knew they would be shot, just as had always happened. Every now and then Father Paul did shoot one. Usually early on a Sunday morning, the gunshot and yelp …

But now. Murray felt the mission was losing clout. And that meant he was in danger somehow.

So, what had happened?

It was on the Saturday afternoon. Murray and Gerrard were sitting out the front of the little house in which Murray lives. It is down past the store, the bakery, along the path that goes past the gardens, past the chickens, ducks, pigs. There were still feathers scattered around the chicken pen where some dog had recently claimed a victim.

Murray and Gerrard were sitting there, in the sun. Maybe they were having a drink. Gerrard was talking about what he was going to do when he left, and they were telling each other how hard it was to work here. They felt taken for granted, used. But the fishing was good, and these beers in the heat.

They saw two dogs come up from the creek down there, in the distance, and slink under the fence at the far end of the horses' paddock. Gerrard and Murray looked at one another, and they recognised the dogs all right. They knew that one of them belonged to Milton's mob. They grabbed a couple of rifles and walked through the gardens toward the paddock.

They saw the dogs, and the horses, on the other side of the paddock. The two groups of animals stood facing one another, as if about to begin some elaborate ritual.

Then the dogs saw the men, and turned immediately back to the creek. Murray knew the camp was at his back, so it was safe to shoot. He raised his gun and aimed at the second of the loping dogs. Gerrard said, 'No! Not from this far.'

Murray smiled, and bang! he shot at that dog. The animal jerked, and fell. Its front legs folded up first. Murray felt triumphant, and was about to brag to Gerrard. But the dog got up, staggered, and ran clumsily, yelping yelping yelping, in the direction in which its partner had disappeared. The two men ran a few steps, and fired again, but they couldn't hit it.

They were worried now. They went back to the mission buildings, and they were swearing.

The dog went through the camp, bleeding and whimpering. It snarled at the people, who stepped away from it and watched it walk past. Some of the children followed it, squealing with excitement and concern. It limped on a front leg, and there was blood on its short mangy hide and spattered in its trail.

It came to a stop, swaying, in front of its home. Sebastian sat in the shade, leaning against the front wall of his house beside the remains of a small fire. He was sick this day, weak and shaking badly, and so his family had left him behind when they went fishing. He looked up and saw the dog come to a halt, and fall over. He saw the children gathered a few paces behind it, staring as the dog lay there, in the dirt, whimpering.

People gathered around, angry with what had happened. They moved close, and the dog snarled at them. Sebastian stroked and patted his dog.

Raphael came, and spoke with Sebastian and some of them there. He swore at the mission, and went away, and came back in Milton's old ute with Araselli and Alphonse. He shot the dog, right there in front of the hut and all the people and kids. He threw the dog in the back of the ute and he and Alphonse and Araselli they drove away and into the mission grounds. No one followed them.

They drove through the grounds, down the path past the banana and mango trees, the leafy shady green, past the cackling chickens and snorting pigs and the rich scents. They stopped with the front wheels touching the front of Murray's house. There was no one there. The house was locked. They threw the dead dog down at the front door, and its blood spilt over the mat and on the door.

If it was not locked they would have thrown the dog on his bed.

Araselli came marching over to the school early on the Monday morning. She was wild. It was before most of the kids had got to school. She asked Liz, angrily, if she had told Murray to shoot dogs. Liz said she'd spoken to Moses about it. She spoke softly.

They sat down. Nobody really wanted trouble, but was it fair?

Araselli, she was wild still. She was nearly crying. She said she had heard the dogs over that way earlier that morning, but she didn't go and see or call them. It hurt her that their dogs could be shot just like that. That dog belonged here. They just don't care, some people, gardiya like that Murray. And Gerrard.

She sat there a long time, and they started to talk friendly. Some of the kids coming to school saw her in the room and they didn't come in because they thought there might be trouble, and they did not want to see trouble between their teachers and Araselli or anyone. They were happy to see Araselli leaving and talking softly.

When Murray went away Jasmine walked out to the airstrip to see him off. There were just her and some people from the mission to watch as he noisily dwindled into the clouds.

When they offered her a lift she said she would walk back. But then, as she walked into the dust left behind the mission vehicle, and Murray was still a buzzing speck in the eastern sky, Milton was suddenly there in the dust with her. His old Hilux was idling noisily, and he was grinning at her. He was going to dump some rubbish from the school. She got into the car with him.

It was later in the day, and they were driving back, coming a different way. They were a couple of hundred metres from Billy's place, near the paddock where the dog had been shot, and they could see young Alan, in his bright shirt and on his bicycle, over on the flat by the powerhouse. They saw him wave, and at the same time saw the pack of dogs rushing at him; saw him try to flee, and the leading dog leap, the dogs tear him down. And then they were bouncing over the flat, they themselves shouting and the horn tooting motor roaring. But still, even in all that other noise, they could hear the boy screaming.

The dogs fled, and the boy was sobbing with pain and fear when they got to him. They rushed him to the clinic and sister called the flying doctor.

Milton slipped away. Alex and Annette came rushing over, and said they were calling the police to kill those dogs, they were leaving this place, Alan couldn't come back here, they would not, this was too much to expect anyone to put up with ...

Some people said, later, that it was the boy's fault. He should not have gone so close to the dogs, not when they was eating. He should not have screamed and tried to get away, that just made them dogs excited like they was hunting, and he should not have been on his own, and the dogs didn't know because they never saw him anywhere.

But Milton said nothing.

That boy had very many stitches. Alex came back later to pack away all his office things, and he left again quietly. He looked very bad. A truck came to drive away all his family things.

We are Not as One

Ah, they all leave, these other people. Let them go, we getting rid of them. Gone. Father Paul, the builders, Alex and his family. Murray too. Some of them see their world slipping slipping the longer they stay, and they struck out before they marooned and forgotten.

So Liz became the boss of the school, one new teacher come in, and Stella became a teacher with them. A trial for her, to see if she could do a good enough job, and then Liz could say to the Ministry of Education, 'She is a teacher already, this one.'

But this time was a trial for others too. For Liz, as a boss. For Billy.

This time of the year, when this was happening, it is getting hotter. Late in every day the sky comes low, it sags down like it is swollen and bruised. The flies are sticky drinking your sweat. Over on the edge of the sky the lightning stabs the hills. But no rain comes yet. It will.

All day nearly, small willy-willies form, sucking up dust and paper and the kids run nm to catch them as they skitter-scatter dance away. The kids run hard to catch them, run with them; get inside them and you might fly.

Mostly, this time of the year, people wait for the rain.

Then the roads will close, and there will be no tourists and not much drinking. Sometimes, on Christmas Day, the mission used to give us one, maybe two, cans of beer for every man.

But waiting can be a hard thing. The fat nasty sky; sweat oozing; the earth so dry, burnt, and thirsty. The grey river grows green in its shallows. People get tired and cranky, and will drink too much too quickly of the last beers that come in overland before the roads become river and mud. The people drink, sniff petrol, empty themselves. Kill the world.

Milton is at the tip with that woman Jasmine. They are together, alone there, by the river, in the heat of day.

Milton drives back with Jasmine. They have been gone a long time. He lets her off where she lives. She should be working, you know, in the office, for us. Not going off with school rubbish and school gardener. Some of the women are calling her names. Slut. Annie's sisters say they will teach her some things.

And Raphael's two wives, later on that day, were sitting in the quiet schoolyard, in the blue shade under the mango tree.

Fallen mangoes — the last ones, bat-bitten, overripe, half-eaten, split and broken —were scattered on the ground around them. The bright fruit spilt flesh and the air was sweet with decay.

Stella and Gloria sat with their heads bowed, but they were watchful, and sat with the tree between them and the community's other buildings.

Billy and Liz were walking home from the school when they saw those two women sitting there, hiding. They knew that Stella was married to Raphael in the church, and that Gloria is like a girlfriend to Raphael, but they all live together. Stella is Milton's sister. Those women do not go away from their own house much, except that Raphael lets Stella go to the school each day, and then straight home again; special quick on payday.

The four of them talked. Stella's face was swollen. Gloria's eyes moved quickly, and she was nervous like a kangaroo, watching out for her attacker.

Raphael, you know, he bashes them. And he will, again, this day, when he finds them. He has told people he is looking for his wives. He is drunk. And they are in the safe grounds of the school.

Billy walked away. He went home thinking, 'This is not my business, what can we do anyway? I do not want to get involved.' But Liz stayed. The two women were afraid. What can they do? Sometimes, they told her, they have stayed with the Sisters at the mission for a day, a night. But they worry now even about the Sisters, for they are getting old themselves. People are not so frightened of the mission any more. Raphael beats them even the more when they go back. Anyway, he's told them not to go there.

'What are you going to do? Stay here all night?'

'Yes. Maybe the river.'

Billy watched the three of them cross the green lawn. Behind them, as the sun inserted itself into the earth, the sky was spattered with red. His wife walked upright with her shoulders thrown back; the two other women were hunched, and looked around as if expecting a figure to leap at them from some hidden spot. Liz's hair blazed with the dying sun, her white skin gleamed. The coming darkness seemed to coagulate in the other two women.

After the meal Liz, Stella and Gloria sat at the kitchen table. They had the lights very dim. The women told Liz how they were beaten, sometimes with a stick, sometimes in front of

Raphael's family. He beats Gloria the most. They listed injuries for Liz, and lifted skirts and tops to show their scars.

Billy sat in another room, looking at a book and listening. The light was bright.

Once, twice? A vehicle drove noisily around the track which ran along two sides of their block. The headlights swept across the windows. The first of these times, Stella and Gloria rushed into the darkened passageway which led to the bedrooms.

Liz remained where she was, and sat up straighter. Billy clenched his jaw.

Gloria and Stella sat together in the dark passage and continued conversing with Liz through the doorway. Liz told them of restraining orders, of contacting the police, of leaving Raphael. But where could they go? This is their home. The police? When will they help black women? And anyway, they in Wyndham, Derby. And Raphael, he is not always so savage and so wild.

The women stayed the night, and early the next morning, they gathered in the kitchen in a fug of cigarette smoke and stale clinging dreams. Eyes stung.

This day holds dread, so Billy thinks, and he wants them to go now, and leave him to rest. He has spoken to them but little, and watching them inhale on their last cigarettes he realises they will soon have to go, if only for more tobacco.

He watches them walk across the lawn, through the various gates and the schoolyard toward the camp. He hears Liz speaking of the shame and violence of their lives.

It is as if they were exhaled from the house, and now the doors slide open and they return, inhaled again. The curtains are pulled across the doors and windows, and the women slump at the kitchen table once more.

Billy stands at the sink. Watches through a gap in the curtains. Washes the cups. Ashtrays. Grey ash on his fingers, floating in the waters, whirlpooling down the drain.

Stella and Gloria have no plans for the day. They have just now been to Stella's family's house. Sebastian and Milton gave them some cigarettes. They asked them where they had stayed for the night. But the women have no plans for this day. Liz cannot think of a plan for them.

Raphael will have plans.

And then, there he was at the door. Stella and Gloria, warned at the last moment, had fled into the bedrooms.

Raphael had knocked. Raphael was dishevelled. His shirt was unbuttoned at the sleeves and chest, and hanging out. His eyes were large and bloodshot. He stood outside the doorway, and looked past Billy when the door slid open, and saw the chairs pushed back from the kitchen table, the ashtray, the smoke where two bodies had been.

'You got my women here Mr Storey.' It was not really a question, but was a cautious statement. Billy was pleased he had the protection of a title.

'I'm mad, you know … Sebastian tell me … All night looking for my women, looking looking. What you doing this for? All night. I've got a three o'clock brain here, you know?' He put an index finger against his temple. 'I'm crazy-kind now. Where they?'

He looked past Billy, throwing his gaze aggressively through the room, but Billy stood in the doorway and was relieved that Raphael did not seek to force himself into the room.

'Raphael, I …'

'You can't do this! Who said you a big boss like god?'

Veins protruded from his throat. His eyes held tears.

'We can't let them go, we can't give them to you as if they were … They're frightened, Raphael. We must help them, even if that means …' Billy's voice was soft, perhaps whining.

Raphael raised himself onto his toes with tension, and lifted clenched fists to his face. Billy fought to remain calm and slouched.

'Raphael, of course we can't keep them forever, but if you go we'll …'

Liz listened. She thought if she had a gun she would shoot the man. The women listened.

And Billy and Raphael, they walked together across the lawn. It was still soft, early morning. They walked out of the small fenced yard, and stood fifty, a hundred metres away.

Raphael stopped at the gate which lead to the mission, and turned around.

'Don't go back that way, Raphael.' Billy was pleading. He didn't want to focus Raphael's anger on himself.

The women, heads down, gazing at the ground before them, walked tentatively out of the house and onto the lawn. Liz remained in the doorway. The women moved as silently as shadows.

From across by the front of the house Raphael watched them. 'You fuckin' sluts! Sluts!' He laughed and sneered at them. 'Hide from me, eh? I get you, you see, I show you.' He shook his fist at them, but he did not move.

Stella glanced up briefly. Raphael swore at her again, and then turned, flung open the gate and was gone, of in the other direction. The women glanced around, and circled for a moment, not stopping. 'Thanks Liz,' they mumbled, 'maybe we go see Sisters.'

There was defeat everywhere.

Billy and Liz retreated. They locked their doors again, moving without speech. The roar of the air-conditioner seemed very loud.

Liz shouted. 'What could we do? Sebastian told him where they were, didn't he? What father, what love is that? That bastard! Bastards!'

A pounding at the door. A pounding. Even through the curtain they could see that it was Raphael. Billy went to the door, and opened it. Raphael had not tried it, and Billy didn't want him to know they had locked it.

'Why you doing this, Storey? You got them here, again, them women. They leave their children behind! Call 'mself mothers!'

In one hand he held a thick piece of wood, a club. At his other side stood two small children. Raphael had the hand of each of them clasped in his own. The boy was grinning.

'You can't come to me with weapons.' Billy surprised himself with the tone of his voice. 'You can't bully your way in here, it's not might is right here.'

But he could if he wanted to, it could be right.

'But you, eh? You hide my women.'

'They're not here.'

Raphael was bobbing about, now tapping his club in the palm of his hand. He looked over Billy's shoulders, trying to see around the very corners of the room before him. When would he shoulder Billy aside?

'Raphael — leave your weapon, there will be no weapons in my house — come, see for yourself.' Billy stepped aside, and ostentatiously swept his arm into the room. Almost before Billy had completed the movement, Raphael had placed his club against the inside of the doorframe and was across the room.

Billy fastidiously grabbed the club between thumb and forefinger and propped it outside the door.

Raphael, having raced through all the rooms in the house, was back. He looked to where he had left his club, and erupted. 'My club! Where …?' Billy pointed to it outside the door.

'No clubs, I said …'

Raphael turned from him and grabbed the club. 'Don't touch my stick. I know where they …' He ran around the corner of the house, muttering and cursing.

The children looked after him. Even when he did not return they continued staring in the direction he had gone. Billy and Liz welcomed them in, and the four of them went to the front verandah with cordial and biscuits. They sat there in a numbed silence. The children slurped. Across the yard the new teacher peered out of his door for a moment, gave a little wave, and withdrew again.

The boy pointed in the other direction, his face lighting up. There was Raphael, jogging across the track toward the paddock where the horses were kept. He still carried the club. He was shirtless, and his stomach jiggled above the belt of his dark nylon trousers.

Suddenly he quickened his pace. He put one hand on a fence post and swung himself heavily over the barbed wire, stumbling as his feet touched the other side.

'Got you bitches,' he yelled as he sprinted into the paddock.

Then they could not see him because of the trees in their front yard and that edge of the paddock. Raphael's son leapt from the verandah and ran to the fence. He stood there, grinning excitedly, trying to see through the trees. The daughter followed. They thought perhaps they could hear screams.

'Come. Come away. Let's go inside and watch a video.'

Oh yes, the children were happy to do that. But, 'He teach them, eh?' said the grinning boy.

A few days later Liz saw Gloria in the store. Gloria did not look directly at her, but whispered as she limped past, 'He said we never talk to you again.' Her face was swollen.

Billy heard that Raphael had proper caught them all right. Hit them around the legs with his club, and half-dragged, let them limp, home.

Hit them again there. Later he dragged Gloria screaming from the shower by her hair. He slapped and hit her in front of his family; men, women, boys, girls, and all. She fell down on the ground in front of them naked and slippery wet and crying, and all the sand and little sticks stuck to her skin and tears.

Gerrard visited Billy and Liz, to say goodbye. 'Raphael's been at it again, did you hear?' They said nothing. 'His wives hid from him all night apparently. No one knows where. We thought with the Sisters, but it must've been by the river.

'I saw him chasing them with a stick, he looked pretty wild.

'I heard it, I was in the workshop, when he caught them in the paddock there. I could hear. It sounded like torture, them begging for mercy. Whack, whack. They were screaming.'

They tried to seem not interested, to change the subject.

'Anyway,' said Gerrard, 'I'll be glad to be out of here. I'm leaving in a week or two. Got a little business to run in Carnarvon.'

What? Running a bus charter? Selling artefacts made by silly Aborigine?

'Glad to be out of this mad place.'

True, this be a mad place, in some ways. But we can fix that. Maybe. This one was a real story, but should not be. This bashing to try show he is a powerful one, and to have control.

Words …

Milton's battered and coughing Hilux left from one side of Billy's yard as Jasmine, having walked through the school grounds, arrived through the opposite gate. She greeted them, and her eyes followed Milton's smoking vehicle. He didn't appear to look back.

'He reckons it's not worth leaving it here any longer,' said Billy.

'He's probably worried he'll bump into me,' said Jasmine.

Their heads turned to her like those of puppets on shared strings.

Oh.

'You know I've been with him, sleeping with him.'

Oh. We thought. We knew.

'I'm pregnant I think. I'm out of here.'

They went into the roaring house, pleased to share this information. They must have tea, coffee, some ceremony. Find out more.

'I've decided. I just want a baby. A black baby.' Oh yes?

'I like Milton, but … He's married, kids. His family's giving me a hard time. I've gotta go.'

From outside the house you wouldn't hear their voices, just see mouths moving. All you hear is the air-conditioner roaring.

Jasmine's bangles slid up and down her forearms. She

brushed the hair from her face, wrinkled her brow. Sighed. Lit a cigarette. Looked at it.

'Have to give these up.'

Smoke above them now like spirits quietly watching.

'Is it true you kept the women here the other night?'

Oh. Yes. But.

'I've gotta go. I'm out of here. Tomorrow. With Gerrard, he's driving out while he can, before the rain. Otherwise it means the expense of flying all the way to Perth.

'Bloody old Samson, you know he scored Gerrard's fishing net? He gave it to him.

'Tomorrow. I'm going home. Live with my mother, me and my baby. I hope he's dark, dark like they are here.'

She got to get away but. She wants to own one, herself, safely. Maybe she right.

Jasmine says, 'And Bill, what has happened with your baby?'

Puzzled expressions. She continued. 'Can I say that? You were so keen early in the year, I thought. Your writing, you know, you were going to collect stories from Fatima and that.'

Oh yes.

'Yes, but … Just for school. And I have no time. They don't read well, not without a lot of editing.' He shrugged his shoulders in resignation, bowed and danced a little defence.

'Another failed project. You've gotta have failures.' Liz's intention was encouragement, and she leaned to him.

'It's problematical, see. I write for the kids, but I edit. So, do I change it too much? Do I write only for the kids here? Who speaks? Have I the right to …' He almost clasped his hands in front of his face, almost looked melodramatically offstage.

'Piss off, Bill.' Like a club smashed on the table. 'You're making excuses. Excuses. It's simple. Look at me.' Jasmine patted her stomach. 'You just do it. That's all that matters.'

She seemed so fertile, and so healthy now, glowing and growing before them. She sat, already, like a heavily pregnant woman, with her knees apart and her shoulders back. She held her head high and angled, mocking Billy.

Billy felt crowded and closed in. The two women exchanged glances like lovers. He was scrawny, already wizened, hollow within, and Jasmine was expanding, suddenly not the nervous and bothered woman of such a short time before. Liz moved closer to her, and Bill had to go.

'Anyway, my fishing time. Only a few hours left 'til dark.'

'It might rain.'

'We should be so lucky. I'll walk down and hope for that.'

Billy went diagonally across the schoolyard, heading for the river. He saw Sebastian and Gabriella slowly approaching from one side of the yard, Fatima and Deslie from the other. The five of them met. If you were to see this from above, to trace the footprints of the walkers from the moment they entered the school grounds, their combined paths would form an arrow, pointing to the river. The stem, a single set of footprints, would appear weakest. The tip of the arrow-head would be where they met, and now stood, at the gate exiting the school and closest to the river. They were not, at the time, aware of this design, but they saw the coincidence, and smiled just because of that.

'Are we all heading in the same direction?'

'I want to see you.' Sebastian was puffing. 'Not come in school, other time, never.'

They detoured into the workshop, because Sebastian had

wanted to borrow a tool, a wood plane.

'Goin' fishin', eh?' said Deslie.

'Yep.'

'Good time. Hot, rains coming soon. Soon be barramundi time. Maybe you lucky!'

'Hope so,' said Billy.

'We all call them barramundi, eh?' said Sebastian. 'Same, it's Aboriginal word. Not ours but, we say …' He laughed, and, looking at Deslie and Gabriella, said it was almost like they were doing a naming ceremony here. 'Young men,' he said, 'come into a circle of old ones, after they been in the bush a long time, and they say the true names of things.'

He grinned, and nodded at Billy. This was important. This was advice. This was true. 'We show them, on a stick, the picture, tell them the name, they eat some of that one. Name for this; we tell them the word. And they say the word, touch that carved stick in the proper place, eat the food. Then emu, kangaroo, goanna; same thing all the time. Give him the power, see.'

Gabriela observed intently.

'Soon, he do that, maybe.' Sebastian indicated Deslie who, standing against the brightly lit window, was dissolving at the edges.

'It's not right to speak too much. You, Gabriella … Me, I don't do that now, I'm a Christian, see.' For a moment he looked nervous, guilty.

'But sometimes that's the same, little bit, isn't it?' asked Fatima, but it was not really a question.

Sebastian looked particularly small and frail today, and was shaking even more than usual. 'Maybe you. You do that. You could maybe be Aborigine.'

'Maybe. Like one arm of me is.'

'That not everything. You believe you is, you feel it, you can be Aborigine all right. You believe, you belong. But, yes, maybe too late for you.'

Yes, Sebastian was visibly shrinking.

'I'll have to learn a new language,' said Billy. 'That's a lot of words, just for food, eh?'

Gabriella continued the tangent, 'That's like what I said to my tutor the other day, "You people have too many words" — speaking about English.'

Deslie nodded his agreement.

'Maybe.'

'Those stories,' Sebastian asked, 'you want some more?'

Billy shook his head. No. Yes. But. No time.

'You sing a story like Walanguh could,' said Fatima, 'that'd be a proper powerful one. Write about it all here. I'd help you. What you say?'

Sebastian nodded for Billy, and mumbled approval. He meant to say, 'The old people, they couldn't read or write, but they had their stories in their mouths and they had them in their hands. They danced and they sang all their stories ...' But his words came out broken and jumbled, perhaps because he was shaking so much. He had shrunk, and Billy felt himself looking down upon him as if he was a child.

'You look tired,' said Gabriella to Billy.

'No. A bit. Some time by the river, fishing, will help me.'

Sebastian had become solid again. 'Maybe catch you a barra, eh? Some people are lucky. After all this time, now you know the word.'

'Maybe.'

… And Knowing

He first saw the bronze and silver flash in the black water, as the barramundi swooped from invisible depths to investigate his lure. Swooped? It was as if it appeared, disappeared. Was there, an arc of it about the lure for an instant, then … gone! It was a big one, he'd seen it snapshot clear.

Now he knew it was there.

So he cast again. Let the lure settle. Let it be a sick fish, that's what he had been taught. He made it twitch, paused, twitched.

There!

He felt the strike run along the line, the rod, into his shoulders. The line was tight like a blade the rod bow-bent the reel singing. The great fish leapt and shook itself and the tiny fluorescent lure rattled at its jaw. The fish hung there, in the air against blue sky bloody cliffs, it dark with the river depths, silver scales engraved and shining like stars, the fame in its eyes.

Invisible again it sped and circled in the depths. He saw it a moment below his feet as it tried to drag the enchanted lure from its jaw. Now unseen, out to the centre of the river, the water bulging above its own deep power. Then launched again, shaking, about to take flight, shaking, shaking itself, shaking that lure. Which did, slowly, tumble free. And the line went limp and folded like a scribble in the breeze.

A fish splashed heavily. Ripples lapped the rocks at his feet. Defeat.

He retrieved the lure fitfully. He was robbed of the power, just a man and pieces of plastic. So close. Such terror for a fish, such a big fish, as big as he surely.

Of course he tried again, continued to cast, but no. Not today.

Find another place. He packed up his bag of craft and lures and moved on along the water, his eyes keen and looking, looking all the time for signs.

But his nostrils were working too, working overtime, and there was a heavy stench of death upriver. Something large had died.

He moved on faster, wanting to find that death and get past it, making that the first thing in his mind.

He stepped to the top of a rocky outcrop beside the river, into a buzzing cloud of flies, and looked upon the death. All at the same time. It was difficult to breathe.

There, trapped in the fishing net slung across the river was a large crocodile. The net was the one Gerrard had given Samson. Samson the ranger. The crocodile had torn the net away from one bank and wrapped it around itself again and again in a great tangle, and now was stiff, half in half out of the water, belly up, with its great jaws thrusting at the sky and its white teeth bared. Flies moved across and above it in dark patches.

Billy looked down. He was standing in ash. Clots of dried blood and the large curled scales of barramundi were scattered across the rocks. Billy felt his own blood banging in his ears, and his chest was tight with the stench and the heavy heat.

Those bruised clouds, that oily dark river. The bloated

crocodile, its head grinning at the sky. The hot day was pocked with buzzing black patches. Billy scuffed through the ash scales dried blood and moved away, his head spinning as if become a planet, alone, orbiting away from us into the dark deep spaces in the sky.

He moved away, almost retching, moved away upriver inland upwind to get away from this this death this death.

Billy made his way along the bone-dry bank, moving in and out of shade, stumbling across the uneven rocks which radiated heat. The river here, at this late time of year, was motionless and narrow. In many places it was possible to walk across it. River black, rocks glowing red with heat. Green algae blurred the edges of the dark river. Thunder broke and rolled across the sky. Sometimes the river valley held its course and Billy saw the distant horizon, the hills like a smudge, blurred and fusing with the sky, the vicious lightning twitching.

There, not so far from the camp, just down from the High Diving pool, was a shallow crossing. The river ran rapidly here, but was only ankle deep. Billy left his shoes and fishing gear on the rocks and walked into the water. He crouched in it to cool himself. The sound of the running water helped soothe him. He wedged himself among some rocks, and lay down. With his head in the water he could hear, within the rushing bubbles, the clicking of pebbles as they rocked and moved.

He stood, tall and revitalised, and felt the breeze breathing against his damp skin, the small rapids tugging at his ankles. On the other bank there was a faint track. This seemed a place that you could drive a vehicle across at this time of year, but the track was old and faint. Billy approached it. As the thunder rolled along the river toward the sea, and the distant lightning tongued the earth, he started along that path.

And, still barefoot and wet from the river, Billy was suddenly in a clearing. There were large boab trees, some sheets of corrugated iron rusting on the ground, and the remains of a few very small huts among the dry grass on the clearing's edge. This was the old people's camp, the old site where the people had stayed years ago in the early days of the mission and before.

He turned and beheld a view of the river, the entire mission and community. He had not realised that he had walked up such a slope. The mission grounds were exposed and vulnerable. The dark leafy green of the gardens, the darker shaded poultry runs, the pig pen. He could even partially see into the monastery courtyard. There were people sitting around a table in there. It could be Father Paul, Gerrard, Alex, Murray, Jasmine. Some others. They seemed to be having a meeting, making plans. But, of course, they were no longer all here. They had left, were leaving.

He could see the coconut palms lining the road into and through the camp to the mission gates. The rows of huts, the dusty tracks; the river snaking from far inland, the rain clouds moving along to the deep pool in the river beside which the mission squatted. The shallow sluggish rapids. Just down from them, on the far side, he could see even the speck of his fishing bag and shoes where he had left them.

The site was far superior to the other side of the river, except perhaps for tilling and working the soil. From here a youthful Fatima had carried her crippled father to the mission and back, and it was here that all the wild nights of dancing, and the many depraved scenes complained of in the school and mission journals had taken place. The place had, then, finally been successfully evacuated.

The high slope provided a cooling breeze. Boab trees and

grass worked to conceal the rust and rotting timbers, the frames of old huts, and the ashes of long-gone fires. For a moment the sun broke upon the site, washing it in rich afternoon light. The thunder continued to roll along the black river.

Billy peered inside one still-standing hut. The doorway forced him to stoop as he entered. He felt trapped, even within a ruin. It was a tiny enclosure. Wire mesh shelving sagged from the walls that remained.

He found another faint trail leading away from the clearing. Was it a path? It showed itself with each firm step; a patch of bare earth, a curve around a tree stump, and yet disappeared again behind him.

Billy moved into the bush, parting it with his hands, imagining and making a path. As he left the clearing the heavy clouds and thunder rolling along the river crushed the light.

He moved, still following the curious trail, among a group of rocks the size of houses, small cliff faces, concealed caves.

As he came out from among them another rusting hut stood before him. It was larger than the others. Billy approached. The door was closed with a large bolt, which slid smoothly. Billy peered in. It seemed windowless, dark, stuffy, and hot. He stepped inside, smelled timber and sweat. There were wire mesh shelves along each wall, leaving only a small corridor down the centre. On the shelves were wooden objects, carvings, engraved and ochred wood. There were tapping sticks, didgeridoos, spears ... other things. He looked at them, held some. They were smooth and worn, and fell into the hand readily.

The rain startled him. A few taps on the corrugated iron, as if of inquisitive fingers, then a loud drumming. Inside the shed it was deafening. The wind started up, was suddenly roaring.

Billy smiled. Caught in this shell, and yet within the roaring wind and rain, he felt a part of it all. Within it, but sheltered and safe. The door banged shut, opened, banged again with the wind. Billy turned on his heels, around and around, and laughed aloud in the deafening roar. He stood in the doorway, holding the door, and although he was on the lee side of the shed, the twisting wind blew the rain back at him in great fat drops.

He closed the door and waited peacefully in the dark roaring heat. Outside, the rain pelted and lashed the bush. Silver thorns were leaping in the deep black pool of the river, which gathered itself inland, and now came rushing, rushing with the rain. Water swirled around the shed where Billy sheltered, it curled, collected mud, and flowed away down the slope. The rapids rose, and flexed. Billy's fishing bag and shoes, they were swept away as the river and the darkness came.

This rain was not going to pass. People would worry about him caught out in it.

Billy left the hut, bolted the door. He was already drenched again, his hair and clothes flat against his skin. Rain stung and wind tore. He slipped down the pathless slope, through the clearing. He splashed across the space — high trees tossing, boab trunks black. There was no view.

Yes, for a moment. Dimly, the mission grounds, the coconut trees; the camp dissolving and blurred across the white water. Gone. The river was now a frothy tumult. Great sinews of water tore at the rocks.

Unusually cold already, and shivering, Billy stood at the river's edge. He entered the river slightly upstream from where he had crossed a short time ago. The water slapped his knees, grabbed him. Pushed and pulled him. He slipped. He turned back because he knew he couldn't cross, but slipped again. The river coiled around him, took him, wanted to swallow him.

Billy knew it as a snake. It threw him about at the same time as it wrapped around him, pulling him to it and deeper, stilling his struggles. Then free, he bounced of rocks, gulped air, swallowed water. A second coughing breath. Twisting. Muscles spinning him, holding. Light distant, a circle of light at the end of a long tunnel. It was a throat. Quiet, warm, soft darkness. He was swallowed and within.

Three figures in the grey glide down the slope from the camp. Perhaps Fatima, Moses, Samson; thin and black spirits in the grey diagonal rain. And, behind them? Sebastian, stumbling, and Liz, hesitating and led.

Billy, limp, his brain quiet, floats out of the rapids, and the thin spirits drag him to the frail, pale djimi on the shore. They stand in a circle around him.

The roaring and drumming. Water running through the hard places. Such a sound and yet to feel so warm and dry.

This bed — it's seen from above — this bed in a small room. Dark people come into the room, look, speak to the pale woman with flaming hair who sits beside the bed.

The dark people, the pale one, white ones, listen to the patient's sentences rambling and breaking. The words bounce around the room and fall softly, broken, to the floor. Those watching listening smile, wrinkle brows at one another.

At the foot of the bed, his long-dead father in work clothes. Like the photo of him leaning on the front of his grader, with his white sleeves rolled up over his dark arms. Grandmother too, white hair and dark skin, tickets from the horse races bunched in one hand, flowers in the other. Sebastian, Fatima, Gabriella there also.

Billy feels Walanguh beside him, they're mute and grinning, they're drifting out the window together. Lifted by a desert wind, high in a moonless sky, they're drifting in silence, each as if alone, but all the time looking, trying to see, searching for a place to land.

Billy in a blue sky, clouds cobwebbing his vision, sun on his back, the air sharp, the shadow of clouds gliding across the scrubby ground below. The shadow of him. He cannot take his eyes from his shadow. The sun shining right through him, warming burning charring insides to black coals as his shadow fades. And he knew who he was, he recognised the land below him. The river snaking across burnt earth sprouting bits of green, that pool in the bend of the river, the green mission grounds, the cross of the airstrip …

The rain spat in the window, onto his face.

I felt it.

See? Now it is done. Now you know. True country. Because just living, just living is going downward lost drifting nowhere, no matter if you be skitter-scatter dancing anykind like mad. We gotta be moving, remembering, singing our place little bit new, little bit special, all the time.

We are serious. We are grinning. Welcome to you.

Acknowledgements

The quoted material appearing in the chapter 'Preparations' is from *Kalumburu: The Benedictine Mission and the Aborigines, 1908–1975* by Fr Eugene Perez OSB, published by Kalumburu Benedictine Mission, 1977.

The quoted material appearing as epigraphs on page 11 are from: *Diesel and Dust* by Midnight Oil, courtesy of Warner Bros, and *Affinities* by Charles Boyle, 1977, courtesy of Carcanet Press.

The author

Kim Scott is a descendant of people who have always lived along the south-east coast of Western Australia and is glad to be living in times when it is possible to explore the significance of that fact and be one among those who call themselves Nyungar.

Kim Scott began writing for publication shortly after he became a secondary school teacher of English. *True Country*, his first novel, was published in 1993.

Kim Scott's second novel, *Benang: From the Heart*, was published in 1999, followed by *Kayang & Me* in 2005. *Benang* won the Miles Franklin Literary Award and the Western Australian Premier's Book Award. Kim Scott has been short listed for the Queensland Premier's Award and the Tasmania Pacific Literary Award, long listed for the Dublin Impac Literary, Award and was winner of the Kate Challis Award.

He lives in Fremantle, Western Australia, with his wife and children.

First published 1993 by
FREMANTLE ARTS CENTRE PRESS
PO Box 158, North Fremantle
Western Australia 6159
www.fremantlepress.com.au

Reprinted 2000, 2008. This reprint 2010.

Consultant editor B.R. Coffey
Cover designer Tracey Gibbs
Cover photograph of Paul Clement by Reenie Scott
Printed by South Wind Productions, Singapore

National Library of Australia
Cataloguing-in-publication data

Scott, Kim, 1957–
True country / Kim Scott.

2nd ed.

ISBN 978 192136152 4

Subjects: Aboriginal Australians — Fiction.
Western Australia — Social life and customs — Fiction.
Western Australia — Race relations — Fiction.
A823.3

Publication of this title was assisted by the Commonwealth Government
through the Australia Council, its arts funding and advisory body.